SUZANNE
MACPHERSON

In the Mood

AVON BOOKS
An Imprint of HarperCollins*Publishers*

This is a work of fiction. Names, characters, places, and incidents are products of the author's imagination or are used fictitiously and are not to be construed as real. Any resemblance to actual events, locales, organizations, or persons, living or dead, is entirely coincidental.

HarperCollins*Publishers*
77-85 Fulham Palace Road
Hammersmith
London W6 8JB

ISBN: 0 00 775075 7
www.avonromance.com

This edition published 2005
First Avon Books paperback printing: July 2004

Printed and bound in Great Britain by Clays Ltd, St Ives plc

To Lucia Macro,
for your warmth and support,
and for knowing every old movie and
every 1940's song I can ever dish out.

And to the real Tutu,
Sydna Mac, we love you.

1

Sexy Dexy—Money Can't Buy Him Love

Allison Jennings read the newspaper society page headline once more. The center photograph showcased one Dexter Needham III, and wow, behind those quarter-inch glasses lurked an extremely handsome man. No wonder all these women went big game hunting after his hand in marriage. Sexy Dexy was right!

She had to admit, she held a strange fascination for Dex Needham, and she was compelled to read the details of his trail of broken hearts. There were four photos of various socialite types around him, and each of them had a tale to tell about the reclusive billionaire.

"Mom, we've got to leave early."

"Okay. I'm ready to rock and roll." She reluctantly folded up yesterday's *Bellevue Register* and stuck it in her bag. Later, Sexy Dexy. "Got your books?" Allison gulped down the last of her tea and scooted out of the built-in breakfast nook.

She dragged her steno pad across the table and ticked off her morning list with blue pencil: duck landlady, start car, Ethan to school by seven forty-five, work by eight forty-five.

By seven-thirty none of those things was even near happening. Her Nova coughed like it had bronchitis, and farted a gray cloud of exhaust out of its tailpipe. Mrs. Reed was watching her out the window, framed in ruffled sheer curtains, shaking her head. So much for ducking the landlady; Eagle-Eye Reed was on the case.

"Mom, this car is shot."

"She's never let us down yet, hon; say a prayer."

"Dear Lord, put this car out of its misery."

"Ethan, don't *say* that! We can't afford to buy a car. We'd be bussing it for the next five years."

"There are worse fates. I gotta get to school, Mom, this is an important day for me."

The Nova sputtered into a rumble. "See, there? We're fine." Allison patted Ethan's arm.

He looked at her through his glasses and smiled a ten-year-old insincere smile. "Why don't you have Dad fix it, Mom?"

"Even your dad needs parts, and I think we're talking new engine here. But I'll speak to him today. Now hold on, we're going to do the dog-day dash."

With Ethan deposited at the front door of Roanoke Elementary, Allison headed to work. *Worse fates than bussing it for five years?* Ethan was getting that preteen edge.

Of course, there *are* worse fates. Allison felt a shimmy in her steering wheel, and an odd, very loud, pop. Her hands went clammy, and her heart started racing faster than a cornered rabbit. She was halfway across the bridge.

Oh yeah, she thought, a *worse fate* for a Seattle girl, by far, is to have your 1988 Chevy Nova die smack in the middle of the 520 floating bridge during morning commuter traffic. *Not* here, not *now* please God. Allison Jennings pleaded with heaven. She even bowed her head against the steering wheel. As if in reply, it began to pour down rain. June. It was June.

The car came to a dead, rolling stop. She tapped the brakes a few times to warn the car behind her, which, lucky for her, had a guy with some coffee in him behind the wheel. He managed to avoid rear-ending her by a few inches, then jumped out of his car and waved frantically to the oncoming traffic. Allison scrunched down and waited for the sound of a sixteen-car pile-up, but it never came. That must be the prayer kicking in.

Snotnose Tim was going to kill her.

Two hours later Allison slogged into work. Her hair was dripping wet. She slopped to the back room and peeled off her jacket. Everything that had formerly dwelled inside her Nova was now in a plastic garbage sack that the big scary tow driver had supplied her, so she could give the car to Rusty. She kicked it into her locker, hung the jacket to drip on it, and changed into her sensible white old-lady sneakers. For once, she was glad they were available—and dry.

It had been one humiliation after another. She'd gotten a ticket for her car dying on the bridge, her debit card wouldn't go through for the tow man, big surprise there, and if it weren't for the fact he took last-minute pity on her, seeing her very cute kid's picture in her wallet, she'd have had to sell him the Nova for scrap.

It'd also helped that he'd showed her a picture of his two ugly teenage girls who definitely took after him, and she'd gushed about them. That, and it seemed to make him nuts that her ex-husband Rusty was a mechanic and had let the Nova fall into such a state.

She slammed the locker door closed.

"You're late."

She jumped. Her boss had snuck in behind her. He was sneaky like that. "Right you are, Tim."

"Clean yourself up and head to my office. Ten minutes."

Ten minutes. How generous, you asshole. She didn't say that. "Gotcha." She said.

Why didn't they have towels in this bathroom? Roller towels even? Allison stuck her head under the hand dryer and wrung out her hair while the obnoxious noise rang in her ears. Speaking of obnoxious noises, she'd better get herself into Tim's office, fast.

When she was done she examined her reflection in the shiny metal fake mirror. Frizz over easy. Her charms weren't going to get her out of this one.

"Miss Jennings, you are late." Tim sat behind his fat metal desk and pressed his thumbs together. He stared at her with his watery fish eyes.

"My car broke down." She plunked down in the chair across from her boss.

"That's the same excuse you used last week."

"So it is. But it'll be the last time I use it, because the car is no longer living. How about I get to work now, Mr. Percival? I'll get things set up fast."

"I'm going to have to dock you for the time. I'd rather not do that though, Allison." Tim leaned forward and smiled. His teeth were crooked.

Allison leaned on the desk and eyeballed Tim straight on. *Here we go again*. Tim's little bag of sly remarks. "I'd rather you didn't do that, too, Tim; you know what a tight budget I'm on."

"I could make things a little easier for you around here, dear; you are my favorite, you know." He reached for her across the desk and patted her arm.

Echhh. The hairs on her neck creepied up. She stood abruptly. "Of all the managers we've gone through in these many years, you're my favorite, too, Tim. Now let me get to the counters."

He was behind her as soon as she moved toward his office door.

"I'm your favorite? Why, Allison, after all these years, it's just natural that we'd become fond of each other."

Allison took bigger strides. Her skirt clung to her damp pantyhosed legs. Her white blouse felt damp, too. She was soggy, crabby, and really *not in the mood*. "That's not quite what I mean, Tim. What I mean is, since I've been passed over for manager four times and watched a string of useless men related to the owner be put in the position I could do blindfolded, you are the least obnoxious of them all. That makes you the fourth least obnoxious creep I've worked for, get it?" She really did say that. She heard herself. Oops. Obviously, Tim was too stupid to sort it out because he kept moving toward her.

She nabbed a bottle of chocolate sauce just as he put his hand on her ass. Then she grabbed his fingers and twisted his arm sideways until he screeched like a girl. Her little brother, Ben, had taught her that move from wrestling.

The next thing she knew, the squeeze bottle of chocolate made nice swirls all over his balding head, and yes, it was her own hand that squeezed it. My, she was truly an artist.

Tim's bulgy eyes bulged further out. Allison finished her art project and slammed the bottle down on the counter, leaving chocolate spatters everywhere.

"You are *fired*, you crazy bitch!" Tim bellowed.

She still had his arm pretzeled up. "No, I am *not*

fired, *Tim*, I've had a very bad morning, *Tim*. My car died on the bridge, I got a ticket, and I'm due for my period. I'm going to clean the counters now, and you are going to go back to the men's room and clean up, then stay out of my face for the rest of the day. We are *both* going to forget this ever happened. Otherwise I'll call your uncle Ernie and have *you* fired for handling the help. Are we clear?"

Tim shut his hanging jaw and nodded in quick nods. Tiny little tears were at the corner of his eyes. She let go. He vanished, leaving a trail of chocolate syrup in his wake. Tsk tsk. She'd have to mop that up.

Allison took a deep breath. *Fired, my ass*. She swept two hands over her scraggly hair and marched to the closet. Her newest red and white striped apron hung on the same hook it had hung on for too many years, right above the mop. She pulled it down and tied it on. Her cone-shaped badge with *Alli Jennings, Assistant Manager* crammed on it scratched at her through the thin cotton of her damp blouse. She pulled a scrunchy out of the apron pocket and shoved her hair into a ponytail, then rolled out the mop with its roller-bucket following her like a dog.

Let the cleanup begin. The string mop slapped against the black and white vinyl tiles. She whacked the floor particularly hard today. That made her feel better.

What an idiot she'd been to stay at this job for so many years. It was time for a change. Which always brought to mind her favorite subject. Why hadn't she gone to college, or at least trade school? Why had she been marching to work for ten years without stopping to think?

And the answer is? Bingo—because of stinkin' money. Allison played game show host in her head. She wrung out the mop in the bucket and slapped it back on the floor. Three squares to go.

After she mopped up Tim's dribbles, she scrubbed the counters until the stainless steel gleamed. She finished her cleanup quickly and moved to her next task.

Allison started filling napkin holders with fresh paper napkins and muttered to herself. Money. Money was like a gene. If you were born with it, life went just a little easier. You had the designer clothes in high school, the car, the senior trip to Mexico, the college waiting for you no matter how your grades turned out. After all that came the great job in Daddy's firm and, finally, the husband—the one with his own money. What a nice little setup—if you didn't blow it.

Money was that thing that her mother never had, even before Daddy ran off. Not even up to the day she died of cancer. Thank God her mom had managed to take out some cheap term life insurance through work. She hoped her mom had looked down from heaven and saw the pretty baskets of flowers everyone had sent for her funeral, and the white satin rent-a-casket they viewed her in; Mom would have loved it. She was much loved by all her coworkers at the hospital, even if she was just cafeteria staff at Bellevue General Hospital.

Allison stopped filling napkin holders and leaned against a booth table for a minute. She missed her mom. Or maybe she missed her childhood.

Then there was Rusty, good old Rusty. She'd reached for him like a life ring right out of high school.

They had it all figured out back then. She'd work full-time, Rusty would go to mechanics school, her brother, Ben, would finish high school and go to college on the rest of the life insurance money.

She'd counted on Rusty to help her create a family for Ben after Mom had died. The flaw in that plan was counting on an eighteen-year-old boy to be a man. They'd made it only two years. Poor Rusty. No matter how hard she tried, she just couldn't get mad at him for falling in love with the drive-through bank teller. A woman who handles money all day is a powerful draw.

Even when Allison found out she was pregnant shortly after he left, she worked it out with Rusty pretty well. She also got Ethan, who turned out to be the best thing that ever happened to her; and Rusty, well, he'd turned out to be an okay dad.

Well, to hell with it. It was what it was. She snapped out of her thoughts, marched back behind the counter, grabbed her dance partner, and rolled the mop back into the closet. Allison flipped on the big overhead lights, turned on the OPEN neon sign, and went to scrub one leftover chocolate spray off the wall.

She took pride in her work most of the time. No matter that this job wasn't her dream job, it paid the bills. But today it was all getting to her. This day just could not end fast enough as far as she was concerned. Calgon take-me-away was waiting for her: a hot bath, a romance novel, and a Three Musketeers. Oh shoot; she'd have to take a bus home, which would take twice as long. Not to mention she'd have to rearrange getting Ethan to school in the morning. Why couldn't anything ever, ever be easy?

Welcome to Headacheville.

2

On the Sunny Side of the Street

"Who wrote this trash, Dexter?"

"One Mr. Stevens, freelancer for the *Register*."

"I think we'll just have to have our lawyer give Mr. Stevens a call. Better yet, that snake Ted Banning, the owner of this rag."

"Mother, sometimes that just puts fuel on the fire. Let me handle this."

"We're a family, dear. Anything that affects one of us affects all of us." Naomi Needham poured herself a hot tea refill out of the art deco silver service pot. She picked up her gold-rimmed china cup and put it to her lips.

Dex saw her hand shake a little. The article must have affected her more deeply than he supposed. He'd have to read it more carefully later. "I'm sorry about all this, Mother. It's my fault. I've thought of a few ways to make sure it doesn't happen again."

Her cup clanked into the saucer. "How, by not

dating? By not having a social life? I hardly see that as an option, Dex, you'd make a wonderful match for the right young woman. We just need to screen them more carefully."

Not dating sounded better to Dex than having his family screening prospective women. Besides, that was no guarantee; look at Mimi. She probably passed the screens with flying colors: wealthy family, excellent education, finishing school. You can't screen for being a lying, cheating, dishonest bitch.

Dex raised his eyes to his mother's face as if she might have heard him. She smiled a weak smile.

"Dex, I know what you're thinking."

No, she didn't.

"You're thinking it's easier not to date."

Yes, she did.

"I can't force you to see it my way, dear, but it would make me very sad to think of you alone for the rest of your life."

"I'm not alone. I have all of you."

"Oh us. We're boring and eccentric. You'll find someone again, Dex, and this time we'll see to it she's trustworthy."

Exit stage left. "I'm sure you will, Mother." Dex gulped down the rest of his Earl Grey tea and rose from his chair, setting his napkin on the white linen tablecloth. "I've got to run. I have a date with some spores."

"I know the brush-off when I'm getting it, son. Go on then. I'll see you at dinner. Cook's making salmon."

"On a Monday?"

"Radical departure, isn't it?"

"So droll, Mrs. Needham. You are such a comedian."

"Thank you, dear. Here, take another piece of toast with you." Naomi slathered even more butter on a whole-grain toast half and handed it to Dexter.

Dex took the toast and gave his mother's shoulder a soft touch on his way out of the room. The scents from the vase of his grandmother's June roses and the Earl Grey tea mingled and followed him out the French doors of the morning dining room into the hall. His mother could be having breakfast in the solarium if it weren't for this drizzling rain they'd been having. Dex looked at the toast as he walked, carrying it, but not eating it. Too much butter.

What his mother didn't understand, and probably never would, was that some people just weren't cut out for marriage. She didn't see the disaster with Mimi as anything except a setback. He saw it as a sign. He passed the kitchen and heard the voices of his father, his brother Edward, and his grandfather Dexter Sr. arguing about the apple crop at the summerhouse. They'd all managed to find wives. His younger brother had skated through a parade of women a mile long before he found Nora. It hadn't been an easy journey for Edward.

The fact was that Dex didn't have the dedication to the hunt that Edward had. His work had always been far more important to him. Perhaps when he felt satisfied with his project and had made some headway, he'd reconsider.

But until then, he had work to do. He had people to help. Not everyone was as privileged as his sister Celia to receive the best medical care in the world when she fell ill with Shimner's disease. If they hadn't had the money to have her treated in a French hospital by French specialists, using a drug that wasn't even approved in the United States, she wouldn't be alive. There were many drugs that could be reformulated to make them more affordable, and acceptable to the FDA. It would take him years of work, but he might be able to help someone in the future.

Somehow the thought of taking time out to date instead of pressing forward to prepare for clinical trials—well, it had always sounded ridiculous to him. But lately he'd been feeling a lack of balance in his life.

Dex took the flight of stairs down to his lab at a fast pace. He stepped into the vestibule, ditched the piece of toast his mother had forced on him, exchanged his sport jacket and its crumbs for a clean lab coat, and went to the stainless-steel sinks for a hand scrubbing.

He slipped on a surgical hat and stepped on the water pedal. The scrub brush brought the lather up on his hands and arms. He looked up into the mirror while he worked. His wire-rimmed bifocals made him look older than thirty-three. The blue paper hat on his head didn't do much for him, either.

Dex finished up and peeled into a pair of thin latex gloves. He backed up to the sealed door and hit the release with his elbow. The air pocket made a whooshing sound as it opened, then closed automatically behind him when he cleared the static pad. Dex stepped into his pristine lab. The light played on the rows of test tubes and beakers like crystals refracting the sun. He liked it in here.

He walked beside the long lab table with row upon row of petri dishes lined up, numbered, producing their various results. His ring binder was marked open to the last day's work. In here there was order. In here there was adventure and mystery. In here he was safe.

She set her mind to solving the car problem. She was sure Rusty could find a used engine for her. But of course he'd use that as a reason to keep several support checks. Allison frowned. That was not a viable option.

Checks, that reminded her. It was the first week of June.

Speaking of the once-handsome devil, Rusty walked in the door. Behind him was pregnant Pamela. Now, every woman has two heads when it comes to her ex. One is the soft head, where you remember being in love with the lout and feel jealous of the new wife. The other is the completely itch-ridden pest-infested irritated head where you snap out of it and he annoys the hell out of you and she's welcome to him. Allison felt like both of them hit her at once.

"Hey, Alli."

"Hey, Rusty."

"What's with the Nova? It smells bad."

"It's the stench of death." Allison slipped a loose strand of hair behind her ear in an automatic gesture of "spruce up in front of the new wife," and it irritated her even more that she had done it. Pamela waved her Miss Strawberry Festival wave and threw in a smile, then parked her pregnant ampleness behind a table. Rusty and Pamela had produced two girls so far, and the one in the oven was girl number three.

Rusty came over to talk to Allison, and she put on her best begging puppy-dog look. My goodness, she'd used that a bunch today. "Rusty, couldn't you please take the Nova in and see if an engine comes around?" She batted her eyes. One stuck closed from her mascara getting all clumped in the rain. She rubbed at it until it unstuck.

"Oh Alli, what a pain. That Nova's body is rusted out. You've got a smudge under your left eye."

She picked up a napkin and rubbed under her eye to remove the mascara smudge. "Rusty, I need a car. Ethan and I need a car. You're a mechanic."

"Look, I'll take it in and get it out of your hair

for a while, but I'm not promising anything. I'll look for a decent car for under a thousand."

"Under a hundred would be more like it. You know I love the Nova. Fix her, Rusty." Allison stopped the puppy routine and got normal. "Are you here to deliver a check?"

"Pamela had a craving."

"Why else would she be here at eleven in the morning?" Allison said, and walked past Rusty over to Pamela.

"Hi Pam, what can I do for you?"

"I can't live another minute without a banana split," Pamela said. She dipped her sleek, blond, ponytailed head backward in a dramatic gesture.

"Banana split it is, then." Allison smiled. *Oh, let me serve your every need since you stole my husband and tied him down with a seemingly never-ending stream of children, hampering his ability to pay anything but the most meager of child support*. She didn't say that out loud. She sure didn't say most of what went through her head.

"Extra cherries. K?"

"K." Allison wished for gum so she could smack something.

"I called Troy. He'll get the Nova towed to the shop." Rusty sauntered over. He always sauntered.

"Thanks, Rusty. Ethan only has a week of school left, you know. Are we all set to go for summer?"

"That's one of the things we came over to talk

about, Alli. Pamela here is due at the end of July, and it's getting pretty darn difficult to chase a bunch of kids around."

Oh no, not this. Please. Allison pulled up a white plastic chair and waited intently for the other shoe to fall.

"So we were thinking maybe Ethan could spend the summer with my mom."

Not old lady Trask. She was cranky and watched game shows all day long. Allison watched Pamela and Rusty exchange premeditated glances.

"What are you doing with your two?"

"Pam's mother is going to come to the house and help out."

"Ethan can help out too, he's ten. You know he'll be bored out of his mind at your mom's, Rusty, come on. We can't afford day care for three months, it's like eight hundred bucks a month."

"We could go in half with you," Rusty twisted his thick gold wedding band around his ring finger. His famous nervous gesture.

"My car just croaked, I'm behind on the rent, I just don't have that kind of money."

"My doctor recommended I take it easy for the last two months of the pregnancy. Remember, I was early last time." Pamela said this very carefully, then cocked her head in a way that told Allison she was not going to budge an inch. She had a point, of course.

"Why don't you ask for a scholarship to the summer school program?" Pamela suggested.

Allison closed her eyes and rubbed her forehead. Asking for charity was like getting a root canal for her. She could feel her body knot up imagining it. She'd done it before, just so Ethan could be in some special programs, but God, how she hated it. And even at ten, Ethan had encountered a few pointed references to the fact he was a "charity case."

She could get a second job, but that just defeated the entire goal. So she'd work ten hours a day and end up with no quality time with Ethan? It all made no sense, and she was sick to death of it.

Allison cleared her throat and raised her head to look at Rusty and Pamela straight on. "Okay, I get the picture. Rusty, you are still taking Ethan every other weekend and on Wednesday evenings."

"Umm. I can still do the weekends, but I'm taking a night class Wednesdays starting this week. I'm upgrading my certificate to work on diesel truck engines."

Allison took a deep breath. She would figure this all out. She would take care of Ethan. She didn't need anyone. "Any other announcements?"

"No, that's about it. I do have a check for you for June, but I'm fifty short. I'll do your towing and see about a salvaged engine and we can call it even."

She was getting a really bad headache. The kind that shoots lightning streaks around your eyes and across your temples. Allison got up from the chair. "I'm going to make Pamela's banana split now. Rusty, you come and make coffee."

Rusty had spent many hours in the Tasty Freeze

before and after they were married and unmarried. He could damn well make coffee, because he was going to want coffee, and she wasn't in the mood to serve it to him without pouring it down his pants.

"Sure." Rusty got up and followed her back behind the counter.

Allison pulled out a boat dish and scooped up some vanilla. "Rusty, Ethan is still your child. I want you to remember that. You've been fading out on me here, and it's Ethan that loses out."

Rusty lined the big coffee filter and scooped up some crappy generic coffee. "Alli, I'm a man of limited means and brains. I'm trying to juggle all of this two-family stuff the best I can. It would help if you got remarried so I didn't have two wives, you know."

"I'll keep that in mind, and you keep what I said in your limited brain there."

"Shut up." He laughed.

"No, you. It was you that said it, dork," Alli said as she repositioned the bananas and shook the whipped cream can.

"Smart ass."

"Watch it, I've got whipped cream here, and I'm not afraid to use it." Allison aimed the whipped cream can at Rusty.

"Okay, okay, you win." Rusty put his hands up in the air.

"Now fork over the check and come up with the extra fifty by Saturday. I have to pay Mrs. Reed the other part of June's rent. Ethan entered some science fair and I had to pay the entry fee."

Keeping his one hand in the air, Rusty reached in his back pocket and slid the check to her across the counter. "I surrender. I'll get the other fifty by Saturday."

Allison grabbed the check, stuffed it into her apron pocket, and redirected the whipped cream to Pamela's banana split. Three-point squirt, three cherries, and extra nuts. Like Pamela didn't have enough nuts on her hands.

"Here ya go, take this to the Mrs. I'll holler when the coffee is ready." She slid it down the counter to him. "And I'll make you a deal. I'll get remarried if you get a vasectomy."

"Ouch. You drive a hard bargain there."

"Take it or leave it."

"I'll let you know." Rusty instinctively covered his goodies with one hand while carrying the ice cream dish with the other. Pamela was squawking by now, undoubtedly hearing too much laughter in the background between her and Rusty.

She and Rusty always just flipped back into being the teenagers they were when they first got married. It made things easier between them, but it sure didn't solve any of Allison's grown-up problems. She swiped down the counter with her cleaning cloth and plunked the scoop into its water bath. She hadn't even gotten around to her good deed she'd promised the tow driver she'd pass on today.

Hmm, maybe making her ex-husband's pregnant wife a banana split without sardines qualified as a good deed.

Science fair. That's right, Ethan had been hauling stuff to school all week, and the big event started right after school. Rusty would have to pick her up and she wasn't taking no for an answer on this one. She'd asked Tim yesterday to leave an hour early. He'd have to cover until Heather, their high school employee, arrived off the school bus. Which meant she'd have to speak to him again. Oh, wouldn't that be a thrill.

The coffee hissed into the big glass pot behind her. She reached underneath the counter and grabbed her favorite mug. It had been hours since she'd had a cup of java. She poured herself a nice cup, picked up the whipped cream, and put a swirl on top. She took a long draw off the coffee. It tasted like dirt. Damn. What a freakin' horrible day, as Ethan would say.

"Rusty," She hollered across the room. "Your coffee's ready." Bad coffee was sweet revenge.

Later, Rusty and Pammy waved bye-bye and got into their nice new red Jeep Grand Cherokee. Rusty had promised to come back for her at two o'clock and get her to the science fair on time. He was right; he did have two wives. But he'd made his choices like hundreds of other men who couldn't seem to keep their tiny brains focused on one woman at a time. They'd even had that last little roll in the hay the week they broke up, which created Ethan. But Pamela won the toss in the end.

Allison peeled six skinny hot dogs out of a package and stacked them into the rotating steamer. Or was it men's tiny *brains* that were the problem?

She thought about what Rusty had suggested to her earlier. Remarry. What a laugh. Who had time? She never went anywhere, she hadn't even thought of dating for years. It would be a miracle if any decent guy noticed her. Heck, the only way she'd ever remarry was if the richest man in the entire state of Washington fell to his knees at the Tasty Freeze and proposed to her. Why not? It was just as likely as any other guy finding her.

3

Sentimental Journey

Dexter Needham had a craving. A craving to crawl out of his lab and live a little. Naturally, he went back in time to the memory of when his life wasn't so . . . deliberate . . . structured . . . boring.

He headed down Bel-Red Road, the old familiar route he and his college friends used to take to the Tasty Freeze. Back then all his friends had been stoned on weed and trolling for junk food. Except for him, of course. He'd been the designated driver his entire life. He vaguely remembered a few beers in that equation, but not while he was driving.

He pulled his comfortable old Mercedes in toward the old white, flat-roofed building with red trim, a huge plastic ice cream cone, and giant red Tasty Freeze letters. It looked even more run down now than it had before.

Now what was that thing he used to have here? He

parked the car, got out, and hit the lock alarm button on his key chain. The Mercedes tweeted at him.

Inside a stout guy about forty with a very shiny bald head and wisps of brown hair on the sides was behind the counter. He stared at Dex without blinking for a really long time and said nothing until Dex looked at him hard—a back-down stare contest. Strange guy.

"I'll have a hot fudge sundae, please, and coffee."

"Nuts?"

"Sure."

"Six ninety-five."

Dex gave him a twenty. Seems like it used to be a lot less expensive to have a sundae and a soda in his youth. The bald guy counted Dex's change back to him the old way.

"Have a seat, I'll bring it to ya."

"Thanks."

Here he was in the middle of the afternoon retracing his college days. He unzipped his suede jacket and hung it on a hook, then slid into a booth. Man, those days were the best. Life was so easy, girls were so easy, and he and his three buddies had been on a smooth, easy ride. Considering they were the four nerdiest guys in both high school and at the UW, they did pretty well.

It was so bittersweet in his mind. Sweet with the carefree feeling of being young; bitter with his sense of wanting it back. He hated that. Maybe coming back here was a mistake. It could never be the same as he remembered.

"Here ya go." The counter guy set up Dex's sundae and coffee and interrupted his thoughts.

"Thanks." Dex took a spoonful of hot fudge and vanilla. It was good, but it didn't have the thrill that his memory did. There was something missing. Maybe pot fumes. Maybe the feeling of a girl sitting across from him who was truly interested in him for himself—not his money or his name or his social status. He plopped a blob of whipped cream into his coffee.

When did life get so dull? He loved his work; he loved his family. It wasn't as if he wanted a big change. As a matter of fact, every time he'd ventured into big change it had been a bona fide disaster. Take Mimi Burkheimer. Dex shuddered. Must be the cold ice cream. He took a sip of his coffee. Wow, that was bad coffee. Either that or everything about Mimi left a bad taste in his mouth.

The bell over the door dinged and a noisy crowd of high school–aged kids poured in the door. They filled several booths in front of him. They were loud and obnoxious and swore like sailors.

One of them, a cute, tall, blonde, went behind the counter, pulled out a red and white apron, and tied it on. She had a conversation with the counter guy and he took off to the back.

Dex watched her move around from task to task until she came walking toward him with the coffee carafe in her hand. She looked to be about eighteen, and something about her reminded him again of being a carefree college kid.

"Refill, sir?" She held the pot dangerously close to his cup. God save him from a refill.

"No thanks." Dex smiled. "It's like bilge water."

"Oh, geez, I'm sorry. The owner buys the cheap stuff and tries to use as little as possible."

"That's okay, the ice cream is still good." The girl stared at him. What was with everyone today, did he have ink on his face?

"Oh my gawd, aren't you that guy in the paper?"

Dex's nerves went on end. He'd hoped the newspaper piece would just sort of vanish. "I don't know, I read the *Post Intelligencer* today. Am I? What's your name?" He tried to distract her.

"Heather. It was in the *Sunday Bellevue Register*. It was next to the arts calendar on the society page. I read the arts and entertainment section. I'm an artist."

"Oh really? Are you in college yet?"

"No, I'm a senior at Bellevue Central."

"Great school. I grew up in Bellevue."

"That's what it said in the paper. Wow, it is you. What's it like being the richest man on the West Coast?"

Dex sighed. "It's a mixed blessing."

"I'm sorry about that chick that dumped you at the altar."

An embarrassed heat tinged with extreme irritation rose up his face. He hadn't actually bothered to read the details. "Maybe you better show me the article. Do you have it here?"

"Sure, hold on." Heather started to walk off.

"Heather, wait."

"What?"

"Let's keep it quiet, okay? There's a big tip in it for you."

"Wow, cool. You bet."

Heather returned with the paper and then moved over to the rowdy booths full of kids with her order pad and pencil in hand.

It only took a minute to hunt down the article. SEXY DEXY—MONEY CAN'T BUY HIM LOVE. Why did they do this stuff to him? There were pictures of the last four women he'd dated, with short quotes from each one, including a paragraph on how Mimi Burkheimer had left him at the altar. No quote from her; a passable picture of him in his bow tie and tweed jacket, and his old glasses.

Was he going to have to have his attorney draw up a nondisclosure agreement for anyone he asked out—as rare as that was? Dex adjusted his new wire-rimmed glasses and read all the dirty details he'd avoided reading before. He felt anger rise up and throb in his temples.

Carefully folding up the page containing the offending article and placing it next to him, Dex set the rest of the paper aside, and pushed his sundae away. His appetite for nostalgic moments had vanished. He rose, pulled on his coat, and walked over to Heather behind the counter. She was running a mustard line down a row of hot dogs.

"Find it?" she said in a low voice.

"Yep. Thanks for your help." Dex held out his

hand and she wiped hers on her apron. He pressed a fifty-dollar bill into her palm. She smiled big.

"Thanks, sir, come back any time. I'm saving for college."

"Thanks, Heather. Take care." Dex made his exit and got back into the safety of his black Mercedes-Benz.

He drove back across Bellevue, back down the pristine landscaped neighborhood that bordered his family's estate, stopped at the huge black iron gates, and punched his code in. The wide gates swung open, and the neatly trimmed boxwood hedges of the Needham property enveloped his car. He glanced in his mirror as the gates swung closed. Dex felt his own unfortunate, but realistic relief as they locked behind him. But this time he felt something else. An aching emptiness.

Allison wished with every little hair sticking out of her head at a bad angle that she'd stopped and changed her clothes before she walked into the science fair. All the other mommies had nice slacks, or those perfect jeans, and matching sweater sets or just some sort of good-mommy clothes on. She had on running shoes, black stockings, a short black skirt, and a rumpled white blouse. It clung to her funny because it had been wet most of the day. She crossed her arms to cover up her freezing cold boobs. She'd hung her stupid jacket in with the other mommies' nice raincoats. Her hair was just as stupid; she could feel it.

"Hi, Mom, hi, Dad! You made it!"

At least Ethan didn't care what she looked like. "I wouldn't miss one of your big days for anything, Ethan." She held out her arms, but Ethan headed straight for Rusty.

"Dude!"

"Dude, back atcha," Rusty countered. They did some sort of hand-jive thing. "Show me the science, my man."

"Right this way, Dad. Mom, I got a blue ribbon, and Mr. Kerns wants to talk to you."

"Great, honey." Oh God, Mr. Kerns was probably going to bawl her out for not contributing enough volunteer hours to the science fair or something. She followed Ethan to his table. As usual his project was tagged with a blue ribbon. There were charts and graphs and diagrams and computer printouts. She saw the squares of wood representing extremely expensive stuff like platinum that they had strung on wire and formed into some kind of a model. Pretty cool. She ruffled his soft brown hair as he stood beside her.

"Cool, Ethan. It looks terrific."

"Thanks, Mom, hey there he is, Mr. Kerns, over here!" Ethan waved his science teacher down. It was really lucky for them that Roanoke Elementary had a science specialist. It was Ethan's favorite subject.

"Mrs. Jennings, I've been trying to reach you."

Here it comes. Allison wanted to crawl under the display table. "Yes, well, I work, you know."

"Oh dear, I should have gotten your work number from the office. It's been a bit hectic these last few weeks. My apologies."

Why was this teacher apologizing? Rusty and Ethan had wandered off to look at the working volcanoes and teeth soaked in cola around the room.

"Mrs. Jennings, we need to have a really serious talk."

Shit. That would cap the day. Ethan had probably blown up the lab or something. Again. "Is there some problem?" Her stomach twisted.

"Well, now is as good a time as any. Ethan has some . . . rather unusual ideas."

This guy was just killing her. She backed up one step and reached for the table behind her, braced for the news, braced to defend her child. Who was this boink anyhow?

"Are you aware of what Ethan chose for a project?"

"Um, some kind of sci-fi thing? It sounded okay to me."

"Well, Mrs. Jennings, as I mentioned to you last quarter, Ethan is very gifted in science. I've sort of taken him under my wing. You see, his project was so beyond his grade level, I took the liberty of entering him in the national science consortium a month ago."

"Oh you did, did you?" Allison said. Then she realized she was moving down the wrong path. "I'm sorry, Mr. Kernel, I've had a really nasty day and I'm not grasping what you are trying to say. Can you just cut to the chase?"

"It's Kerns, Mrs. Jennings."

"It's Miss."

"Oh, I see."

Heard that one a thousand times. After she and Rusty had divorced, she'd returned to her maiden name and given it to Ethan as well. It just seemed right, since she and Rusty weren't married when Ethan was born. So why did she have her back up anyhow? This was Ethan's favorite teacher. It was such a habit with her to be on the defensive at these school things, but she needed to snap out of her Harper Valley PTA moment and extend herself. She wasn't the only single mom in the universe, or even in this school.

"Okay, so you entered Ethan in this thing. That was very nice of you, thank you. Do I owe you money?"

"Heavens no, it was my pleasure. Besides, as Ethan's science teacher there is a certain amount of recognition I get just for being the one that found him. He's going to bring the entire district into the limelight, and basically, his achievements will justify the existence of the science specialist and extend our funding into the next five years."

"Found him?" Allison was catching partial phrases of Mr. Kerns' delivery. My goodness but this guy was verbal.

"I know I should wait until you get the letter, but

I just felt you would be so thrilled, and there will be plans to make, so I'm going to tell you myself. Ethan won. He took first place. This is phenomenal, you realize. He's only ten."

Her Ethan won some contest? Well, of course. He was a whiz at science. "What did he win?"

"He won a sizable amount of money to put toward his education, of course, but more than that, he won a full scholarship to the consortium's two-week summer program for gifted scientists of the future."

"Summer program?" If her premenstrual hormones would just release her from brain hell long enough to be able to sort Mr. Kerns' stream of information into orderly rational thought, she'd be much happier. So far he must be highly unimpressed with Ethan's parental genetics.

"*Rusty*!" Allison gave up and just shouted at the top of her lungs for the nearest available person who could help her get it all down.

"Of course you will be getting written confirmation of all of this. But the program begins one week after school gets out. I'm surprised the letter and airline tickets haven't gotten to you yet."

Allison realized she probably threw it in the bill basket and ignored it.

"Science camp? He's only ten."

"Oh. They take excellent care of their little scientists at MIT."

"MIT? In *Massachusetts*?"

"Miss . . . may I call you Allison?"

"Sure."

"Allison, this is a once in a lifetime opportunity for Ethan. You understand it might lead to a full college scholarship if he keeps his general grade point up as he goes."

Rusty and Ethan found her in a slack-jawed state of shock. She couldn't begin to explain it all, but she was beginning to understand. Her kid was a genius. She knew he was smart, but she'd sort of figured it was like, oh-he's-one-of-our-best-students kind of smart.

"What up, Alli?" Rusty had his hands in his jeans pockets and was dancing to some unseen music. Sheesh, it *must* have come from her side of the family. Her brother, Ben, was pretty darn smart; he was a navy pilot now. That took some brains. And who knows, maybe old Dad was smarter than he acted, the idiot, running off on Mom like that, leaving her two children to raise alone. 'Course she'd only been five so she didn't remember him that well.

"Ethan won a prize!"

"Yeah, he got a blue ribbon, I know."

"No, no, it's bigger than that. I'll let Mr. Kerns here explain it to you. Ethan, did he tell you?"

"Yes, just tonight. Way cool, huh? Mr. K, this is my dad, he's a mechanic. He knows all about cars." Ethan was very calm for a boy who was going to MIT for two weeks.

Allison found herself a metal folding chair and let Rusty listen to Mr. Kerns' news without her. She leaned against the wall and let her heart catch up with her breath, and her brain.

Ethan was hopping up and down like any overexcited ten-year-old buzzed on science fair soda and cookies. He looked so young. They had never, ever been apart for longer than his little weekend overnights with Rusty every month. This would be two whole weeks with him clear across the country. She shivered and pulled her jacket closer around her. What was she going to do with herself? Allison didn't know if she could survive two weeks without her boy's sunny funny face there to greet her in the morning.

Her heart ached. She shouldn't feel this way. It was selfish to let her own feelings get in the way of Ethan's opportunity. Rusty was giving Ethan a high-five. He obviously didn't have any problem letting him go; fathers were so much better at that.

Ethan was her whole life. Everything she did, every action, every reaction centered on Ethan. But she'd boxed herself into a corner. If he was this gifted, there were going to be more opportunities. Opportunities took money. Even for this trip she'd have to scrounge for Ethan's traveling money. Just think if she'd been asked to come up with airfare? Just think if that would have been the only thing holding him back?

She was going to have to move their life to another level. Suddenly she felt panicked. She could take night courses, try and improve her job skills, but who would watch Ethan while she was at these classes? How long would it take her to accumulate a new certificate, and in what? How would she pay for school?

This would take years. Ethan didn't have years. Allison felt sick. She should have started this thinking five years ago. Every day she'd trudged to her assistant manager job because it paid a monthly salary with benefits. It had covered their basic expenses for all of Ethan's early years.

But lately everything had gotten so much more expensive. Food, science fair entry fees, shoes, and her rent was higher. Anything extra just wasn't there anymore. Any emergency spun her into a nosedive.

She'd also been passed over for manager four times while the owner gave the job to men who didn't know their ass from a teakettle. That manager job would have meant a five-hundred-dollar-a-month raise. She should have smartened up and smelled the bad Tasty Freeze coffee years ago, but she'd hung in there because they'd let her work Ethan's school hours instead of a late shift.

She needed something to drink. Allison got up and headed for the refreshments. A smiling young teacher was behind the table. She was probably twenty-three. Perky.

"Can I help you?" she asked.

Allison surveyed the paper cups of soda and the plates of M&M's–laden cookies. Rusty had already bought Ethan a cookie and a soda. They looked good, and she was hungry. She pulled out her wallet. Seven dollars left. She'd skip the cookie. She put all but one back in. Better save the rest of it for a stop at Burgerville for Ethan's dinner. A celebration. She could buy him a meal deal and a shake and still get herself a budget burger if she had six bucks.

"I'll have a cola."

"One dollar, thanks for supporting your school," Miss Perky said.

Allison sipped her soda and tried to remember the teacher probably made about the same or less than she did, poor thing. But by the looks of the extremely large shiny diamond on her left hand, it wouldn't be long until Miss P became a Mrs. and joined her tiny income with a husband. An economic partnership.

As she walked back to Ethan and Rusty she tried to imagine herself in love with some man enough to actually agree to wash his stinkin' socks and let him *do* her once a week.

Despite the hardships, there was a freedom she and Ethan had. They could stay up late playing Scrabble or watching Animal Planet specials, and they could go to bed without doing the dishes. What more could she want?

Money. A better job.

She walked through the crowded gym watching couples. Dads in suits and moms in expensive black or beige summer outfits with great shoes and handbags made up a good half the crowd. The other half was where she fell; Tasty Freeze uniform, scraggly hair untouched by a salon. And there stood Rusty with a blue zip jacket embroidered with his name in orange letters. Beside him stood their genius son, Ethan. Allison choked back her emotion and swallowed it with her last gulp of soda.

"Ready to go, Ethan? Dad's going to give us a ride."

"What happened? Did the Nova die for good?" Ethan, childlike, blurted out in front of Mr. Kerns.

Allison winced. "Yes."

"It was a piece of junk, Mom. Don't worry, I'll get the early bus and get to school fine."

"Let's roll, sport." Rusty saved the day.

Mr. Kerns had that look of concern on his face. "I'll call you tomorrow after school, Miss Jennings. Ethan, great job."

As they walked out together, the three of them, she remembered how she used to long for this picture; a real family. Not necessarily Rusty, but any guy who would fill the number three spot in her line-up. When did she give up that dream? That little bit of hope was why she'd chosen to go by Miss.

But that was ages ago. Now she found it annoying. Hello, Miss Unmarried Mother of Ethan Jennings.

Ethan and Rusty were chattering.

"Hey, I've got enough for the two of us for Burgerville if you can throw in your own, Rusty. Can we give Ethan a congratulations double-cheese Burgerville special?" She knew it was kind of manipulative to ask in front of Ethan, but somewhere along the sidewalk she realized she wouldn't be able to transport them there alone. No car.

"Sure." Rusty raised his eyebrow at her. "Hey, I'll treat."

She shrugged a *sorry*. But she wasn't. Pammy could wait another hour. It was Ethan's night.

4

High Society

"Dexter, honey, don't you pay this thing any attention. Why, when I was young they plastered some society article up about your grandfather and me before we were married. *Who was that red-haired young lady seen cavorting with Master Needham on the veranda of Millie Critzmiller's spring party*? Made me sound like a harlot. No one will remember in a year." Grandma Needham took a slurp of her coffee and winked at Dexter.

"Your grandmother is right." Dex's mother said firmly. "I've looked into suing the paper, but I feel it's better to let it fade away. We strongly suggested to Mr. Banning that there be no follow-up articles."

"I completely agree about letting it fade off," Dexter said. "Let's just forget it ever happened. I'll be more careful about who I date."

So why were they still talking about it days later? Dex thought to himself.

"Good. It's forgotten," Naomi said. "We'll all keep an eye out for unscrupulous young women. Now, we are knee-deep in plans for the Fourth of July party. Would you please sit here with us for a brief time? We are going over the guest list and menus, and we need a young person to help us come up with some ideas more suited to your set." His mother set her cup down as serenely as a queen and took up her gold pen and pale ecru notepaper with *NN* in gold script at the top.

"I'm afraid I'm not much good at these things." Dex felt restlessness descend on him. He had work to do. "Horseshoes, volleyball, a tennis tournament, that sort of thing. Why don't you ask Celia?"

"Tennis tournament. That's jolly." Grandmother poured herself another coffee.

"Tutu, ease up on the coffee. It's not good for you."

"Forget it, Naomi, I'm an old lady. I'll do as I please. Get a big trophy for the tournament. Have Mrs. Fisk order that."

"She's too busy with the menus. I'll have Edward order one."

"Sounds grand. I hope you ladies will excuse me. I've got work waiting." Dex rose and placed his napkin on the table. He gave his mother a kiss on the cheek, and one for his grandmother.

"You work too much, Doodles," Grandma said.

"I like it. Have a lovely afternoon. I'll do whatever task you assign me for the party. Let me know."

"Your brother and sister are coming for dinner. Please set your buzzer so you can join us. We'll talk about things more."

"I'd love to. Now I'm going to check my spores. I've been making good progress lately."

"That's good news, dear. Just be sure and schedule in Grand Island the week of the Fourth." Naomi gave Dex a wave and went back to her list.

"Sssssss he's gone." Lucille Maude Needham hissed at her daughter-in-law. "What did you want to tell me?"

"Tutu, we've got some work to do. You've known everyone in this area for many years. We've really got to stack this party up with eligible young ladies or my son is going to be a bachelor forever. I've got at least three. Bunny Barnes Winchester Parker is on there. I told her to bring a girlfriend if she likes. I think Bunny is engaged, but I'm not sure. That woman just has to stop getting married. I can't decide which name to put on the invitation. Who can you come up with? Marcus Tinsdale's granddaughter?"

"Bunny's engagement is off. Naomi, you can stack the deck, but Dex will have to pick out his own queen of hearts," Lucille answered.

"Since he never gets out, we can at least provide some potential candidates. 'Money can't buy him love.' Those bastards. How dare they mock my son?" Naomi's handwriting got darker. She was so utterly steamed about the article in the *Bellevue Register*, she could hardly stand it.

Lucille's eyebrows rose.

"Excuse me."

"Tsk tsk, such language from my well-bred daughter-in-law. You *know* that it is a true statement. His money is not going to buy him love. If you are going to meddle, let the boy have his own pick of your candidates at least. You can present them, but he's got to find true love on his own."

"It's like he has some girl in the back of his mind that doesn't exist, and even he realizes that, so he's given up. Well, I haven't. At least the ones I bring in will have their own money and we'll be sure they're not out for his. We want suitable girls here. If he's going to be in that lab of his all day long and never go out, we'll deliver them to his own territory. And Grand Island is perfect—he only has a mini-lab there."

"I'll leave this to you, darling. You seem very determined." Lucille dabbed her lips with the linen napkin and pushed her chair back. "I'm off to my garden club meeting. We're going to dish the dirt. Get it? Dirt?"

"So amusing." Naomi's gaze fell back to the list before her. "All right, Lucille, but if you think of anyone, let me know. And keep an eye out at the party for opportunities."

"Oh, I will do that. Opportunities will arise. Don't work yourself into a snit, dear. Dexter will find his own way through this. He's a super kid." Lucille straightened her overalls and stuck on her large straw hat decorated with a big blowzy pink rose over her gray curls.

"Take it easy, Naomi," Tutu said.

"Yes, I will." Naomi watched her mother-in-law leave the room. Must she wear that getup? Naomi might not be able to make Lucille be sensible, but there was no way she was leaving Dexter to his own devices. He just wasn't making good choices. That article proved it. Naomi bent over her guest list and started making notes to hand over to Mr. Pinkerton, the family's favorite private investigator. These beauties were going to be screened and preened and ready. She'd personally see to it that Dexter found a suitable wife. That would stop this horrendous gossip for good.

Allison put down the phone and scanned the notes she'd taken during her conversation with the people at MIT. That was going to be some long-distance charge. She'd needed to hear it all from the college just to be sure; no misunderstandings.

She had a list of things Ethan would need. The students would be staying in dorm rooms, and meals were provided. He'd need some new clothes, and some spending money, but basically the entire trip was paid for. The airline ticket to Boston had been sitting in her bill basket along with the confirmation letter for at least two weeks.

She was just lucky this time. Lucky they'd picked up the tab. What was going to happen next time?

From what they told her about his entry, a boy like Ethan belonged in private school getting a top-notch education. She'd gotten lucky again with Mr. Kerns. Ethan could have easily dropped through the cracks of budget cuts and program cancellations that public school had to contend with.

Allison drew out a long piece of black licorice from the open bag in front of her. She chewed vigorously. Licorice made her stomach feel better. It also calmed her nerves.

"Dibs." Ethan walked in and caught her.

"Just one. It's my private stash." She handed him two pieces of licorice.

"So how do you feel about all this science camp stuff?" She chewed and talked with her mouth full.

"I know you're all worried, Mom, but it's going to be totally cool. Mr. Kerns is going along, and we've started an e-mail loop at school of all the kids that have been invited. There are kids from all over, even Europe."

"I heard. But you are the youngest."

"Looks like it." Ethan chewed and talked with his mouth full, too.

"I'll miss you terrible."

"I'll miss you, too, but you'll be at work and I won't miss hanging out watching *Wheel of Fortune* with Nana Trask."

"Oh, so true. Sorry about that."

"By the way, Mom."

Allison swallowed a ball of licorice. Whenever Ethan said that, she knew something was up. "What?"

"I signed up for the summer day program for the time between when I leave and school gets out."

"Oh Ethan, I can't afford to send you to that."

"I put in for a scholarship. I just filled in the forms myself. I know how you hate that stuff. It got accepted. Just for the first session."

Her Mother of the Year trophy was fading fast. The licorice was no longer helping her stomach, which seemed to be in a constant state of emotional turmoil lately. "I should have done that for you, Eth."

"It's no big deal. No one knows but the program director."

"Thank you. Well, now you've managed to escape Nana Trask for the first part of the summer, but from now on could you please ask me first?"

"Okay. What's for dinner?"

"Licorice."

"I'll make some mac and cheese on the side."

"Okay, you get the box, I'll put the water on," Allison said.

Ethan went to the cupboard for his box of macaroni and cheese. Allison rattled pans around and filled one with water to boil. She turned on the old stove. At least two burners still worked. She'd have to remind Mrs. Reed about it, but not this month, with her being late on the rent and the power bill due or die.

She leaned against the wall next to the stove and watched the water heat. When would this end? She'd have to make it end.

5

"A"—You're Adorable

Bunny Barnes Winchester Parker took her well-manicured nail out of her matching lipsticked mouth and spoke. "Root beer float."

"Coming right up. How are you, Bunny? How is Trish?" Allison set up the float glass and scooped a generous helping of vanilla ice cream into the bottom.

"She calls herself *Tiger* now," Bunny replied. "She's turned into a totally snotty child. I'm beside myself. Last weekend I heard her climb up the trellis after I grounded her for the day. I'm glad I didn't realize she was gone, or I'd have called the cops on her. She's twelve going on sixteen."

"You and I used to sneak out all the time. Remember how Rusty and Race waited a few blocks over in that loud car and we all went to Jill's party? I can't believe our parents never caught us. We were so bad at sneaking out." Allison let the root beer fill up slowly until the float foamed to the top. She put in a striped straw, a long spoon, and two large maraschino cherries on top. Just because she knew her old pal Bunny loved them.

"Well, we *were* sixteen. At least she'd only gone across the street to her little pal's house, and it was during the day. Yum." Bunny picked up the float and took a big sip through the straw. She stared at Allison in a funny way while she slurped. "Can you take a break?"

"Sure, it's quiet. I'll take a coffee break."

"I guess not many people hit the ice cream at eleven in the morning."

"It's pretty dead for a Friday. It'll pick up when school gets out. It's the last day. We stocked extra ice cream.

Allison poured herself a cup of coffee she'd made herself, so it wasn't swill, in one of their thick, white, rounded cups and put it on a saucer for fun. As they walked toward the booth she admired Bunny's sleek outfit: slim white linen slacks, a pale yellow sweater set, and chic white woven leather shoes. Bunny's rich brown hair had that perfect swing to it, cut in a chin-length bob with a thick white headband holding it in place.

She'd always envied the color of Bunny's hair. Even in grade school.

"Love your outfit, Bunny." Allison slid over to the far side of the red leatherette booth bench and poured sugar into her coffee.

"It's just basics from Ann Taylor. I hit a great sale. I picked up a black set, too, and a sort of pale green. Hey, we should go shopping. You look a little down in the dumps, girlfriend. Not only that, your hair looks like crap and your nails are monstrous. What's new?" Bunny slid into the booth opposite Allison.

"Oh thanks! I can always count on you to brighten my day. You, of course, look fabulous. See, *I* can be nice."

"You're always nice, Allison, too nice. How's your son-shine?"

"He's great. Ethan is going to this amazing science camp. He won a scholarship."

"That's terrific! You must be the proud mama now."

"Turns out he's pretty much a genius. Obviously he gets that from my side of the family." Allison slapped the table and laughed hard, making her coffee slosh into the saucer.

Bunny snorted her root beer float and coughed a laugh.

"Well, we know Rusty, although a kind soul, isn't the brain donor here. What are you going to do with him?"

Allison stopped laughing. "Exactly. What am I going to do with a brilliant son?"

"Quit frowning like that, Alli; your brow is getting all creased."

"Gee, here I thought the hamburger grease was keeping my skin lovely."

"How's your love life anyhow?" Bunny nosed in. Boy, she was good.

"Nonexistent. Rusty's wife is expecting again. He says I should get remarried. He's tired of having two wives."

"He's right. Look what it's done for me."

"Made you nuts?"

"No, made me *rich*, silly."

"You already had money."

"I had level one money, family money; enough to get the right look to snag Daddy Big Bucks. Of course it helped I got pregnant by accident, and that Race was so good with money, and had some to start with. But now, I have level *ten* money thanks to Colonel Parker, that dawg."

"Bunny, you are bad. Bad Bunny." Allison pulled her ratty navy sweater closer around her and sipped her hot coffee.

"Don't go getting all chilled and withdrawn, Alli, I've seen you do that before. You can't hang that big 'private' sign out with me. We need to work this idea through.

"It's been too long since we hung out. We've been ships passing in the night, and I want back into your life. I had a feeling about you today, and I came in here to see if your ass was still stuck in this nowhere job. Talking on the phone once a month isn't enough anymore. I want more of you." Bunny gave her that very intense stare she was famous for, then crossed her eyes.

"Ass is still stuck." Allison laughed at Bunny's cross-eyed goofy face.

"Allison, Rusty is right. You need to remarry. I'm just the person to get you there. I've managed to catch two husbands so far and I was just engaged again, briefly. I just wasn't in the mood for another wedding. But obviously this is still my best skill."

"Where am I ever going to meet a wealthy, single man, Bunny? At the Kmart? Tar*zhay*? Wallyworld? Hey, how about here at the Freeze? I just said to myself a few days ago that the only way I'd ever remarry is if the richest man in the entire state of Washington fell to his knees at the Tasty Freeze and proposed to me.

"Oh, and here's the best part, I heard Dexter Needham himself was in here the other day. And I missed him. Damn. Even if I would have been here, oh, I can just see that. *'Hello Mr. Needham, I'm your waitress today, and will you have a side of marriage with that chili dog?'* As if."

"Well, why the hell not?" Bunny slurped.

"Look at me. You said it yourself. I'm just not going to be drawing Mr. Big Bucks' eye."

Bunny stared at Allison, one penciled eyebrow arched high, with a measuring-tape-total-evaluation-head-to-toe gleam in her eye. Allison squirmed.

"Stop that, Bunny, I feel naked."

"That would help. That uniform is a fright. Can you come over to my place after work?"

"Actually, I did have an errand, but for you, I can dump it. It can wait. Rusty's taking Ethan after school for the weekend. They have their traditional last day of school thing. Rusty takes Ethan bowling or biking around Greenlake, or something fun."

"Then pack a bag, honey, you're spending the night. We'll have a slumber party. Just us girls. Let's rent movies and paint our toenails." Bunny finished up the end of her float and burped.

"Oh my God, Bunny, was that a belch?"

"Don't be insane. Ladies never belch. I covered my mouth. It was just a momentary escape of excess carbonation."

"You are amazing. All right, I'll be there. I haven't done anything fun in years. Not since the last time you dragged me out, come to think of it. I get off work at six. But if you want me I'll need a lift, because my Nova is having a new engine put in, I hope.

"Also, we don't want to cross the bridge back to my house at rush hour, so let's just head to your place and forget my overnight bag. You can loan me those flannel Lucy pajamas and a toothbrush. I'll throw my dirty stuff in your washer," Allison said.

"Sounds perfect." Bunny patted her lips with a paper napkin and slid herself out of the booth.

"Are you, like, stiffing me on the tip?" Allison slid out laughing, feeling better than she had in a long time.

"I'll give you a tip; don't forget to wear clean underwear in case you get hit by a car."

"Classic. Well, I'll consider the ride my tip. I'll see you about six-fifteen, Bunny. We'll hit the video store. Hey, go reserve *Mr. Blandings Builds His Dream House*. I love that one. '*I just wanted a little drain in the potting shed, nothing fancy, just a little flagstone with a drain.*'" Allison imitated Myrna Loy's movie voice.

"I actually own that now. Trish joined some video club and stuck me with a membership, so I bought fifty old movies on DVD rather than let her fill the house with *Scream XVII* or something. We're all set. See you six-fifteenish." Bunny gave Allison a little hug as she left. Allison detected some deviousness on the part of her friend. Probably she'd end up with purple glitter nails after all. Oh well.

Bunny probably needed someone to talk to as much as she did. This was going to be great. Girls' night out.

"Shrieeek!" Allison screeched and pushed open the Tasty Freeze door. A stretch limo was parked sideways and Bunny's dainty foot was emerging from the back door, which was being held by one heck of a hunky driver in a gray uniform. Talk about quittin' time! This day had taken forever.

"Ma'am." He tipped his hat to Allison.

"What have you *done*, Bunny? Wait there, I have

to lock the door." Allison hastily inserted her key and twisted the lock. It stuck. She rattled it into submission.

"Oh calm down, Alli, what good is having all this money if I don't get to play with it once in a while? Welcome to girls' night out! Your chariot awaits." Bunny had two champagne flutes in her hand.

Allison juggled her tote bag and sweater until Hunky Driver took them out of her hands and smiled a hunky smile. Bunny handed her the champagne glass, and they both climbed into the limo.

"Slide in, honey! It's gonna be a smooth ride."

Bunny stood behind Allison and stared at their reflection in the huge full-length mirror leaning against her bedroom wall. "All right, here's the plan. First, we're going to overhaul your entire body and wardrobe over the next three weeks. Then you got me thinking about the Needhams', what with him making a rare appearance at your place of business. I've decided you are coming to the Needhams' annual Fourth of July house party with me."

She must be kidding. Meet the actual Needham family? Allison couldn't think of anyone richer in the whole area. She'd be a complete frog in the koi pond. She'd stand out like a nudist. "I might as well be naked." Allison was focused on the mirror.

"You said that before, and now you are naked, and it's still an improvement over that uniform, sweetie. We're going to make it so you never wear a uniform again, unless it's some officer and gentleman's and he's in your bed. Those are the butt-ugliest panties I've ever seen. Where'd you get those, Ugly Panties R Us?" Bunny was taking notes. Notes, mind you. Allison crossed her arms over her ratty bra and stared into the mirror.

"Pretty much, and that's where most of my clothes came from: Ugly Clothes R Us. There is no way I can blend in with that crowd, Bunny."

"And that bra has to go. It's ill-fitting, and just . . . nasty."

"It's my favorite!" Allison adjusted the straps to pull her boobs up a notch, but one side broke from the effort, leaving her clutching the dangling grayed cotton cup. "Fine. I'll use my other one."

"We're buying you new undergarments, something with some actual support in them. Now, your figure has held up surprisingly well considering your lack of a personal trainer. If you start some basic weight workouts, your upper arms should get some definition in a few weeks."

"Thanks. I think. Bunny, I hate to break your bubble, but I don't have the money to buy myself new undies right now, or clothes, or anything."

"Your birthday is coming up. My gift is going to be a little shopping trip."

"My birthday isn't until January."

"So what. In January I won't give you anything. It's your damn thirtieth birthday, and I can give you whatever I want, whenever I want. When I put my mind to a project, missy, I make sure it succeeds. You are my current project." Bunny pointed her pencil at Allison.

"What if I decline your offer?"

Bunny put down her notepad and matching pencil, opened up a dresser drawer, took something out, and came over close to Allison. She fussed with Allison's broken strap while she talked.

"You won't. You know perfectly well it's time for you to make a change. Look at it like this. If you come to the Needhams', meet some extremely rich man, and get married, you'll thank me forever. If you don't meet someone, we'll have overhauled your entire look and you'll feel better about yourself *before you turn freakin' thirty.*"

"Augh. Stab me, why don't you? Ouch! I didn't mean that literally!"

"Sorry, I'm just pinning up your strap with a safety pin."

"Oh. Don't forget, Bunny dearest, you're on the verge of three-oh yourself. I believe your birthday is after mine by only a few months."

"Pfffft." Bunny waved her off, ignoring the facts. "First thing we need is a master plan. A wardrobe plan, a hair plan, and a game plan."

"The rain in Spain falls mainly on the plain."

"By George, I think she's got it. I think hair, first. I'll put an emergency call into Kenneth and we'll do a morning blow-out."

"No, Bunny, I can't let you do this." Allison

walked over to the fake leopard chaise and grabbed up the silky robe Bunny had loaned her.

Bunny came and sat beside her, taking up one hand. "I'm going to be extremely blunt and indelicate here, Allison. I've known you since fourth grade. I've seen you raise your chin and be tough to make up for having no lunch and wearing ill-fitting hand-me-downs all through school. I've watched you support your brother after your mom died. I'd hoped you and Rusty would find some happiness, but still, there you were taking care of everyone else; Ben and Rusty both going to school, and you working two jobs.

"Then just as he's making some money, he takes a powder on you with Pamela, that dawg, and just when I was thinking you could springboard out of it all and maybe start to have a little fun without Rusty, you two have a little moment and you turn up pregnant."

"That turned out to be a good thing," Allison said firmly.

"Yes, Ethan is a doll, but here you are still working yourself to death and getting nowhere. Just like your mom."

Allison pulled her hand away. "I've just had a different path than you. Not all of us have it easy. I just can't let you treat me like a charity case, Bunny."

"Different path? Rusty is right, Allison, you should have remarried long ago. It wasn't getting divorced or pregnant; it was curling up in a ball afterward and letting your life go fallow. A good healthy marriage can do wonders for a woman. I had one, I know. You've cut yourself off from one of the basic paths—the path where two adults care about each other and create a home and pay the bills together."

"I've just never met anyone."

"You've never tried. You've let yourself go. Look at you." Bunny gently turned Allison's head back the direction of the full-length mirror. "It's time to snap out of it and pretty up. Someone needs to wake you up, Alli; you only have so many more years of beauty left to use."

Allison looked at her dry, scraggly, dishwater hair and the dark circles under her eyes. She let out a tiny, unexpected gasp. Bunny handed her a tissue. Even the tissue box matched the room. It had one of those fancy covers. This one was faux gold leaf.

For some reason the Kleenex box just pushed her right over the edge. A huge wave of emotion rolled up inside her and made her start to cry. She tried hard to hold it back, but it wouldn't stop. She flopped onto the leopard chaise and grabbed a hot-pink pleated silk pillow, sobbing into it uncontrollably. Bunny pushed a large wad of tissues under her hand and rubbed her back in a comforting gesture.

"I'm sorry, Alli, someone had to tell you. I'm your best friend. I have all this money. You've refused help from me time and time again. You've kept your life and your struggles so private that I don't even know how bad it's been, and that's just not right. I'm your best gal pal.

"This time I'm not taking no for an answer. The joy I will receive from giving you a chance to change your life is repayment enough."

Alli hiccupped. She couldn't talk. Everything Bunny was saying was true.

"Do it for Ethan."

That made Allison stop crying for a minute, then wail more. How could she find someone right for both Ethan and her? It was impossible.

"There are some great men out there. Even my second husband was decent. He gave me great stock tips and left me richer than he found me. He couldn't help it if he had to flirt constantly to appease his fear of aging. Come on, Alli, snap out of it now. I didn't mean to hurt your feelings this bad. Besides, you're water-staining my silk pillow."

Allison lifted her head off the pillow long enough to see streaks from her tears all over the hot-pink fabric. Shit. She started to raise herself up all the way, and Bunny offered a hand.

"Wow, your hands are rough. We'll get a manicure, too."

"You're so, so . . ." Allison mopped her face with a tissue and took a deep breath. "*Persistent.* And you are so right about everything. I've been thinking about it all, but I just couldn't see a way out."

"Well, guess what. I see the way. Follow me." Bunny pulled her off the chaise and made her walk to the adjoining bathroom. She pulled a pink washcloth out of the linen cupboard and turned on the pretty gold faucet, warming the water. The glistening pink marble counters gave the whole room a beautiful, expensive, very *Bunny* look.

Allison looked around through blurry eyes. She'd always loved Bunny's house. It was the house Bunny and Race had lived in together. When he died, she'd inherited the entire estate. Race had left her very well off. Bunny's style was in every tiny detail and corner: fun, elegant, and rich. Not excessive, but enough so you felt like you were in a luxury hotel. It wasn't like she envied Bunny, but the contrast between their lives was so striking, it always made her feel a little odd.

"Here, honey." Bunny handed her the warmed washcloth. Allison laid it on her face and let the heat soothe her.

"Thanks," she said through the wet fabric.

"Let's go downstairs and have a good meal. Tad came in special and made us a terrific dinner. I've got movies and we can get crazy and dance. I'll have Tad make up a batch of daiquiris or something before he goes."

"Can we actually eat in our pajamas?" Allison took off the cloth and faced the soft lights of the bathroom mirror. Not too bad, just red and puffy and dark circles and bad skin.

"Yes, I believe we are allowed, you goose." Bunny led Allison to the walk-in closet and handed her the black velvet lounge pajamas that matched the silky gold paisley robe Allison already had on. The edges of the robe had the same black velvet. It was probably the most elegant thing Allison had ever put on in her life.

Bunny pulled out a set of leopard print pajamas and a matching robe for herself. Her slippers had a pouf of feathers on the top. So *Bunny*.

Bunny's dining room had a sort of Tuscan yellow plaster look. This year. "I like this color. But the purple was really good, too," Allison remarked. She settled into the plush chair at one side of the table and took a deep breath. She'd calmed down enough to come down to dinner, but a nice glass of wine would help a great deal.

"I got into this Italian thing." Bunny pointed to a large statue in one corner of a very well-proportioned man—with a fig leaf.

"I see. Anyone we know?"

"Oh, some gentleman I met in Rome." Bunny giggled.

"A gigolo probably, after all your money, Mom."

Allison was startled to see Bunny's daughter, Trish, framed by the pocket doors on one end of the dining room. She'd Jell-O dyed her dark hair with pink streaks, and wore a typical teenage garish outfit. Trish, at twelve, was truly a preteen now.

"Joining us for dinner, darling? That's wonderful. I thought you were eating at Mary Kathryn's house. I'll have Bridgett bring another place setting." Bunny folded her hands together and smiled a strained smile.

"Her parents decided to go out. I'm starved. Hi, Alli, are you still working at the ice cream place?" Trish parked herself in the midsection of the long marble table, opposite Allison.

"I'm afraid so. How's school, Trish?"

"I go by Tiger now."

"Oh. Tiger. How's school?"

"Boring."

"Tiger here is interested in drama. She's in the school play," Bunny interjected.

"That's great. What's the play?"

"It's a sociological examination of the oppressed child within us all and our obsessive quest for the basic love and affection we were never provided by our dysfunctional parents."

Allison looked at Bunny, hoping for an explanation.

"*Our Town.*"

"Oh. A classic." Allison smiled at Trish.

"She got the lead role. I'm very proud of your talent, dear."

"Why should *you* be proud? It's my place to gain reward from my own developed talents. I'm not doing this for you, *Mother.*"

"Yes, dear." Bunny rang a crystal bell, and in a few moments a handsome man in a chef's uniform appeared through a swinging door, wiping his hands on a dishtowel.

"Good evening, Mrs. W. Are you ladies ready for dinner?"

"We are, Tad. We're famished. Thank you for coming over tonight. I wanted my friend Allison to meet the man who cooked his way into my heart."

Tad gave a little bow to Allison and waved as he vanished through the door again.

Bridgett, the kitchen helper, came out in her black and white uniform with a place setting for Trish. She then proceeded to serve their meal, making trips back and forth to the kitchen. Allison could hardly stand that, but she was enjoying her meal so much she finally stopped worrying about Bridgett, who seemed quite happy.

Dinner was fabulous—and awkward. Trish and Bunny, Allison noticed, disagreed on just about every subject. The food was haute cuisine Southwest, with an amazing mole sauce and melt-in-your-mouth dishes. Bunny and Trish fell into noncommunication, which left her to make chitchat with the sullen teen.

Allison finally hit a subject that made Tiger perk up. The Needhams.

"Did you see that article in the *Register*? I can tell you the entire dirt on Mimi Burkheimer. I go to school with Bettina Dunford. She's related to the Needhams and she knows Mimi's niece Madison. Mimi like *boffed* the best man, one of Dex's back-east college friends that had come over for the wedding. They ran off like an hour before the ceremony. Bettina can't believe Mimi was actually going to go through with it and just sleep with the guy on the side. What a ho."

"Trish, that's crass." Bunny said.

"No, Mimi was crass. I'm just honest."

Allison listened intently while she took bites of her mole sauce–smothered chicken. Tiger was so much more teenlike than Ethan. It scared her to think that two years made that much difference. Of course, growing up with Bunny as a teenage mom was part of it.

And poor Dexter Needham. Allison knew what it was like to find out the person you trusted was cheating on you. By the dates in the *Register* article, it looked to her as if after Mimi, there were no more contenders for his circle of girlfriends. All the girls in the article were pre-Mimi.

"Dex's brother, Edward, was a total playboy before he got married. Dex will probably get back in the saddle and marry another one of those rich bitches just to keep the bloodlines going. Bettina says the Needham family is totally inbred and completely mentally deranged."

"That's enough, Patricia Winchester. The Needhams are not deranged. I know Dex's sister, Celia. She's a complete peach of a gal. And you can just take that language back to the girls' locker room. If you open your mouth like that once more at my table, you'll be eating oatmeal in your room for a week—the same batch even, and with raisins.

Mommy Dearest has nothing on me, missy. Now apologize to Allison this instant."

Tiger actually looked slightly embarrassed. "I'm sorry, Allison. I'll wash my mouth out with soap later."

"Apology accepted, *Tiger*," Allison said, giving Tiger a sarcastic smirk regarding her half-assed apology. "Where does she get this stuff at this age?" she redirected to Bunny.

"Girls talk. Don't you remember? Well, it's worse now. They watch soap operas when they get home from school."

"No, we don't, we just listen to you guys." Trish had picked all the green pepper bits out of her dish and piled them on the side of her plate. She was now talking with her mouth full of the last bites of her chicken.

Allison smiled. Trish was so different from Ethan. But it had been absolutely a ball being Bunny's best friend when she got pregnant with Trish in high school. There were two years separating their pregnancies, and they'd helped each other every step of the way, emotionally. Not all of Allison's life had been bad; she'd had Bunny.

"Okay, girls, what's for dessert?" She distracted Bunny and Trish from their ongoing argument immediately. Ah, the power of chocolate.

Over flourless chocolate cake, a delight that made Allison swoon when her silver fork reached her mouth, Bunny told Trish about the Needhams' house party and the *plan*.

"I want to come, too. Bettina will be there for sure and she and I can hang out."

"How can I keep track of you and Alli, too?"

Allison rolled her eyes at Bunny. "Excuse me, I won't need keeping track of. I'm simply going to enjoy myself and meet nice people and, um, maybe get a glimpse of that Dexter character. I'm not going there to be sold to the highest bidder, you know."

"Now that is a really brilliant idea. Maybe we could have one of those picnic basket auctions. That'll really tell you who is interested, and who has the money to back it up! I think I'll just call Naomi Needham and suggest it."

"Are you *serious*? That only works in movies. I'll end up with the bad cowboy—like in *Oklahoma*." Allison sipped her port. It was heady and sweet and made her feel very *smoooooooth*.

Bunny leaned back in her chair and surveyed Allison. "Honey, if the bad cowboy has the best horse and a big ranch, he's your man."

"Specially if he's cute," Trish added.

"All right, you can go with us. It is the Fourth of July after all, a very family sort of holiday. But right now Alli and I have some grown-up stuff to talk over. Would you like to invite Mary Kathryn over here for a sleepover?"

"I'm going back over there. They just went for dinner. She said she'd call when they got back."

"Well then, are you asking me to spend the night there? Because you still have to ask permission. You are only twelve."

Trish made a disgusted face. "Mother dearest, may I please go to Mary Kathryn's for a sleepover?"

"Yes, you may. Why don't you go pack up your things and let me know when she calls. We'll walk you over."

"I can walk myself, it's four houses away."

"Yes, but then I can see Mary's parents with my own eyes and make sure you are delivered properly. No more arguments, go pack up your overnight bag. You are excused."

"*Fine.*" Trish did a rather good imitation of a huffy teen on her way out of the dining room.

When Trish had cleared out sufficiently, Bunny turned to Allison.

"*Fine.*" Bunny twisted her face up like she'd sucked a lemon.

Allison couldn't contain herself. She let the laughter bubble up like champagne. It felt wonderful. "*Fine.*" She did her own version, by far the huffiest.

"My mother would have smacked me if I mouthed off to her like that." Bunny took a sip from her port.

"Your mom still would!" Allison laughed.

"Now, getting back to our grown-up plans. Tomorrow we are going to Kenneth's for a day of beautification. We have three weeks left to train you, and basically only weekends available with your work schedule. Let's see. You'll need some tennis lessons, some wardrobe help. Good thing we are about the same size; you can borrow from me after you drop a few pounds. We'll Hollywood Diet you down and get rid of some of that water weight. Oh, I've got to write this down." Bunny got up and went over to a large built-in banquet where she rummaged in a drawer.

"Bunny, aren't we getting a teensy bit carried away?" Allison was feeling very mellow from her port, but Bunny was starting to worry her. She could see going to this house party, and maybe she'd meet someone nice, but no matter what Bunny said, she wasn't going to sell her soul to the nearest rich devil just for money.

She had to tell Bunny that very clearly. "Bunny, I'm not selling my soul to any old rich devil, you know, I'd have to like him. He'd have to be nice to Ethan. Ethan would have to approve. I'm only going to make you happy and see what it's like to socialize again—meet people."

Bunny came back armed with a notepad and pen. "Of course, dear, but you have to go into the adventure with the mindset of a big game hunter. You are there to bag your prey. What you bag is purely up to you, and what you do with him is also. You can stuff him or do a catch and release. I'm just going to make sure the selection is the top of the herd. Do you know how to play croquet?"

Allison had a vision of herself in safari duds with a croquet mallet pursuing a runaway billionaire over the grounds. What had she gotten herself into?

6

There'll Be Some Changes Made

"Bye, Mom, don't blubber. I'll call you the minute we land. I love you." Ethan gave her one last hug.

"Don't worry, Allison, I'll take good care of him." Mr. Kerns—Bob—stood patiently waiting.

She and Bob were on a first-name basis now since she had insisted on meeting his entire extended family and had spent at least three evenings with him going over the itinerary and grilling him on his personal beliefs until they both laughed. But she'd felt good about him. Her instincts were soothed.

And of course it helped her feel better that she'd done an extensive background check on him through Mark Lubovich, Rusty's cop friend. Allison figured since Officer Lubovich took his task very seriously and had tailed Mr. Kerns for several days, there was pretty much nothing more she could do. He was actually a very nice guy.

Even so, Allison had given Ethan specific instructions on how to reach her at any moment. She'd made Rusty supply her with a pager. She ruffled Ethan's hair and turned him around to the airplane gate, holding him by the shoulders. "You are going to have a wonderful time. I love you. Bob, I'll kill you if anything happens to my boy, and you know I mean that sincerely. Now go get on that flight. Bye, you two."

Allison let go of Ethan's shoulders, then pretended to wind up an invisible key on Ethan's back, an old joke of theirs. He picked up his backpack and walked like a mechanical man toward the gate, turning once to give her a mechanical wave. Bob Kerns gave her a human wave. She jostled people aside to be able to see the last glimpse of them as they went down the airplane ramp.

Suddenly she was glad Rusty was working instead of having come with her. He'd said his goodbyes to Ethan yesterday.

Allison walked through SeaTac airport, adjusting to the feeling of being completely alone. It felt so . . . odd. She caught a glimpse of herself in a gift-store window reflection. Her new reddish-blond hair was still shocking to her. Bunny's hairdresser Kenneth had taken her strawberry-blond. He'd said with her pale skin she was a natural redhead just waiting to come out and play. They'd played a lot—with face goop and makeup half the morning—and they'd come up with a great combination of earth tones.

Between the facial, new makeup, and the hair, she looked ten years younger. Well, five anyhow.

Really, she looked her actual twenty-nine instead of thirty-nine. Even her old jeans and her white sleeveless sweater looked better on her. Even with her own slightly worn-out white cardigan tied around her shoulders, she actually felt . . . elegant.

The aroma of Starbucks drew her in to the corner coffeeshop. She gazed longingly at the pastries, but Bunny had her on a diet. If she was going to borrow Bunny's clothes, she'd have to keep to it.

She must be nuts to have agreed to this. The only way Allison could wrap her mind around it was by convincing herself it was just a vacation. Something she hadn't done since she and Ethan took an impromptu drive down the coast to Seaside, Oregon, years ago. Back when the Nova was trustworthy.

"Single nonfat lattè," she told the gal behind the counter.

"You sure know how to make coffee here in Seattle." A man's voice came from behind her. She turned to see a gray-suited, good-looking fellow smiling at her.

"We have to do something to stay zippy in all this rain." She smiled back and picked up her coffee. She hesitated for a minute between the man and the sugar and cream station.

"You look to be zippy enough already. Would you like to join me for coffee? I've got three hours before my flight leaves."

Allison looked the guy full in the face. Was he actually hitting on her? He had a faint accent. "Where are you from?"

"Texas. I'm an oil baron. No, I'm just kidding. I'm in software. Computer software. I come up here once a month or so. Are you a local?"

"Yes."

"May I ask what line of work you're in?" He was being polite enough.

Allison paused. Should she lie? There was a silence hanging three feet in front of her in the space between his question and her answer. "Management. I'm in management. I'd love to take you up on your offer, but I've got an appointment to get to. Have a good trip home."

"Can I get your phone number? Maybe I could take you to dinner some evening I'm in town. I know I'm being forward, but how's a fellow going to meet any nice women keeping his mouth shut?"

"That's true." Allison laughed. "I won't give you my number, but you can give me your card."

"Okay, hang on, let me put this down." He set his coffee down and pulled a business card out of his jacket pocket. "Terry Kjornes. Nice to meet you . . . ?"

"Allison. Well, thank you, Terry. You never know, I might give you a call." Allison smiled and pocketed his card in her jeans. Terry stood and chatted while she finished stirring fake sugar into her coffee and popped the lid on. She gave him one more smile and left.

Wow. When was the last time someone put the moves on her? It was fun. It was flattering. She walked the rest of the airport and back to the loaner car Rusty had come up with. She had a date with Bunny for private tennis lessons. She had some guy's business card in her back pocket. She was lookin' good.

She located the Ford Blandmobile, whatever model it was—a generic blue box—so indistinguishable she had to tie a scarf to the antenna to be sure she'd find it in the parking garage again.

When she got in the car she looked in the rearview mirror and saw the new improved her staring back. Ethan had been thrilled to see her pretty herself up for a change. Suddenly Ethan's absence stabbed at her. She fought back the tears and gathered herself. He was going to be fine. She was going to be fine. Hopefully.

As she exited the parking garage the circular ramp made her dizzy. One thing was for sure. She was going to have to look for a new job. Her Tasty Freeze life was like having a pair of shoes you know are comfortable. They've worn out to the point of holes, but you wear them anyway. She'd fixed her Tasty Freeze shoes just one too many times. Like her Nova. It was time to face the fact that she'd outgrown the job. Long outgrown.

Her needs, Ethan's needs, everything was different now. Ethan needed a mom who could help him get the best opportunities in life.

She would get a better job. And she'd open herself up to the possibility of meeting some rich schmuck. She'd do it on her terms, though. Not some big game hunt. She'd just open up her life. He'd have to have a decent personality, that's for sure. And surely she could become interested in someone who just *happened* to have a good financial foundation on the side—couldn't she? *I'll take portfolio with that personality, please. And a side of stick-around.*

Allison sighed. She felt like Sleeping Beauty, and Bunny had just grabbed her off the bed, smacked her in the face, and rudely awakened her. Where was that damn prince? She'd forgotten to look around past the briars for the last ten years.

As much as this new thought intrigued her, it wasn't her way to plot to trap some guy. She had to find someone genuine who would make Ethan a wonderful stepdad. Someone fun. Someone stable. Someone who would stay. What were there, about ten of those in the entire city, and five were taken? She'd better focus on getting a new job first. The odds were better.

7

Don't Sit Under the Apple Tree (With Anyone Else But Me)

You Are Cordially Invited to Attend
the Needham Family Annual
4th of July Celebration
Grand Island
July 3–5

It was one of those engraved invitations you read about in novels. Gold letters with a little American flag underneath the last line: very tasteful. Allison put it back in her new purse and gazed out over the water. Bunny was filing a nail, sitting across the ferryboat booth from her.

She would have fallen into a miserable state of loneliness with Ethan gone if it hadn't been for Bunny. Bunny distracted her endlessly, showering her with gifts that just popped up here and there along their path of self-improvement. This was undoubtedly the best prebirthday she'd ever had.

Every one of her muscles ached from the exercises Bunny had forced on her. The damn videotape should be called *Let's Cause Extreme Pain in Your Fat Butt* instead of *Let's Get Tight Buns*.

Her head ached from meditating on positive self-esteem statements droning in the earphones of the portable tape player Bunny supplied. I *deserve* a break today. Oh, wait that was fast food. I deserve *happiness*. That wasn't such a bad concept. No one had ever said that to her in her entire life, let alone saying it to herself. By the end of the second week she'd actually started to believe it.

Now here she was about to masquerade as a socialite. Just when she'd started to feel good about herself, she had to be someone else. Ironic.

The ferry docked as Trish came back from her jaunt around the boat and joined them.

"Don't forget, be vague." Bunny whispered to Allison as they got up to leave.

"What if I meet someone and get interested? What if I want to date them? What happens to my fictional background?"

"Gone with the wind, dear. Once they fall for you, they don't care who you are. Hormones take over at that point. Just be vague. Vague is good. Are you ready?"

"As ready as I'll ever be."

As they exited the ferry ramp Allison could see a

driver beside a silver van holding a sign up that read PARKER.

"*Hoo hoo, Celia*!" Bunny waved wildly. A tall, lithe woman with long dark hair stepped out of the van and waved her arms in the air. "That's Celia Needham. We went to Washington Prep together, my one horrid year of high school without you, remember? I told you scads about her."

"Scads. I remember." Allison was struggling with a rolling suitcase the size of a foreign car, trying to keep it from tipping over. The driver swiftly relieved her of it, and all the rest of their hand luggage. Was she supposed to tip him?

"Look, darling, here's my friend Allison. Allison, shake hands with Celia."

Allison's straw hat started liftoff so she grabbed her head with one hand and stuck her other hand toward Celia. Her thin white cotton dress blew high on her legs. "Oh! Nice to meet you, Celia."

"Yikes! The wind kicked up. Let's get you two in the van." Celia shook hands firmly and put her arm around Allison protectively. "Have you ever been to Grand Island before, Allison?"

"Never. It's beautiful."

"I adore it. Come on, you two, I can hardly wait to catch up with everything." Celia led them to the van.

Allison sat back and let Celia and Bunny chatter together. Trish pulled out her Game Boy and got involved in saving Zelda. Out the window Allison watched the boats skimming the harbor around the ferry dock. The fir trees and natural underbrush painted a picture postcard of Grand Island for her. There was a very relaxed feel to the surroundings. People strolled instead of rushed.

They drove along the main street past antiques shops and fishing gear stores, and lots of tourists.

"We've brought out the sunshine for you both. My gosh, it's been a dreary spring. I wanted to run down to Palm Springs or something in April but no one would go with me. Warren's been busy with work. Besides, we've been trying to get pregnant." Celia rolled her eyes a bit and elbowed Bunny.

"Oh my God, Cece, did the doctors say it was okay?"

Allison listened closely. This beautiful woman had medical problems? No life was perfect, obviously.

"Yes, yes. It's been a full year. They gave us the go-ahead. We've been at it like rabbits for three months now. I think Warren is enjoying this way too much. I'm sorry, Allison, I had this wretched disease and the only way I could get rid of it was for my family to ship me off to France for an entire year for this treatment they only do over there. That was quite a while back. Seems it did the trick, and I'm a fit person again."

"We almost lost her. I'm sorry I didn't fill you in, Alli, sometimes I just pretend it didn't happen and that makes me feel better." Bunny gave Celia a hug as best as her seat belt would allow.

"I'm so glad you recovered," Allison said. "It sounds like your family was very supportive."

"They are. My brothers are horribly protective of me. Warren was lucky to make it through the guard dogs and marry me. If you ask him, he had to fight them off with a tennis racket to get near me. Of course, it helped that he worked with my father. Married the boss's daughter and all that." Celia kept a straight face, then laughed and slapped her knees. "You must think we're a comedy, Allison. Actually we're just like everyone else. I swear."

Allison relaxed and joked with Bunny and Celia for the rest of the ride. She hardly noticed the long tree-lined drive that led to the Needhams' summer estate. When they pulled up to the huge house it was as if it appeared out of a dream.

"Here we are! Girls, I made sure you had the blue room. You remember the blue room, don't you, Bunny?" Celia elbowed Bunny in the ribs. She turned to Allison. "It's my old room here and I just love it. The windows open to the bay, and, really, it's just so relaxing. We're all going to have a good time this weekend."

Here it comes. Allison took a deep breath and stepped up the stairs to the open doors. She could see guests in the foyer and over to her left a huge living room with a river rock fireplace and more guests. She felt like Anne of Green Gables, red hair and all.

So this was the country house. She tried not to gape like a tourist.

"Bunny Barnes, darling, how are you?" A slender woman with dark hair swept over to them. This could only be Celia's mother. Allison hadn't heard Bunny called by her maiden name in ages.

Bunny went into action. "Naomi, you look fabulous, as always. This is my friend Allison Jennings. And look, here's Patricia."

"My goodness, she's grown like a weed. Trish, Bettina's been pacing the floor waiting for you. I think she's in the kitchen, that direction." Naomi pointed left.

"Thank you, Mrs. Needham." Trish took off at a run.

"She may be growing up, but she's still a kid in many ways." Bunny shook her head. "I can't believe Trish actually managed a thank-you. Oh, she goes by Tiger now."

"She's a good kid. She'll grow out of it, just like Celia did. Didn't you, darling?"

Several entering guests had distracted Celia but she smiled and nodded at her mother when she heard her name.

Naomi turned her full attention on Allison, taking her hand between her own and speaking directly to her. "Well now, Allison, where are you from?"

Deep breath. Allison launched her story. "Bunny and I went to Bellevue High School together before she transferred to Washington Prep." Allison did a little dodge and weave with the statement she and Bunny had prepared. *Where am I from? Currently, a run-down but charming section off the Roanoke overpass. The odd fact that I attended Bellevue High was due to geographics rather than the income of my family. My mother had a horrid apartment in Bellevue to be close to her cleaning customers she serviced when she wasn't working the hospital cafeteria.* She didn't say any of that.

"Oh, that's great. Old school chums. Bunny, I'm delighted you've brought her along. You'll have to tell me all about yourself this afternoon. Let's get you two settled. Celia's put you in her blue room. You'll love it. It's a bit rustic here, but that's sort of the charm of the island.

"We'll have your bags brought up. There's a lunch buffet still going on the front veranda, and dinner is at seven." Naomi Needham let go of Allison's hand and graciously led the way toward a large staircase. Her melon-orange silk slacks, matching top, and flowing silk scarf looked designer divine with her dark hair pulled up in a sedate bun.

If this was rustic, Martha Stewart's Connecticut place was rustic, too. How charming. Allison adjusted her face to seem less cynical and more "brainless twit." A terrible stereotype on Allison's part, but it was the only thing she could use to trick her mind into a "society girl" face.

Naomi actually seemed like a nice lady. She had a good smile. But she also seemed to take in everything around her with a fine, discerning eye. Allison straightened her hat and smoothed her dress. She'd have to gear up for telling Naomi more about herself "*this afternoon.*" Under that remark lurked an order, Allison sensed.

Allison was feeing as if she blended in pretty well in her lovely frock and hat, anyhow. She felt so 1920s. Bunny had insisted the classic flapper look was a great one on her.

"Oh look, here's Dex." Bunny called and waved to a man descending the staircase.

So, here was the man himself. The jilted, scandalized, reclusive . . . Allison paused her thoughts as Dex got closer to their group. Tall, well-built, sandy brown hair, *really* looking good in those navy slacks and that white oxford button-down collar shirt, and that bow tie and . . .

Allison stopped being able to think as Dexter Needham came within a foot of her. He had a very intense look about him, and it was focused completely on her. He stared right into her. His eyes were deep blue and almost familiar behind those gold-rimmed glasses.

"Hello, Bunny, you look well," Dex's voice was radio-announcer sexy. Deep and low. He spoke to Bunny but kept his eyes on Allison. "Have we met?" he asked her.

"Dex, this is my friend Allison Jennings. We went to Bellevue High together." Bunny interjected their standard line. It was funny how that seemed to get her in the door.

"How do you do, Mr. Needham; I'm delighted to be here." Manners 101. Allison stuck out her hand. Her purse strap slipped off her shoulder and clunked on the floor. Damn that long strap. He took her hand.

"Oh, for heaven's sakes, Alli, call him Dex. There're already enough Mr. Needhams to keep track of."

"All named Dex, too. It's a pleasure to meet you, Miss Jennings." He shook her hand firmly and let it go, where it remained in mid-air until Bunny bumped her.

"You can call me Allison."

"Allison."

"Yes."

Dexter's right eyebrow twitched up above his glasses rim as he let go of a strange smile. Allison couldn't take her eyes off him. She felt an odd sensation surround her. Confusion, almost. Who would have imagined the elusive Dexter Needham would come off as such a dynamic force in person?

No wonder he was the focus of that newspaper article. He had that thing . . . larger than life . . . like a movie star. Not a pretty boy, a big-screen heartthrob who happened to be wearing wire-rimmed glasses in this particular role. Allison took a breath. Well, she might as well move on to the other male guests because Dexter Needham was just way out of her league.

"Yes, well, upstairs we go, we're holding up the

show here." Bunny put her arm around Allison and pulled her by the waist toward the stairs.

Naomi Needham had been politely silent while Dexter and Allison met. Allison looked over her shoulder to see Naomi still at the base of the stairs having a few words with Dexter.

Somehow she got the sense her ears should be burning.

"Come on, I know the way." Bunny kept up in front and directed Allison down a large corridor at the first landing.

"Wow, this place is huge. How many bedrooms?"

"Ten. Their estate in Bellevue is much bigger. Twenty or so there, I think. It has that convention center feeling. I like this place much more. Grand Island has so much character."

Allison caught glimpses of bedrooms through open doors. A yellow floral chintz–draped room with a canopy bed, a spring-green room with white matelisse bedspreads embroidered with green vines. All very tastefully done. Unless Naomi was extremely talented, it had that interior designer feel.

"Here we are." Bunny pushed open the white painted door to a charming cornflower-blue room with twin beds. Sheer curtains billowed at the windows, lifted by sea breezes off the bay, which was indeed just beautiful.

"Silk gingham duvet covers. This is so Celia. I spent a few weeks here for several summers. We had a blast. You can actually climb across the roof and down the trellis from the far corner. Only when you are a teenager and in love, though; today I'd break my neck."

"It's all just amazing, Bunny. Thank you for bringing me." Allison sat on one bed, dazed.

"Try not to look like you haven't ever seen an estate before, will ya?" Bunny said. She stood by the open window. "Race made love to me in this room. Celia helped me sneak him in."

"Oh Bunny."

"He would have to go off on a business trip in some stupid private plane. He was always so intense and rushed. *Had* to be in Hong Kong by Friday." Bunny was gazing out at the water.

Allison knew Bunny was thinking about Race's plane crashing into the ocean. She went and stood beside her.

"Come on, hon, let's go get some lunch. We haven't eaten since coffee and muffins in Seattle." Allison put her hand on Bunny's arm gently.

"Yes, yes. We need to eat."

A burly-looking young man came in their open door with suitcases and bags balanced everywhere.

"Thanks!" Bunny brightened up and chatted flirtatiously with the way-too-young man.

Allison knew it made Bunny feel better to be distracted by whatever male was handy.

Dex watched Bunny's friend attempt to balance a buffet plate on her lap and drink lemonade out of a punch cup at the same time. There was something very compelling about Allison Jennings.

Those eyes of hers, for one thing: amber as cat's eyes, with a little too much black mascara. Dex could have sworn he saw the spark of a true human being in those eyes. She was quite a contrast to the well-groomed, well-prepped group that surrounded his family. And he was fairly sure she had no idea she stood out.

Right now her knees were together holding the plate, but her feet were wide apart like a kid's. It made him laugh quietly inside.

What was Bunny up to? Maybe she'd brought her friend to meet some wealthy prospects. Well, you couldn't blame her for that. He'd hate to see Miss Allison stuck with someone like Reggie or Alan, though. Maybe he'd have to step in and save her himself.

Oddly enough, Dexter found himself interested in her. She was so different from the usual fare around here. She had something special. And damned if he wasn't up for an adventure. He'd grown quite restless these last few weeks. As he watched her he felt an oddly familiar feeling take the place of his restlessness. Oh yes, he was definitely feeling something. Dex leaned against the wall and watched her shift her pretty legs around to balance that plate. She was delicious.

•

A very short Corgi dog was perched on the edge of Allison's chair with its pitiful *feed me* eyes trained on her slightest move. Well, good, because this dreadful stuff on this cracker could just *be* dog food as far as she was concerned.

"Oh, Peaches loves you!" Bunny was having a very hard time keeping a straight face, Allison noticed.

"Peaches loves this *stuff* more, I think." Allison slipped the dog another gross lump of whatever.

"You're feeding the dog pâté. Why don't you give him caviar while you're at it?" Bunny choked down her laughter.

"Peaches is welcome to the caviar. Bleah. Fish eggs; don't rich people eat normal food?"

"Sure. I saw some tarragon chicken breasts over there, and some genuine salad."

"Is that the chicken with the little smelly green bits all over it? And here's the salad," Allison stabbed a ragged-looking leaf. "Whatever this is, it ain't lettuce."

"Radicchio."

"Exactly. Tastes like the bitter stuff I had to drink for a cough when I was a kid."

"I see your point. We'll have to raid the kitchen late tonight and make a decent ham sandwich."

Allison tried to nudge Peaches away with her leg, but Peaches took it as a come-on and tried to strike up an amorous relationship with it.

"Akkk, I thought Peaches was a girl!"

"Apparently not. Peaches, stop that." Bunny started to set down her plate and punch cup to help.

Allison stood up and tried to extract Peaches. She started to lose her balance.

Suddenly Dexter Needham stood in front of her, outlined by the afternoon sun. He took her arm and steadied her.

"You'll have to excuse my grandmother's dog. He's completely without manners." Dex let Allison go and scooped Peaches up in his arms. The dog licked at Dex's face and seemed quite happy with himself.

"Oh, that's all right. He's adorable." Allison stuttered. Dex made her nervous. She set her lunch plate down on a side table and straightened her dress. Allison looked up at Dex and felt a whole bunch of butterflies whomping her in the gut. She ignored them and tried to be nonchalant. She put some glib in her smile.

"My, what a lovely place you have here."

"I'd be glad to give you a tour."

Well, heck, she didn't mean to get roped into a tour, but maybe he'd introduce her to some other men. Some plainer, less amazing men. "Great. Fine. I'd love to. Bunny? Are you coming along?"

Bunny, Allison noticed, was staring at a large group of people just emerging from the French doors that led on to the veranda. "Oh no, you go ahead, I've got to check on my daughter and I'm going to help Celia sort out the new arrivals." Bunny rose and smiled a knowing smile at Allison. "Run along now, you're in good hands with Dex here."

"Quick, let's ditch the incoming madness." Dex surprised Allison by hooking her arm in his and walking fast. She put a hitch in her step to catch up.

"Whoa there, cowboy. I've got funky heels on."

"Oh, my apologies. Funky heels?" Dex slowed down and looked at her feet. Indeed, she had funky heels on her beige sandals, sort of inverted parallelograms. And bare legs; those pretty ones he'd been staring at. "You might want to slip those off, the grass is soft here." He reached out and took her hand while she balanced on one foot to remove her sandals.

"There, shoe-free."

He pointed toward the orchard at the far end of the expansive lawn. "That's our test orchard. We'll head that way."

On the edges of the lawn his grandmother's perennials were bursting with color and fragrance. Vivid orange lilies mingled with tall white phlox and Tutu's favorite yellow roses. Dex glanced over at his guest. Her reddish-blond hair caught the sunlight and made her face light up. She was quite pretty. He saw a smattering of freckles across her nose. Her lips were full, with a peachy pink lipstick color.

Her golden hazel eyes caught the light and danced like the sea. She was looking toward the orchard, with its lush trees and wild rhododendrons. Dex caught a sense of amazement in her. Most of the girls who visited here had seen plenty of beautifully landscaped estates, and didn't have much of a reaction to the gardens. Allison Jennings seemed to be drinking it in. She ran ahead a little, shoes dangling from her fingers, like a kid, over the ridge, and down toward the trees.

Dex was going to say something to her like *slow down*, but it was too late. Miss Jennings, in her excitement, hit a slick patch of grass and went down sliding.

"Shit!" she hissed.

"Ehh, I was going to tell you there are a few damp spots on the way down. The sprinklers come up here and there." Dex strode to where she lay in the grass. "Any damage?"

"Just my pride. Excuse my language, please."

"Here, let me give you a hand."

"No, no, I'm fine. I can get up myself. You could have warned me, you know." She waved away his hand and gathered herself up off the ground.

"I was going to, but I got lost in thought. I get very focused sometimes. Besides, you just ran off."

She brushed off the back of her dress vigorously. "I just lost my head. It's very lovely here. I had a moment."

"Yes, I see." Dex stifled a laugh as he watched her walk ahead of him. Through the semi-sheerness of her summer dress, before she managed to yank her slip into place, he could see hints that her delightful panties with their subtle pink floral design were streaked green with grass stains.

They made it to the orchard and he did his tour-guide thing. "Now here are the Gravensteins, this row, and over here are the Kings. We've got a hybrid over here, a cross between a Golden Delicious and a Rome. It's my favorite."

"They all just look like little green apples to me. When do they get edible?"

"Fall. But we've been having a bad year."

"Really?"

"Yes. Tent caterpillars. We're trying to deal with them without using chemicals. See those green bands around the tree bases? We're testing them to see how well they inhibit reinfestation. We've also tried a soap spray. They don't actually pose a high-level threat, but the defoliation really affects the trees if they've had several repeat years. This is the third year we've seen a bad bunch, very unusual. At this point the caterpillars are about ready to cycle out. See here? They are going into cocoons and will emerge as moths in late July to mate, lay eggs, and then die."

"Wow."

Dexter looked over at the charming Miss Jennings and was surprised to see a most interesting fact. She was actually listening to him. He stopped in mid-thought and stared at her. She had plucked a cocoon off the branch of the apple tree and was examining it carefully.

"Little buggers."

A woman of few words. Dex chuckled to himself and walked closer to her. "He's in there all right.

The moth is reddish in color with white bands on the forewings. Females can be double the size of the males, with a wingspan of two and a half inches."

He reached under the palm of her hand and with his other he peeled back some of the silky layers surrounding the pupae case she was holding. She looked up at him briefly, her eyes sparkling. Her hair smelled like flowers. Apple blossoms.

Dexter Needham felt his body stir to life. It shocked him. He felt the warmth of her hand in his. He felt the heat rush through his blood. Biology was fascinating. It was he who was in a cocoon, wrapped tight in a protective layer. It was the first time a woman had peeled through any of those layers in a long time.

"Later tonight all the men in the family come down here with torches and burn the nests out. The caterpillars return from feeding at night."

"Oh, that's . . . so . . . weird."

"Well, we aren't big on canasta or bridge." Dex made an attempt at humor. He removed his hand from below hers and felt some embarrassment creep over him. He was so very close to her. He wanted to reach out and pull her in to him. But that would be inappropriate. And dangerous. She hadn't signed a release form.

He frowned and stepped back. "The rose gardens are this way. My grandmother breeds roses." Dex gestured toward the main house. He needed to move them back with the other people. Witnesses. Chaperones. Anything so they weren't alone.

"I love roses. My landlady let me plant a few in the walkway of our building." Oops. Allison blew it. Damn. Landlady. Building. Now she was going to have to lie.

"Which ones did you pick?"

Wow, he missed it. Saved by the plants. "Chicago Peace, and a bright pink called Promise. I tried a white variety called Honor, but it died when we had that cold winter."

"J&P roses are about the only brand that grow the stock well enough to take our zone seven climate. You've chosen two very hardy hybrid tea roses there. They should be fine. JFK is a good white hybrid tea that might hold up if you purchased a particularly healthy one, but you might look into the floribundas. They're a touch more hardy and can really give a good show. Just spray any of them with a combination of dish soap, water, and baking soda. That keeps the aphids off and helps with black spot. Plus a systemic-combination fertilizer insecticide, if you must."

Allison figured every man in the universe would rather talk about himself and his work than anything. She kept questioning him about his plant knowledge as they walked up the hill to the other side of the grounds. He was an interesting man. And she could certainly be polite to her host, even if he was out of her league.

The rose garden was spectacular. This was the peak of bloom and Allison moved from rose to rose reading tags and testing the fragrance. She really did love roses. The garden was laid out in a large circle, with an outer row that included six or seven upright trellis structures with climbing roses flowing over them. One in particular caught her eye. Its blossoms were a brilliant orange tinged with yellow on the edges.

"This is amazing. What's this?" She dug around the base for the metal tag.

"Playboy."

"Oh, that's perfect for you," she blurted.

"What exactly do you mean by that?"

She heard his voice and looked up from her crouched position to see a very huffy host. "I'm so sorry, I didn't mean anything. I read about you in the paper. It just popped out."

"Rumors of my love life are greatly exaggerated. You ought to know better than to believe everything you read in the newspaper." He stared down at her, towering.

"Well, excuse me. I was very rude." Her tone was sharp, she knew. She stood up and stared into his piercing blue eyes. She'd been ready to go head-to-head with him, but those eyes of his—they made her feel funny. Funny like the bazillion butterflies were back. Jitterbugs.

"Oh Dexy! Dexy Doodles!" A voice from the far end of the garden interrupted both of them.

Over Dex's shoulder Allison could see an elderly woman. The closer the lady got, the more detail Allison gathered. She was dressed in a bright red floral peignoir set that flowed all around her. It had feather boa trim and went very nicely with the huge picture hat pinned with roses. Nice, like the crazy-loonies-in-the-local-nuthouse nice. She also had a trowel, a yellow floral apron, and matching floral gardening gloves. At her heels was the infamous Peaches. Arf.

"Tutu. You look lovely today." Dex turned quickly back to Allison. "My grandmother," he explained.

"Who's the babe? My, my, aren't you a dolly," Tutu said as she got closer.

"Grandmother, this is Allison Jennings."

"Nice to meet you, Mrs. Needham." Allison put her hand out.

"Call me Tutu. It's Hawaiian for grandmother. Harley taught me that. He's descended from King Kamehameha." Tutu took a folded Japanese fan out of her apron pocket and waved it a bit. "Whew. Hot day."

"Harley is Grandmother's head gardener."

"He's one sexy dude, too," Tutu added.

"He certainly does a wonderful job with your roses," Allison said. Peaches was sniffing the hem of her dress. She tried to subtly kick him away with her foot.

"That's not all he's good at." Tutu winked and clicked her tongue.

"Grandmother, please. You'll give Miss Jennings the wrong impression." Dex pulled at his shirt collar.

"Oh, lighten up Sexy Dexy. Say, that was quite a

spread they did on him, dontcha think?" Tutu grinned.

"It was extremely inaccurate," Dex interjected before Allison could answer, thank God.

"Pity." Tutu turned and waved madly at a figure in the distance. "Hoooo-hoooo." Tutu headed off toward Harley, forgetting their conversation. Peaches followed, kicking up a bit of dirt with his back paws on his way.

A white-haired gentleman with deep, beautiful tan skin had his shirt off and was leaning on a garden tool. If that was Harley the gardener, Allison could see Tutu's point. He had an amazing physique. Muscles. Allison looked up at Dex. Dex rolled his eyes and nodded in answer to the unspoken question.

"He's a truly gifted gardener. I have a biochemical Ph.D. with a botany secondary and he knows more about plants than I ever will."

"And, he's one sexy dude, too."

"My grandmother is not having an affair with the gardener. You aren't from the press are you?" Dex moved so he was facing her directly. She shielded her eyes from the sun to see his face. "Because if so, we'd need to cut this pleasant walk right off—immediately. I refuse to be spied upon."

"Heavens no. I'm Bunny's friend, remember?"

"Yes," Dex said slowly. "Yes."

As Allison watched, Dex seemed to get a hold on his paranoia. Boy howdy, this guy wasn't falling far from the family nut tree. Time to head back to safety.

"Shall we head back?" She stared at him.

"Yes. I think Mother has some event planned for dinner. The greenhouse is just up that slope. We can cut through the cherry orchard and get back to the house that way."

The greenhouse was full of orchids. Allison had never seen so many varieties. Orchids and jasmine hung from rafter pots, filling the air with glorious fragrance.

"Allison, I'm sorry I jumped to conclusions back there. I'm very upset about that article." Dex walked behind her. His voice echoed in the greenhouse.

"I understand. I'd feel the same way, I'm sure," Allison said. She really meant that. She made a mental note not to pick a man in the public eye. She was intensely private about her world. She would hate to have the details of her life blasted all over the papers. Actually, the more she thought about it, the more she felt it would be a freakin' nightmare where she was concerned. She could see the headlines. UNWED MOTHER, MANAGER OF BELLEVUE TASTY FREEZE, SNAGS RICHEST MAN IN THE STATE.

She'd better steer her prettied-up self away from *Sexy Dexy* right now.

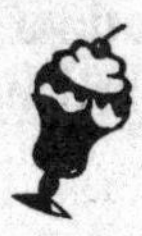

8

Shoe-Fly Pie and Apple Pandowdy

The Grand Island mansion was buzzing with yuppies. Bunny introduced them all in clumps to Allison. Reggie, Midge, Babs, Scooter, obviously all named by Mattel. They all pretty much looked like prototypes for those dolls. The Reggie doll, complete with his tennis sweater tied at the neck, wore hunky shorts to show off his hunky legs, and matching "accessories." Reggie seemed to be flirting with Allison. Either that or having a seizure. His eyebrows kept shooting up, and he winked nonstop.

Well, he wasn't too bad. An accountant in his daddy's investment firm. Low public profile. Allison decided to observe Reggie for a while.

Babs, however, was a barracuda. She draped herself over Dex and played at thwapping him on the butt with her racket. Dex did not look amused. He looked uncomfortable. He adjusted his glasses and got a dark broody look, then vanished. If Allison didn't know better she'd say there was a secret door Dex used to slip out of rooms. He'd done it twice since they'd returned.

"Well, gang," Celia Needham Colby raised her voice. "Mom has planned a surprise for dinner. We're going to auction off each lady to a gentleman along with a picnic basket full of great food. We'll donate the proceeds to the Red Cross as a gesture of old-fashioned Fourth of July spirit."

The buzz in the room rose up a notch. Allison broke into a cold sweat. She gave Bunny a hard look.

"Oh, don't worry darling, it's your chance to meet some nice guy, remember?" Bunny smiled brightly.

Celia waved her arms toward the largest room on the west end of the house. "Let's all go to the living room and see what Mom's got planned. Remember now, it's all in fun, and we're all friends."

Celia came over to Bunny and Allison as the rest of the group, maybe twenty people of various ages, swarmed into the elegant Country French living room. Allison had read enough home decorating magazines to know that style.

"I know Mother did this to get Dex hooked up with someone. I'm just afraid she's pushing too hard with him," Celia said quietly to Bunny.

"Well, who knows? Maybe the prince will meet some Cinderella."

"I suppose. It's not like he hasn't met every woman here. He and Babs have even dated."

"There's always Allison," Bunny said with a flash-of-teeth smile.

"He'd probably feel better with a familiar face." Allison backed a step away. She had made up her mind about the very public Dex already. The fewer spotlights on her life, the better.

"Gosh, I'm sorry, Allison, what was I thinking! You'd be perfect. It looks like he's ditched anyhow, so I'm going to take his place in the auction and win you! Then you two can get to know each other, but it won't put him on the spot since you are such an easygoing gal. Right?"

"Actually, I'm not so sure that's a good idea." Allison took another step backward.

Bunny blocked her way. "Don't be silly. You don't want to end up with Reg, do you? You'll have to carry a fly swatter to keep his hands off you."

"I think it sounds great. You still have all weekend to mingle around, Alli. Dex isn't so bad. He's just driven. And shy." Bunny caught Allison's arm and dragged her off to the living room.

"Bunny," Allison hissed. "I've made up my mind that Dex is just too *in the news* for me. I need a guy that's not hounded by the press. I don't want to have my life flayed open. And more importantly, I can't make a donation to anything but my rent right now, as much as I'd love to."

"Oh, just have dinner with him. Besides, you can see who bids on you, and take it from there. It's the guys who dish the money out. Now put on some lipstick and stop dragging your feet on the priceless French Aubusson carpets, for pity sakes." Bunny pulled her harder. Allison held on to her hat and plunged forward.

"And each basket contains half a roasted chicken basted in lemon and fresh herbs from Mrs. Lucille Needham's garden, pasta salad, hot biscuits, Mother's rose-hip jam, and a surprise dessert, just to tell you the highlights. There's lots more goodies in there than I can name off." Naomi Needham held up a lovely woven basket with a blue-checkered lining and wooden lid. There were what looked like ten more on a caterer's cart on the veranda.

Allison thought she might be ill. She pulled out her old favorite dime store powder compact and applied some more peach lipstick. Bunny nodded with approval, but had her stuff the compact back in her bag quickly. Guess her makeup wasn't high-class enough.

Dex was nowhere to be seen.

"All right, ladies, who is going to be first?"

"Over here!" Bunny yelled. Allison died. "You might as well get it over with, and Celia's going to bid in Dex's place," Bunny whispered to her and gave her a gentle shove from behind.

"Allison, is it?" Naomi smiled and handed her the pretty basket. "Uncle Randall will take it from here.

"Come right up here, little lady. Now what have we here? A wonderful companion to share this delightful picnic supper with! Who will bid fifty dollars?"

"Fifty!" Celia hollered from the back of the room. Allison watched all the heads in the room turn in Celia's direction. "I'm bidding for my brother Dex," Celia added.

The heads turned back to Uncle Randall. He was a stately gentleman with plaid golf pants and a matching sport shirt and hat. Dapper, these Needhams. Weird names, though.

"Do I hear fifty-five?"

"Sixty."

A voice came from Allison's left. It was Reggie. Reggie the groper. Help. Well, he was an accountant type. Maybe he'd behave if she was quite clear with him. Either that or she'd twist his pinky finger till he screamed, like she did to stupid Tim.

Allison sent a weak smile in Reggie's direction and stared down Celia and Bunny. Then she realized she was selling herself off to Dexy. Sexy Dexy, the publicly exposed. She felt very confused. Wasn't there anyone else out there? Some nice dentist? At least she and Ethan could have free dental work.

She scanned the room.

"Seventy!" Celia countered.

"Eighty!" Reggie parried.

"One hundred." A new voice came in. Allison squinted to see who it was. It was Dexter Needham, reappearing from his secret entrance.

"Dex, boy, you're bidding against yourself. Not that we object. Celia, your brother is back now."

"One hundred *fifty*." Reggie stated emphatically. Heads turned.

"Tsk," Bunny hissed. "Cheapskate."

"Five hundred." Dex's deep voice carried across the room.

Bunny elbowed her and grinned. For some reason Uncle Randall moved things quite quickly and Reggie never had another opportunity to rebid. The gavel fell, and Allison went to Dexter Needham for dinner for five hundred bucks.

"Sold to Dexter. Next we have Babs. Now we all know Babs is a great gal and would make a swell dinner companion. Do I hear fifty?"

Uncle Randall went on with the auction. Allison was practically moshed to Dexter's side.

"Um, thanks, I guess?"

"I was merely performing an act of chivalry. Reggie isn't a fit beast for someone like you, Allison."

"Someone like me? Fiddle-dee-dee. I'll just put up my parasol and twirl awhile, sir."

"Oh, very funny. I mean someone as *nice* as you. Although they do take returns, I think." Dex actually gave her a wry smile. "What's for dessert? I'm partial to a nice pie. Maybe I'll keep you if the pie is decent."

Allison opened up the lid of the basket. "Well, it's your lucky day, Dexter, I think we have blackberry pie in there."

"Come on, we'll find a nice picnic spot in the

cherry orchard." Dex grabbed Allison's hand and led her out of the house.

"Oh man, those are sour." Allison couldn't help herself; she spit the offending thing out in her hand and tried to discreetly dump it on the grass.

"Those are the pie cherries. The Rainers are almost ripe. Here, this one looks good." Dexter pulled a single rosy pink and yellow cherry off a branch and handed it to Allison.

She was a little apprehensive, but gave it a nibble. "Mmm, now this is the good stuff. I've only had the dark red ones. So, you net this place over to keep the birds out?"

"Yes, just for the season. I used to love it when I was a kid; it was a great tent to hide in. Not very invisible, but it felt like that to me when I was young." Dexter picked another cherry for himself.

"What a beautiful place to grow up," Allison said. That was a major understatement. Rolling grassy lawns dotted with orchards and gardens. Greenhouses full of orchids and other rare plants, a beautiful house overlooking the water; this was ideal.

"We only spend summers over here, and not as much as we used to."

"Oh that's right, the big house is in Bellevue." Allison tried not to sound snide.

"I'd be perfectly happy here. But I have a great research lab at the other place. I know what you're thinking."

"No you don't."

"You're thinking all these houses, this wealth, it's pretentious."

Dex was spreading out a picnic tablecloth. He'd grabbed a couple of cushions from the patio on their way, and put those down for them to sit on. He put her cushion pretty darned close to his.

"I was not thinking that."

"Sure you weren't. Look at it like this. I was just born into it. What am I supposed to do, renounce my family's riches? Or perhaps put it to some use?"

"How the heck did you get all this money?"

"My own, I took the trust fund I received at twenty-one and invested it. My brother, Edward, is very good at knowing when to get in and out of the market. We both tripled our trust funds. A few times I've created a drug that became viable and sold well. The family has been in the pharmaceutical business for about a hundred years, it seems."

Allison grabbed at a few more Rainer cherries and managed to pull them off the branch. There was no way she was going to comment on this and reveal her roots.

"So," Dexter continued as he pulled items out of the picnic basket, "that's what I do. Put it to some good use."

Well, now, wouldn't that be lovely. Wouldn't it be nice if she could just put her extra money to good use? Allison thought.

"Yes. Of course," she said slowly. Her deep-seated sense of her own poverty-encrusted childhood rose between them. "But many people are out there struggling just to make ends meet and never get to put anything to good use. They work two jobs and barely make enough to keep a roof over their heads."

Allison realized this probably wasn't the best thing to say, but she was starting to get pissed at Mr. I'm-So-Rich-I'll-Pick-a-Cause-and-Scatter-Some-of-My-Pocket-Change-at-It. His freakin' dry cleaning bills could probably pay Ethan's first year at college.

"We've had some hard times, we took a huge hit when the stock market dipped. We almost considered selling this land to a developer."

Oy. A dip. She didn't say that. She'd said too much already. He would start wondering about just how poor she'd been—or was.

"You're missing my point. I didn't ask to be rich," Dex went on.

"No, you didn't. You just lucked into a good womb. Congratulations." Oops. Well, that's all he'd get out of her.

"You seem to have quite a chip on that pretty shoulder of yours."

"With a cherry on top." Allison plopped another rosy cherry into her mouth. Sour. She came over to sit by him on the grass. She better *try* and behave at least. "Let's talk about something else."

Dex brought out a bottle of wine and uncorked it with great skill. He was probably one of those wine people. He poured two glasses and handed her one.

She took a sip. It was strange but not bad stuff. She looked at him. "Pretty good."

"It's our own." He held up the bottle, which read *Needham Estate Winery* on it. It was a pretty label with a picture of this house.

"Where are the grapes?"

"Over on the south end of the property in a large field. We have the wine processed on a different site. It's my grandfather's recipe. This is the first decent year really. Deviled egg?"

"I once buried one in the ground to keep from eating it."

"I'd say that's a no-thank-you, although you've never tasted Cook's deviled eggs. She uses spicy mustard and cilantro: really exceptional. How about melon?"

"Melon would be great." Allison took the container Dexter offered her and picked up a piece of slippery cantaloupe in her fingers, then chomped into it. The rest flew out of her grasp and splatted on her chest.

"Don't you laugh, it would be bad for your health." Allison commanded Dexter as she peeled the offending melon slice off of her.

Dex didn't laugh, but he had to keep his mouth clenched to stop. He handed her a fork and a cloth napkin. She snatched them out of his hand. Gawd, what a snappish, opinionated, impulsive, ill-mannered woman. What fun she was.

"I want to get one thing straight with you, Mr. Needham," she said between melon bites.

"I'm listening," he said, very amused.

"Obviously your wealth is quite enormous."

"Enormous."

"Don't repeat everything I say, please."

"No repeating."

"You're still doing it. Anyway, I'm a very private person. Even though you are a very attractive man, I have no interest in pursuing a relationship with you. The last thing I need is my very own page in the *Bellevue Register*."

Dexter took pause. "Did I indicate in some way I was interested in pursuing a relationship with you?"

"Well, you bid on me." She gave him an exasperated look.

"Remember, I told you that was an act of chivalry?" Dex was talking, but his eyes were watching a little melon juice drip out of the corner of her rose-lipped mouth. He might have to kiss her.

"So you have no interest in pursuing a relationship with me?"

"I didn't say that." He could see the outline of her full breasts beneath the silky summer dress she wore. Dex set down his cantaloupe.

"So, there you see, I'm forewarning you that I don't like public exposure."

"I'm not too keen on having my name in the paper, either."

"But you are cursed. Your family is cursed with a high profile. I can still avoid it." Allison wiped her mouth with the back of her hand and swallowed the last bit of melon.

"By all means, you should avoid it."

Dex had spent the last four sentences shifting nearer Allison. He'd argued with himself in his head every inch of the way. When she wiped her mouth, he couldn't take another minute. He reached over and touched her lips. Her eyes flew open very wide.

He removed his glasses and set them aside. It took quite a bit of body twisting to get into position, but he managed to take her in his arms and . . . kiss her.

It was a good kiss. Hot as hell. His socks were burning. She tasted sweet like melon and . . . her own taste. She melted in his arms for just a brief moment. By the end of it she was on the ground and he was beside her. He'd kissed her flat to the grass. He looked straight into her still-stunned hazel eyes, all golden and spitfire alive. Something about her was very familiar and exciting and magical.

She shoved him away hard so he fell over on his back. Allison clambered up off the ground. "Were you not listening to a word I said?"

"I was listening. I just didn't agree."

"I would have been better off with Reggie the octopus!" She grabbed up her crocheted handbag and sandals and stalked off toward the top of the orchard.

He might have made an error here. Better catch her and do damage control. Damn, she *was* delicious. On second thought, better catch her and kiss her again. He grabbed his glasses and ran for it. She was fast. He was gaining.

"Go away!" She ran faster up the grassy slope, dodging between cherry trees.

"Quit running, I'm not going to bite you." Well, not right this minute anyway. "I just want to apologize."

She slowed slightly, but still kept moving away. Then she turned and started walking backward. "So, apologize already, just keep your distance."

Then the oddest thing happened. She just froze. Dex watched as an odd black cloud surrounded her. It took him only five seconds flat to realize what had happened. She had stepped on a felled bee's hive. The cloud was a swarm of bees.

"Run, Allison!" He kept approaching, but she didn't move. He got to her fast, reached in, grabbed her wrist, and pulled her out. Dex swept her up in his arms and ran like hell. He could feel bees clinging to him, stinging his arms, but he held on. The koi pond was twenty yards away. He dove in as fast as possible with her still in his arms.

Ahhhh, my *God* that felt better. He let her go under the water. Those bees gave it up and floated to the surface. So did she. She sputtered up to a standing position and screamed. There were water lily vines on her head.

"Shhh, be quiet. We're okay. We got away. Look." Dex pointed to the floating bees.

"What the *hell* was that?" Allison swiped at her veil of vines.

"You stepped in a bee's hive."

"My God, this place is nuts." Allison sat back down in the water. A large orange thing brushed by her. She yelped.

"It's just the koi. I hope we didn't hurt any of them."

Allison started to laugh. *He* was worried about his *fish*. Her dress was completely destroyed, she had mud between her toes, and she was starting to notice some very uncomfortable spots on her body in some really odd places.

Dex extended his hand to her. She grabbed on and let him pull her to a standing position.

"Come on, we'll go back up to the house and get patched up. You've got some nasty stings there."

Allison felt above her lip and hit a nasty spot. Her forehead was stung, too. But looking at Dex, she figured he got the worst of it.

"I hope you know a back way in, 'cuz I ain't sloshing over yer mother's fancy carpets. She's a little intimidating. I'm afraid she'll ground us."

"Mother? She's a marshmallow. Don't let her fool you. We'll go up the servants' stairway on the east side. That'll get us to the third-floor bathroom. It's hardly ever used."

The servants' stairs. Allison bit her lower lip. She might as well be one of the servants. Maybe the

Needhams needed an ice cream steward. Look after the freezer goods. “That’s swell. Lead the way, Needham.”

Her dress clung to her like what it was—wet silk. She had on a slip, but it was in the same shape. She curled down a few edges and trudged on behind the Great and Powerful Dexter. Of course it was swell of him to save her from the bees. Speaking of swell, Dexter was really starting to look . . . lumpy.

9

Shoo-Shoo Baby

"Ouch!"

"I have to get the last stinger out. Those were honey bees." Dexter held the tweezers up to the light and nodded in approval to himself.

In the light of the bathroom, stripped to their underwear, Dexter was by far more stung-up than she was. She'd already pink-polka dotted him as much as he'd let her on the spots he couldn't reach himself. He was very stoic—much more than she was being—when she tweezed out a dozen stingers, but hey, it hurt.

He looked like a clown. Maybe ten or twelve stings dotted his arms and face and legs. She looked down at her own legs, and there were really only two stings on each, now blobbed with pink calamine lotion.

Dexter dabbed her with the saturated cotton ball

here and there. She sat on the edge of the sink, cold marble chilling her behind.

The calamine was soothing. The nearness of Dexter was disturbing. He gently turned her arm back and forth, then dabbed at another spot and held her waist with his other hand. He examined every inch of her very carefully.

"I think you are having too much fun," she said.

"That might be true," he replied. His breath was hot against her skin.

She felt the calamine-soaked cotton ball slide down the side of her neck. "We'd better each take a Benadryl. The number of hits we took might make us a bit toxic."

"You really took the worst of it." She tried for lame conversation. "They have a clear version of this stuff now, you know." She could feel her body arouse.

"We prefer the old-fashioned pink," he said in a low voice.

What was it about her life that made her end up here with Dexter in the bathroom with a bottle of old-fashioned pink stuff being dotted on her entire body? Why did everything happen to her? Why was she here in her bra and panties? Damn, she was glad Bunny had made her replace her dingy old cotton undies.

Her mind was slipping up here. She was not interested in Dexter the cursed. She tried to regain her calm while he finished, but his cotton ball was wandering around her body in a way that was just making her insane. She hadn't had a man in so long. *So long*.

He must get out of that lab of his sometimes, because his upper body was amazing, and his abs were anything but soft and pudgy, he had a regular six-pack! She looked down at his firm, muscled body covered only by a very thin pair of boxer shorts. They looked expensive. Silk maybe. They also looked like he was about to bulge out of them. She felt a heat wave engulf her. She wanted to touch him and make that huge erection of his even bigger.

Dexter had lost it. His sexual urges were completely taking over his rational thought. He had to think. He had to take back his brain. Who was this woman? Would his every move end up in a tabloid? Would the fact he was about to put his thumb to her hard little nipple through the cream-colored satin and lace bra she was wearing be in the sidebar?

He did it anyway. She sucked in a rasping, shocked breath. But she didn't slap him. Or push him away. So he put his mouth where his thumb had been. He'd watched her undress, he'd even helped peel off her wet slip. Her body was round and voluptuous and he had never seen a woman so ripe and luscious. He had to taste her. He had to have her. She was sharp and salty and sweet all at once. She made a deep, throaty sound as he moved from one side to the other, this time slipping her breast out of her bra and fully into his mouth.

No, she didn't shove him away this time. Instead

she reached down and stroked him through his silk boxers. He felt his body respond so strongly, it shocked him.

He pulled her close to him and kissed her. This was crazy. He didn't move this fast, *ever*. Brakes. Where were the brakes? He needed to think about baseball or his latest lab results or anything but her arms around his neck, or her smooth legs wrapping around him, or this slow, sweet, hot kiss he was giving her.

And then the door amazingly, swiftly, and unfortunately, opened behind him. In the lovely gilt-framed mirror he could see his mother standing in the doorframe. Her face went strange and then her hand flew up to her mouth.

Instinctively, Dex jumped back from Allison. This unbalanced her from her perch on the bathroom counter, and he ended up catching her as she whooped and tumbled forward.

Well, hell. Had his mother forgotten the fine art of knocking? Then again, had he forgotten the fine art of locking the door?

"I'm . . . Excuse me . . . Oh dear." For once his mother was speechless. She wisely backed out the door and shut it behind her.

"Wow, that was really bad, wasn't it?" Allison leaned her head on Dex's chest and laughed a little nervously. They were both standing up against the counter now, with their arms still around each other. He looked in the mirror and saw a spot he had missed on her naked shoulder blade.

"Well, now, being walked in on by your mother at thirty-three does have its odd qualities." He smoothed her hair back, then put his fingers under her chin and raised her face up to his. "Perhaps we got a bit carried away?"

"Perhaps."

He kissed her lightly on her slightly swollen lips. Swollen from his kisses, not bee stings. "I missed one back here. Turn around."

She obediently turned her back on him. They stood gazing in the mirror at each other. Dex picked up the cotton ball still wet with calamine and dabbed at the last sting. He had that head rush you get when you've done something naughty, along with a bad case of lingering lust. He was shaken up.

He looked up at her in the mirror. She smiled a Mona Lisa smile and leaned her hands against the counter. He had the urge to kiss her neck. Actually he had the urge to do *way* more than that.

He resisted. Time to resist.

"There. You're repaired." Dex set the cotton ball down on the sink side. "I'll grab us a couple of robes. Wait here." He took two steps backward, looked at her again, then grabbed a towel, wrapped it around his waist, and made his exit. Time to put some distance between him and temptation. Time to have a chat with his mother . . . after he got dressed.

Dex Needham was not what she'd come here for. Allison looked in the mirror and sighed. She was a pink-polka-dot mess. She was also completely hot. Dex's strong arms around her had just melted any sense of self-control she'd arrived with today.

Allison turned on the faucet and splashed cold water on her face, despite dislodging some of her pink spots. What was she thinking? This whole adventure would be a waste of time if she zeroed in on Dex. There were plenty of wealthy, decent, good-looking men here who didn't have their names in the paper except maybe for becoming CEO of some company.

But Dex had something. That was for sure. No wonder those girls went after him. Poor Dex. Here he was, prince charming in his castle, with his mother the wicked witch keeping guard, and those broads just nailed him. Allison wondered how they each ended, and if his mother, Naomi, had anything to do with it.

That wasn't fair, though. Naomi seemed nice, but there was just something about her that gave Allison the willies.

For being so sheltered Dex had quite a lot of skill in the lovemaking department. He had a slow, smoldering touch that made her blood boil. His body was just fabulous. Allison grabbed a washcloth from a white basket and soaked it with cold water. She needed to stop thinking about his hot mouth and get back on track.

Naomi Needham sat behind her desk and laughed at herself with her hands covering her face. Her son was a grown man. She was glad he had some sort of life. She was an idiot not to knock on that door before barging in.

Just who the hell was Bunny's friend anyway? Surely she was from some sort of decent background, going to Bellevue High with Bunny and all. Bunny wouldn't presume on their friendship and cart some gold digger in here, would she? The preliminary report on the guest list that her private investigator turned in didn't have any red flags on it.

Naomi sat up and made a quick decision. Her son's happiness was her first priority, and she'd be damned if she'd see him hurt again. Why, it took forever for him to recover from that horrid Mimi Burkheimer running off with the best man, and it'd taken thirty thousand dollars of family money to convince Mimi to do that. Her true intentions became crystal-clear when she took that check out of Naomi's hand. Mimi's family had taken a horrid hit in the dot com disaster, and she'd schemed to marry Dex to replenish the family coffers. Not because she loved him. Dexter deserved better. That hussy was already sleeping with Geoffrey Upton anyway. Harry had found that out.

Naomi nimbly riffled through her Rolodex and found the name she wanted. Harry Pinkerton would make the extra effort she needed to track down the facts on Allison Jennings. She didn't want to interfere; she just wanted to be fully aware of the details that led Ms. Jennings into Dexter's arms. And Harry already had a file started on her from the preliminaries.

She punched the phone buttons with the end of a pen and smiled in relief when she heard a man's voice on the other end. Time was of the essence.

"Hello, Harry? This is Naomi Needham."

Man alive, Allison Jennings had made him lose control. Dex was liking that idea at the moment. He felt wild and alive for the first time in years. He felt his body electrified with desire for her. She was so different from the pretentious well-tended socialites that his mother had stocked the party with. He couldn't figure Allison out. Surely she came from money as well, her clothes were expensive, and she went to Bellevue High School, surely . . .

Dex stopped himself and thought through his own statement. Maybe the reason she was so different was that she *was* different.

Dex tightened his robe belt and rearranged the thick white terry cloth robe he'd brought for Allison from the pool house, along with two cold, bottled peach ice teas. He turned on the back stairway landing, and there stood Bunny.

"What the heck is all over you? And what have you done with my friend?"

Leave it to Bunny to get right to the point. "Bee stings, calamine lotion, and she's locked in the third-floor bathroom practically naked."

"No kidding? I thought you might like her."

"She's definitely interesting."

Bunny turned and fell in beside him as he continued up another flight of stairs. "Dex, don't let your mother drive her off."

"Aren't you being a little premature? I just met her."

"I have a strong sense about the two of you. But Allison doesn't deserve to be toyed with and dumped. Be honest with her."

"When have I ever been anything less than honest?"

"Maybe I'm thinking more like you being honest with yourself for a change. You've got a pattern in case you didn't notice—disappearing girlfriends? Maybe Allison could be special. Take care of that possibility before someone else decides for you."

"I have no idea what you are talking about, Bunny, I'm in charge of my own life. If I like her, I'll go out with her. I'll probably have to have her sign some bloody release form not to talk to the press, but I'll go out with her."

"If you really like her, don't let your family get in the way, Dex. That's all I'm saying."

"I'll keep that in mind. Now do you mind? I'm saving the damsel in distress, and that's always good for a dinner date or something." He held up the robe for evidence.

"Go for it. I'm around if you need back-up excuses. I'll be at the pool with Trish and Bettina."

"Roger that." Dex said, and waved her off. Bunny should talk; she was the queen of disappearing boyfriends—and husbands. Of course any idiot could see she'd never gotten over the one that mattered—Race's disappearance.

"Knock knock, room service." Dexter rapped gently on the bathroom door.

There was silence.

He twisted the glass knob and slowly opened the door. "Allison?" The room was empty. Now how in the hell did she get out of there in her underwear?

Allison swallowed hard and kept up her wall-crawl to her bedroom window. The heavy ivy vines made a perfect support structure to grab hold of. She inched her way along. Maybe it would have been better to face the wall rather than the open, vast, clear air.

The wind off the water made goose bumps on her bare skin. This wasn't her best idea, but she had to get away from Dex right now and think. She couldn't very well flounce through the halls in her bikini briefs and skimpy bra, now could she?

Bunny's description of scaling these walls when she was a teenager to sneak out and see Race seemed a little less terrifying than actually clinging to the old vines at the moment. Allison kept creeping along the ledge one inch at a time. She was sure her bedroom window was the next one over. Just *sure*.

"What in the hell are you doing?" Dexter leaned out his bedroom window and craned himself in her direction.

"Oh! Don't scare me like that!" Allison slammed herself against the wall, startled.

"Scare you? You are three stories up. I'm assuming nothing could scare you. Now come here. I'll help you in."

"No thank you, I'm on my way to my room."

"Your room is four windows down. I'll give you a hand in. I have a robe for you."

"I need to be away from you right now. You're muddling my head."

"Likewise, but let's not end up splatted on the patio over it; the guests will be inconvenienced while they clean up the mess." Dexter cranked the window as wide as it would go. "Now come here this instant." His voice was commanding.

"No. Go away. I'm very attracted to you and I came here just to learn to get out and meet people again. I'd be very foolish to let my attraction to you sidetrack me from starting a new phase in my life. I don't want to end up in the papers."

"Neither do I. But if you keep ledge walking in your underwear, I'd say our chances of the press getting involved are pretty high. I insist you get your pretty little rear end over to me *right now.*"

Little rear end? Allison thought about this a minute and smiled to herself. Figuring in the grueling body-toning regime Bunny had put her on, she decided to take that as a compliment. "Fine. But no hanky-panky."

She inched over to his open window. When she got where he could reach her, he grabbed her and pulled her in so fast she screamed and held on to him. She held on very tight, afraid of the fall she almost took.

"Shhh." He crushed his mouth against hers and kissed her hard. She kissed him back for a very long time, her head reeling, dizzy with adrenaline and . . . lust.

"I said *no* hanky-panky." She gasped for air. Her body, scantily clothed as it was, pressed against him in total contradiction to her words. She felt herself craving his touch; wanting more.

"Now, what exactly is hanky-panky, anyhow?" Dex backed her up until they fell on his bed. He shed his robe and came after her like a tiger. A smooth, sleek, desirable tiger. "Would that be this?" He kissed her neck and ran his hand across the bare flesh of her waist and over her hip.

She responded with a low growl and leaned into his kiss. *Oh* man, she ached to have him. She pressed into him. He let out a primal sound that made her aware he was going where all men want to go—one giant, mindless step into sex.

"Stop that!" She squirmed away. "I know my body is saying something else, but just ignore it. It doesn't know what it's talking about. I'm going now. I'm going to put on this robe and go to my *own* room and get dressed. I've been here a matter of hours. This cannot be happening. I refuse to let it happen." Allison jumped off the bed and grabbed the white robe she saw draped across a chair.

Dex watched her, lying on his side, balanced on his elbow. He looked amused. He also looked very hot and sexy.

"You are amazing. Let me know when you actually *want* some hanky-panky," he said.

"Where did you get that body anyway? That is a lethal weapon."

"Tennis. And running. I run around the grounds here. In Bellevue we have a gym. That about covers it."

"That's just not fair. Bunny makes me do these torturous yoga positions and aerobics and weights and she straps me to machines that do bad things to me."

"Your body is perfect the way it is. Rebel against those machines."

"Frankly, I might. But I've never been very sporty. I better do something to keep it all in place."

"A Bellevue girl that doesn't play tennis?"

Allison better watch herself. She just wasn't in the mood for self-disclosure. "I've taken a few lessons."

"Well, tog up, I'll meet you at the courts. I need some physical activity to distract me from your charms."

Allison rolled her eyes and tightened the robe belt. Her tennis skills would definitely distract him. Probably knock him out cold. "All right, but I'm not very good. Maybe you could give me some pointers."

"Deal. I'll see you down there. I'll be the one with the bee stings."

Allison poked her head out the door and looked both ways. One way clear, one way definitely not. Naomi Needham was charging down the far end of the hall going the opposite direction. Allison decided to risk it. She slipped out the door and ran like hell toward her bedroom.

When she got to it, distinguished by a blue ribbon door hanger so the guests wouldn't get confused, the damn thing was locked. Bunny must be in there. Damn, damn, *damn*!

"Bunny, open the door. Bunny! *Please.*" Allison tried to be quiet, but she really, really needed in there. She pounded on the door. One sideways glance down the hall revealed it all. Naomi had paused on the top of the stairs and was staring directly at her.

Bunny flung the door open. "Well, well, if it isn't my nearly naked friend Allison. What *have* you been up to, dear?"

Allison practically shoved Bunny out of the way and slammed the door behind her. She sighed a very deep, relieved sigh and leaned up against the closed door. Safe. She was safe for a while.

"Okay, spill it." Bunny went back to her station at the nearby boudoir table, sat down, took up a nail file, and started calmly filing her pinky fingernail.

"We went for a picnic in the cherry orchard. I

stepped on a beehive that must have fallen from a tree. Dexter got the worst of it when he grabbed me out of the swarm. We jumped in a pond, my dress got ruined, he took me to a remote third-floor bathroom and stripped me. We emptied a bottle of calamine lotion on each other and boy, am I glad you made me buy new underwear."

"Wow." Bunny sat down on the side of her bed.

"That's not all. We got crazy. *Really* crazy. Then his mother walked in," Allison continued.

"Shit."

"After that he went for a robe. I freaked and climbed out the window, but it was farther than I thought to this room. He stuck his head out of a window somewhere in between. He grabbed me and pulled me in and I sort of really wanted him and we ended up on the bed but I came to my senses. Now I have to get dressed and go play tennis with him. The creepy part is I feel like we are being watched all the time. Maybe that's because Naomi keeps popping up. Any questions?"

"Dexter Needham kissed you? Dallied with you? My God. Unbelievable. It must be mating season."

"Did you know he has an amazing body?"

"Yes, I've seen him in the pool."

"Have I just totally screwed up this entire weekend?"

"No, you've just caught the eye of the richest man on the West Coast."

"Oh Bunny, I wasn't out for that. I told you I'd come along just to get back in the swing of things.

I didn't mean to catch his eye." Allison moved away from the door and grabbed her hairbrush out of her open toiletry bag. She started brushing her hair like crazy. It was matted with pond mud and had a few strands of water lily stuff still in it. How could she have caught anyone's eye like this?

"You better shower. You look like the Bride of Frankenstein," Bunny said, her file poised in midair. "That is so funny, Dex being a mad scientist and all."

"I don't think his mother is too thrilled. Not only did she walk in on us during a rather awkward moment, she also saw me in the hall just now. One could only figure I was coming from Dex's room."

"Uh-oh."

"Uh-oh what?"

"Naomi likes to have the full picture on any girl that comes around her son. That is not good. Well, we can hope she is so busy with her guests, she won't have time to do anything about it."

"Do anything?"

"Like run a background check on you, that sort of thing."

Allison flopped on the bed. "Uh-oh is right. Why did I let you talk me in to this, Bunny?"

"For fun. To move into a new phase in life. You *are* turning thirty, remember?"

"With friends like you to remind me, how could I forget?'

"Sorry, darling."

"I'm doomed anyway, so I might as well enjoy

the food. I'm starving. I haven't managed to complete a meal around here since . . . never." Allison picked lily stem strands out of the hairbrush.

"Don't stuff yourself before tennis. Just drink a ton of water. Eat later."

Allison's stomach growled. She moaned. She stared at the blue-flowered border of the wallpaper. "Okay. I'm ready. I'll shower. Pull me out some tennis clothes, Bunny. At least I can dress right."

"Gotcha. Wash your hair, will you? It's ghastly."

"Yes, dear." Allison pulled herself off the twin bed and headed for their private bathroom. At least she didn't have to traipse around the hall in a robe and undies again. Thank heaven for that.

Harry Pinkerton pulled his handkerchief out of his back pocket and carefully picked the wineglass up off the grass under a cherry tree. The lipstick print was perfect. There were a couple of excellent fingerprints on there, too, in case Miss Jennings had an actual police record. Nice of Naomi to point things out and make his job so easy. He shoed a few bees away, attracted to the leftover food and spilled wine. You'd think the Needhams' staff would have cleaned this up already. Lucky for him they hadn't.

'Course this area was pretty out of the way. Dexter must be hot on this girl, taking her to such a secluded spot.

He slung his camera aside. Those shots he took from his boat were perfection. What were the chances of his being right by the estate on his boat when he got her call? How often do you get to take pictures of a near-naked woman inching across the third-floor ledge into Dex's arms? Some tabloid would pay a hundred grand for those.

Too bad he couldn't sell them. Mrs. Needham was one of his best customers. Maybe after she saw them she might decide to kick in a bonus. Sort of keep him happy. That was pure fate for sure, and it sure as hell was worth something.

Better stay on the outskirts of this party. He'd go stow the fingerprints back in the boat and come back to mingle with the guests. One thing he knew for sure was that he'd learn more from party gossip than any old police file could provide for him any day.

10

Tuxedo Junction

Her tennis ball went into orbit somewhere near an undiscovered star cluster. He'd have to climb up the south hill to the big telescope tonight and try and find it.

"Oh God, I'm sorry."

Dex couldn't speak because he was laughing too hard inside.

"For pity sakes, Allison, get some control on that ball, will you?" Babs Hudson had her hands on her hips with her racket sticking out from one side. Reggie, across the net from Dex and Allison, had thrown himself against the chain-link fence, laughing hysterically.

"I'm really not very good at this."

"Well, that's *totally* obvious. We'll try one more set, and then Reg and I surrender. Dex can give you a few lessons." Babs had a twang in her voice that came only from having life served up to you on a silver platter.

Allison wished she did have some control on that ball, she'd send it into Babs' teeth. There was probably ten grand worth of orthodontic work there. Or maybe aim for the nose job. Allison caught the ball Dex tossed her and bounced it a few times. She wondered what Babs looked like before all the repairs.

"Pony up there, Reg, she's on for her second serve." Dex took a ready stance beside her. He looked mighty fine in those white shorts. Reg disconnected from the fence and lazily took his place with Babs.

She tried, really she did, but she'd had only five lessons, and serving never had sunk in. Allison pitched the ball up for her serve, took aim, swung, and her racket made contact. It sounded right, that nice ping in the center. It headed straight for Reg. It made it across the net! Amazingly enough, Reg moved a quick sidestep and nailed it back over.

Allison ran toward the net and hit the thing as hard as she could: a slam or something. It slammed all right, straight into Babs's nose. Blood spurted. Babs did a very strange twisted fall sideways on the ground, curled in a ball, and screamed through her hands, clutching her nose.

Damn! She hadn't actually meant to smack her. Babs just dove in too close! She ran over to the Babs and Reg side of the court to see the damage done.

"Oops." Allison bent over Babs and tried to be reassuring. "I'm so sorry, Babs."

Dex strode quickly around the net, grabbed a towel, and doused it with ice water. He gave it to Babs. "Here. Apply some pressure." He took a good look at the nose, uncurling her fingers. It was a bridge hit, not broken, but Babs would no doubt have two black eyes. "It's fine, Babs, no break, just a scrape. You'll be fine."

Babs buried her face in the wet towel and moaned.

"Okay, Annie Oakley, I think we'll retire your racket for a while." Dex removed the weapon from a stunned Allison's grip.

"I didn't mean to . . ."

"How about we go for a swim. I can't see you doing much harm in the water. You can swim, yes?" Dex put his arm around her.

"Yes. I can swim."

"Okay then!" Dex patted her back. "You go up and change into a suit and I'll tend to Babs here. Reggie, old boy, grab that ice bucket over there. Let's ice her up."

"She's already pretty icy, Dex." Reg smirked, but headed off to the ice bucket on the courtside as ordered.

Dex watched Allison slink off to the house. Seems as if he was always getting her to strip down. He'd like to see her in a swimsuit for sure.

"Say, Dex, what's the status with you and *killer* there? Are you in for the chase?"

Dexter ignored Reggie in order to let the emotions run through him before he answered. He was surprised to find emotions running through him. He extracted the damp towel from Babs and fashioned a temporary ice bag. "Here, Babs, let me help you up. Let's get you off the courts. There's a chair over here."

"Uhhh," was all Babs could say as he lifted her by her arm and guided her toward the Adirondack chairs close by. She slumped into one and buried her nose in the ice bag. "Oh, *do* answer Reggie's question Dex, my nose is hacked, not my ears," a muffled voice came from behind the white towel.

Dex could see the hint of a smile on Babs' lips, and an intense questioning stare from Reggie.

"She's not keen on being with someone who might jeopardize her privacy," Dex said.

"Well, I'm jolly nobody, I pass that test." Reggie stuck his thumb in his lapel.

"How I envy you," Dex replied, and it was sincere. He didn't know what else to say. He *was* up for the chase, but she was running awfully fast.

"I'm available to either of you idiots. You're always chasing some skirt and never remembering your pal standing right next to you. You'd think you were still in college. Let her go Dex, she's strange. She's not one of us," said Babs.

"That's what I like about her." Dex looked down at Babs. She was really getting to be a snob.

"Refreshing, isn't she?" Reggie added. "Marrying you would be like an arranged marriage, Babs. No offense. We need some new blood around here. Someone to shake things up."

Babs talked through her towel. "That wears off. Then you've got this strange bedfellow you can't take to the Hamptons or to the benefits because she might put ketchup on the pâté or wear white after Labor Day. You'd have to have her trained."

"So you're saying this strange, socially unacceptable bedfellow would just keep you home as her love slave and deprive you of boring parties?" Reg's dry wit surfaced.

"Fate worse than death, I'm sure," Dex added.

"Shut up, both of you. Get me a martini. Very dry, six olives. Make it one of those new ones—lemon or something."

"Yes, madam." Dex waved at one of the staff members and made drink gestures. Look at him. He was as bad as she was. The girl came over, a cute younger gal undoubtedly hired just for the weekend by the caterer.

"Hi, what's your name?" Dex asked.

"Christine," she answered. She had a silver tray and sort of bowed.

"No bowing allowed, Christine, we aren't royal. More like a royal pain in the arse," Dex said. "Could you please bring us three creative martinis; whatever the bartender is up for, very dry, six olives for her?"

"Yes, sir. I'll take care of it."

"Thanks."

Dex was suddenly acutely aware of his own discomfort at ordering servants about and being lord of the manor. He looked around him at the party guests and staff. A pain stabbed across his forehead, and he rubbed at it with his fingers. He had a deep longing to get back to his research.

Worse than that, he realized why. It was his escape from all of this. It was his way of justifying his wealth. If he worked hard and found a cure for Shimner's or at least an affordable drug source, he would be giving something back. It was guilt that drove him. Pure and simple.

Christine returned with the three martinis, and Dex took the tray from her. "Thank you very much, Christine, I'll take it from here."

"I'll need my tray back, sir," she said awkwardly.

"Oh, of course." Dex handed Reg a normal one-olive martini."

"Dex, you all right?" Reg gave him a puzzled look as if he sensed Dex's small inner breakthrough. Or more likely Reg wondered why he'd broken protocol and grabbed the girl's tray. "Mmm, lemon vodka. Very refreshing, Christine." Reg downed it in two gulps, popped the olive in his mouth, and set the glass back on the tray Dex held.

"Here, Reg, hand this to Babs, will you?" Dex heard the edge in his own voice. Undoubtedly he could use a drink himself. Personal insight was a pain. He got Reg to grab the six-olive wonder and helped himself to the last drink, skillfully handing the tray back to Christine. His odd gestures made the entire group stare blankly at him. Never mind. The cold, sharp bite of the martini helped his head immediately.

"Thanks again, Christine, and bring us another round when you get a chance, no hurry." Dex noticed everyone relax again as he went back into the role they all expected. As if they'd all been frozen, then resumed their movements.

All this analytical bullshit was making him nuts. He flopped down on a chair and sucked up the martini. If only he could shut off his mind for a while. If only he could find something to quiet his endless questioning and searching and justifying.

Dex took another sip of his drink and had a very clear thought. He raised one eyebrow and smiled to himself. As if in answer to his question, he looked up to see Allison Jennings walking across the lawn wearing a very, very, sexy black and fishnet one-piece swimsuit. The closer she got, the better she looked. Her light red hair was set off by the black suit and black net cover-up that opened in the breeze. Her legs, while still dotted here and there with bee-stings, were long and sleek and made him think beastly thoughts. She slow-motioned across the lawn like a movie star, dark glasses and all.

Dex had never seen a woman change clothes that fast in his entire life.

It must be the western sun in July or something, because all of a sudden Dex was hot. Very, very hot.

11

All the Way

It was dark and Allison lay on top of the sheets and listened to her stomach growl. She was starving, and hot. The air-conditioning didn't hit the third floor as well, no doubt. All that hot air rising.

Bunny was soundly asleep with a mask across her eyes. The small travel clock on the bedside table between them read 1:45. She'd dozed off for a few hours at least.

The pool had felt glorious on her bee stings, and at least she hadn't made a fool of herself swimming. She did know how to swim. She and Ethan had gone to the public pool quite a bit. It was her way of providing him with some balance to all his study time.

Even when she was young she and Rusty swam in their friends' pools, and at school. She remembered one time they'd snuck in the high school pool after hours and had quite a romp.

But Rusty and their youthful lovemaking didn't hold a candle to the heat Dex Needham and she were stirring up, which was a completely crazy thought.

Allison sat up and stretched her toes toward the cool wood floor. It was dark, but her eyes adjusted to the soft light coming through the curtains. She moved over to the window, curious what was making that much light.

The almost-full moon reflected off the water. She unlatched the window and opened it. The sound of the waves lapping gently at the shore was peaceful. The air felt good, too. She turned her body full to the light breeze and let it caress her. For one full day she'd forgotten all her troubles, and it had been wonderful.

Even the last part of the day, zany as it was, left her feeling more alive. Watching the crazy Needham men carry their torches into the dark orchard after sunset like some ancient ritualistic pagan caterpillar sacrifice only made her laugh harder.

Bunny, Dex, and even Reg and Babs sang some odd fraternal song they all knew, to the beat of Harley's Hawaiian drums. Allison had picked it up and faked it pretty well. It was hilarious, and oddly sweet. Then Harley sang some Hawaiian songs while Dex's brother played the guitar. Harley had a smooth, magical voice.

To see the Needham family go through their strange family traditions, which they undoubtedly had been doing for generations, was something she'd never experienced before. It had made her laugh and cry at the same time. Cry because her family didn't have that when she was growing up. She was tired of crying. She should laugh more.

A wave of guilt washed over her as she stood at the window. She felt the burden of her real life come back and settle itself between her shoulders. At least Ethan had sounded great on the phone. He was basically doing the same thing she was, stepping into a world completely different from what they had been living up to that point. Mr. Kerns had been reassuring, and Ethan said even the food was "totally awesome."

The chronic worry of the last ten years had worn creases in her forehead and made her feel old before her time. Just like her mother. For some reason Allison remembered seeing her mother's peaceful face after she died. But it shouldn't take death to give you some peace. Mom would have loved it here.

Why didn't her mother remarry after her husband ran off? She was alone with two kids, sure, but she was still an attractive woman for many years after. She just seemed to throw herself into working instead. Didn't she ever want a little something for herself, like companionship, or even sex? How about a bingo night at the church? Allison couldn't remember her mom doing anything at all for herself.

A chill went through Allison. She moved away and let the curtain fall back into place. She was doing the same thing. This weekend was the first time she'd let herself have any fun in the last ten years. Adult fun. Here was Rusty, remarried, having babies, taking the family to Ocean Shores for the weekend with Pamela by his side.

She held her arms across the thin silk of her gold nightgown protectively. If she didn't stop thinking about this she was going to cry. Better a ham sandwich than hysterics. She went to the closet and grabbed her swimsuit cover-up. At least she wouldn't be completely indecent if she ran into someone in the hallway. With a deep breath she buttoned the flimsy black net thing over her nightgown and slipped out the door, careful not to wake Bunny.

The servants' stairs were dark, hot, and stuffy. She fumbled for a light switch and found one, but nothing happened. The bulb must be burned out. No matter, she knew the way to the kitchen, and intended to use it. Maybe a cold beer to wash that sandwich down wouldn't hurt.

The servants' entrance to the kitchen was one of those swinging door jobs. Her bare feet padded across the cold tile floor. This was definitely where you wanted to be on a hot night. She thought about lying down naked and getting cooled off completely. A giggle escaped her as she groped her way along the counter toward the huge refrigerator at the end of the room.

Behind her she heard a rustle. She turned as a dark figure moved. Her heart beat fast, and she pulled in a gasp of air. The shadow struck a match.

"Hungry? Or are you after the family silver?"

"Damn, Dex, you scared the crap out of me." Allison watched Dex light several candles on the large kitchen table in the center of the room.

"Such language. The power is out. I'll have to turn on the generator if it doesn't come back on in twenty minutes."

" 'Scuse my French, sir. You frightened me."

"*Seulement vous si vous me donnez un baiser.*"

"What?" Allison only knew one of those words from high school French—*baiser*—to kiss.

"Nothing. What can I do for you, Allison?"

"I'm starved. If you recall, I've been distracted or stung out of every meal served so far." Allison clung to the counter edge. For some reason Dex still frightened her a little. He was very quiet and moved around the kitchen gathering candles. When he was done there were at least twelve candles perched in various areas of the room. The light danced and cast shadows across Dex's face. He looked serious.

"I had the same thought. How about a sandwich?" He moved to the industrial-sized Sub-Zero refrigerator and took out several items.

"Do you have ham and Swiss in there?"

"Sounds good. Mrs. Fisk always has a great ham on the weekends. And we have bread from a local baker: Farm Kitchen Bread. It's almost as good as European."

Allison moved closer. "Count me in."

"To tell you the truth, I usually make myself a bowl of ice cream in the middle of the night."

"Ice cream is my specialty, sir. I'll whip you up something later." No kidding it was her specialty.

"Well, ice cream is my weakness. Now you know." Dex sliced off thick slices of bread and arranged the ham and Swiss across them. Allison saw some kind of fancy mustard go on there next, out of some imported jar.

"Oh. Mustard okay?" Dex paused.

"Pile it on. No onions though. And no mayo."

"Heaven forbid. Tomatoes and lettuce?"

"Sure." Allison sat down across the table and watched Dex assemble sandwiches. He wore only a drawstring striped cotton pajama bottom and no top. Sexy. Very sexy chest. Oh no. Here she was again, alone with Dex, ham, sliced tomatoes, and ice cream.

He put her sandwich on a thick white plate and passed it over to her. Reaching back into the fridge, he pulled out two cold microbrew beers. Fat Tire Beer. The label was very artsy. There was an opener built into the wall, and he skillfully popped the tops, then handed her one. She raised the bottle to her lips and chugged a good long draw on it.

"I was going to ask if you wanted a glass, but I see that won't be necessary."

"Nope." Allison picked up her sandwich and took a large bite.

Now, once in a while food just tastes so good it's practically orgasmic, and this was one of those times. It probably helped that the food was the finest ham, the finest Swiss, the imported mustard, the hand-grown tomatoes and lettuce, and the fresh baked bread, and that she was ravenous, but it was nonetheless orgasmic. She made a sound that indicated just that. Then she washed her big bite down with another slosh of beer. Heaven.

Dexter Needham had been deliberately keeping himself in check for the last twenty minutes, but she was wearing that check thin. She was amazing and earthy and beautiful in the candlelight. The silk nightgown she wore looked so . . . touchable. He loved watching her eat. She was unpretentious, and seemed to relax him in a way no other woman ever had. He leaned back in the kitchen chair and enjoyed her.

"This is my favorite room in the house." Dex took a draw of his beer and fell easily into talking to her. "We used to dig clams off the beach and steam huge pots of them, then eat them with melted butter and garlic bread and corn on the cob. At this house things were less formal and we did more as a family."

"I can see that. This place is great. The beach is beautiful."

"Don't get me wrong, Celia and Edward and I were regular little hellions when we were kids. We got in plenty of trouble together."

"The Needham kids? No way."

"Seriously. But we love each other very much."

"I know what you mean. My brother and I are very close now. He's in the navy and I don't get to see him that much."

"As annoying as my mother is with all her party preparations, one of the reasons I cooperate is so I can hang out with my brother and sister. Time just slips away when we are over here on the island.

"So tell me, what do you do?" Dex asked. He wanted to get to know her better. He needed to, before he went any further with her. She'd better tell him quick though, because her lips were begging to be kissed again. Pretty lips. Tempting lips. He reached across the table, and with his thumb wiped mustard off the corner of her mouth. She paused, surprised.

Allison got up abruptly and put her plate in the sink. It made a clink, pottery against porcelain. Dex was startled at her quick move.

"I'm in management. It's boring."

"Well, if you could have any job instead, what would it be?"

She turned and looked at him. "What a great question! Well, I've thought about being a florist. I love flowers. I haven't actually thought about it that much. You know how it is, you trudge through your job and smile, then one day you wake up and it's ten years later?"

"I know about the ten years, but I actually like being a test-tube geek. It's exciting, believe it or not."

"I believe you."

"Hey, we better eat ice cream before it's all melted in there. Did I hear you offer up your talents as ice cream goddess?"

"You bet. Let me see what you've got, big boy." A quirky smile crossed her lips.

Dex cleared away the sandwich ingredients and pulled out an amazing assortment of ice cream toppings and flavors and other items.

"Wow, you take your ice cream seriously around here. What's your pleasure, sir?"

"To tell you the truth, I've been trying to remember this thing I used to order all the time when I was in college. Of course there was some alcohol involved on several of those occasions so my memory is poor."

"Where'd you go to college, Harvard or Princeton or something?"

"Very funny. Actually I spent two years here at the University of Washington, then transferred to MIT for four more years. Then I came back here and did my doctoral work back at the UW."

"You went to MIT?"

"Yes, but my ice cream days were spent here. Let's see. It has chocolate and vanilla, and little chocolate sprinkles, but I'm missing something."

"A black and white. Geez, for a scientist, you'd think you'd get the formula down. It's marshmallow cream. That's your missing ingredient. Hand me that scoop."

Dex dutifully handed the silver scoop to her. She went to the sink and ran hot water over it. "Good thing the water stays on when the power goes off."

"Oh, I forgot the generator. I'll be right back.

The ice cream dishes are in the second cupboard to the right of the sink."

"Get ready for the best black and white you've ever had, Dex."

Dex stepped out the back door and grabbed a flashlight from the pegboard. The utility room was cool because the floor was cement. It brought his senses back, somewhat. He went about hooking up the generator. It was noisy, but his father and brother had made some fancy modifications to the mechanism, and compared to some he'd heard, it purred like a kitten. Dex flipped the switch. Nothing happened. Damn. He zeroed the flashlight in on the side panel.

He had two choices. He could work on the generator for an hour, or go have ice cream with Allison, then tackle it.

There was something about Allison. When he was alone with her, it felt familiar. As if he'd known her for years. He wanted to protect her, and he didn't even know from what. Maybe from him.

If he was going to protect her he'd better keep his hands off her. Come to think of it, if he was going to protect *himself* he better keep his hands off her. He really didn't know her that well, and he could end up in the *National Tattletale* this time instead of just the local society pages.

Allison opened up the cupboard to a gleaming assortment of ice cream glasses. She pulled out two boat-shaped numbers and started assembling the sundaes. Normally she didn't go for ice cream. She'd reached burnout long ago. But tonight she wanted to try again. Besides, she'd dieted herself crazy in the last few weeks, and she was sick of it.

It nagged at her that Dex might have seen her in the past at the Tasty Freeze. After all, he lived in Bellevue through high school and two years of college, even if he did attend Washington Prep instead of Bellevue Central. She rummaged in the fridge and actually found a jar of marshmallow cream.

Then again, she sure didn't look anything like the girl behind the counter tonight. She was a strawberry-blond svelte socialite for all he knew. She seriously doubted he'd remember her if he'd happened to drop by the Tasty Freeze in his youth.

Allison shed her black cover-up and grabbed a butcher's apron off a kitchen hook. Reaching around her, she snapped the neck strap in place. Then she tied the long strings around her middle and back to her front to protect the pretty nightgown.

For the last forty-five minutes she'd been watching Dex Needham relax around her. He was a very cool guy for a geek.

She'd been wrestling in her head about how attracted she felt to him. No wonder she'd always wanted to meet him; he was everything she'd imagined. Sure, he was cursed with fame and fortune. But maybe they could just have a little fun together and not make it so serious. Maybe go out to dinner. Maybe have a little sex.

She felt the heat rise up her neck in her standard

blush. Ha! What the heck did she have to blush about? She was twenty-nine years old. She was seriously deprived in this area. What was the harm? Obviously Dex was a fairly stable guy with some similar issues. He was also extremely good-looking, and . . .

Allison held the spoon with marshmallow cream in a midair pause. What the hell was she thinking? She would never fit into his world. Stepping into Dex Needham's arms would be the stupidest thing she'd done in, oh, eleven years.

Dex swung open the kitchen door and came over to where Allison was concocting ice cream confections. He felt a strange tension in both of them, as if something had shifted while he was out in the garage. He didn't like that. At least they could be friends. He moved in close beside her and peered over her shoulder.

"I better learn to make this thing if it turns out to be my old favorite."

"Here, have a taste." She offered him up her finger with a blob of chocolate ice cream and white topping. He went for it.

"Oh, *oh* yeah. It was the missing marshmallow," he said with her finger still in his mouth.

Their eyes met as she slowly pulled it out. He could feel her body come alive, even without touching it.

"What happened with the generator?" Her eyes never left his.

"It didn't start." He stared into her crazy amber-gold sparking eyes without blinking.

"Do you want to monkey with it? I can put this stuff back in the freezer."

"Nope. I want to monkey with you." He got rid of the six inches separating them and slammed his mouth against hers with all the held-back intensity he possessed. She met him with twice as much, slapping the spoon she held in her other hand against his naked back as she flung her arms around him, pressing herself into his kiss. She stung his lips—and his back.

"Ouch."

They stepped apart. His breath was ragged. So was hers. Their eyes still locked.

"Oh my God," she said. "What are we doing?"

"I don't know, but let's do it again," he said. This time he drew her close, took the spoon out of her hand, and slowly kissed her full, burning lips the way he'd wanted to for the last hour. He ran his hands up her back, his mouth up her neck, and whispered in her ear.

"I want you to feed me another finger full of marshmallow."

"Kinky," she said. She reached behind them and swiped into the dish.

This time he held on to her hand and licked every bit of marshmallow cream and chocolate off her index finger. A moan escaped her. He pulled at her apron strings and removed the apron in three moves.

As he removed the apron, the thin strap of one side of her nightgown slid down her shoulder, revealing her breast. Allison stood there looking completely delicious. Dex went straight for the jar of marshmallow cream. He piled a large finger full on her left nipple, which was already hard to his touch. With a smooth movement he lifted her round, lovely breast into his mouth.

She dug her fingers into his shoulder and moaned heavily this time. From that moment on things went even crazier. It was like the dam finally broke between them. He crushed her mouth with hot, wet kisses. She gave them back twice as wild.

"Lock that freakin' door!" she gasped between kisses.

Without letting go of her he maneuvered them to the door and twisted the bolt shut. The room glowed with moonlight through the window.

Against the wall he stripped off what was left of her gown and let it fall to the floor. Then he traveled her body like a road map with his mouth. Every hill, every valley, ever little bump in the road. He gently parted her legs and moved his fingers against her, in her, around her heat and desire, and his touch made her scream out as she felt herself release. He put his mouth over her and she screamed again.

She couldn't take it again. She pulled him up. Allison crushed her naked breasts, wet from his mouth, against his bare chest. His mouth sought hers, and his hands pulled her body hard against him. She ground her hips like some crazy woman who hadn't had sex in way, way too long. She didn't care anymore about what she should and shouldn't be doing. She wanted him right now.

Through his thin pajama pants she could feel the heat of his erection like a blazing fire. She wrapped one leg against him and ground harder against him. "Oh *my*," she mumbled through his kiss as she heard a deep wrenching moan escape from the depths of him. "Dex, Dex."

She reached down and undid the tie of his pajama bottoms. He caught them briefly before they fell and grabbed something out of the pocket.

"Wow, you are one prepared man," she said breathlessly. "Give that to me."

"Since you got here."

"Shhh." Allison ripped the condom package open and paused. She lowered herself and let the tip of her tongue touch him. He growled and moaned and leaned his arms against the wall to steady himself. She ran her hands up the hard muscles of his thighs and teased him with her fingertips . . . and her tongue . . . and her mouth until he was even harder.

"*Allison.*" A dark sound escaped him and formed into her name. She decided he'd had enough, and besides she must have him inside her right now, now, right this minute. She then had the extreme pleasure of rolling the condom slowly down Dex's long, beautiful, throbbing erection.

Dex drew her against him, and before she knew

what was happening she was sitting on the smooth wooden table that seemed to be just the perfect height for Dex's evil plan to push her over the edge just one more time. One more. His mouth on her breasts was more heat than she could stand. She was burning. She was caramelized sugar under his touch.

Then just as she was going over the edge yet another time, he pulled her down on him and slid inside her. She exploded around him and clawed his back. He had perfect control. He waited. He moved hard inside her as she rode against him into a wet wave of pleasure. He moved slow and let her feel it even more. She could not think or stop or do anything but move against the heat of Dex's body all around her and inside her.

When she thought she might cry from the pleasure, he suddenly arched back and pressed hard and deep inside her. He growled low like an animal as he let go, and she felt the throbbing so deep inside her, she did cry out. She pulled him as close as their bodies would go. Her legs were wrapped tight around him and they let the waves of their passion roll over and over them until they quieted.

His first movement was to pull her into a kiss. His hands slid up her back and into her hair. He kissed her again and again until she felt him throb inside her once more.

"We have to find a bed. Right now. I have one." His voice was raspy.

Allison laughed a quiet laugh and ran her hands

over his broad shoulders. "Yes, let's do that. I know you have a bed. I've been on it. Do it. Find us that bed."

"We will be required to move from this position," he said as he thumbed her nipples. He stroked under her breasts and brought them to little hard peaks again. He didn't want to stop touching her. He slid out of her and ran his hand between her legs, brushing her most sensitive spot with his thumb and diving into her incredible wet heat with his fingers. She held his shoulders and leaned her head down, watching him touch her, moaning at each stroke. He found that incredibly sexy, that she watched.

He wasn't through with her. He felt his erection rise again and slipped his hand down to remove the condom. He moved away from her to regain his senses, as if that could be done at this point. She looked beautiful in the light coming through the kitchen window. Her skin was pale as moonlight. Like cream.

He took another step back. He threw the condom in the trash under the sink and stood against the counter, just watching her. She leaned back on the table and she lifted her head up to look at him. Her hair had fire streaks from the candlelight, and her eyes sparkled.

"Go to my bed. I'll clean up in here." He moved and grabbed her gown off the floor in the corner, where this had all started. Close to her again, he held the gown until she raised her arms, then slid it over her head and down her lovely body. His hands smoothed the silk across her breasts and down her hips. "Go now." His voice sounded odd and deep and full of the desire he couldn't crawl out of. He wanted her again.

She slid off the table and let the gown fall across her body. The swinging servants' door opened into the darkest side of the house. She made her way to the back stairs and let her eyes adjust. Her body tingled all over. The thought of having him again made her obey his command without pausing. She knew the way to his room. She would be waiting for him in his bed.

Dex ran his hand over his forehead and through his hair. He breathed deeply. He had never wanted a woman this bad. He fit into her as if they were made of the same mold. Bringing her to climax, feeling her body fall headlong into pleasure, he could drown in her. He felt supremely . . . alive.

In ten minutes he opened the door to his bedroom quietly and locked it behind him. He saw her there, lying naked against the bare sheet, no cover. She reached her arms up to him. He stripped and stepped over to her, lying down with her, gathering her into him. In one moment he had opened her like a flower and pushed inside of her tropical, wet heat again. He was going to make love to her again and again. She wrapped around him like a wild orchid vine and pushed him deeper into her perfume. All was lost, and he let his mind split into a thousand stars as he moved inside her sweetness.

12

As Time Goes By

"Thank you very much." Naomi handed Harry Pinkerton a very fat envelope.

"Always a pleasure, Mrs. Needham." Harry turned on his heel and slipped out the door.

That man was a snake. But sometimes you need a snake.

Naomi opened the metal brad on the manila envelope and slid out the contents over the top of her desk. She spread out the photos, and they caught the morning light. Naomi picked one up and turned it into the shadows. Apparently Miss Jennings felt the need to scale the outside of the house in her underwear? And there was Dex pulling her in the window. Now, wouldn't that make terrific tabloid fodder? It gave her a sudden headache thinking of Harry Pinkerton with this in his possession. She'd just beat him to the punch and make an offer for the negatives.

There were several pages of typed information. She scanned them and picked out the most interesting details. Married, divorced, had a child very young: no degree, no skill, and assistant manager at the Bellevue Tasty Freeze?

Naomi rubbed her right temple. This woman was after money. She was dirt-poor, and her only assets were the ones she'd used to entice Dex into the bedroom.

Well, it certainly wasn't too late to fix this. A big fat check would take care of this one, just as it took care of Mimi Burkheimer. Of course, it helped that Naomi had walked in on Mimi and Geoffrey Upton groping each other. Obviously Mimi's goals were not to love and cherish Dex. Well, the Uptons were welcome to her.

Naomi set down the papers and opened the middle drawer to pull out her checkbook when another photo caught her eye. She slid it out from under the others. It was Allison's son . . . what was his name? She checked the papers again. Ethan.

Something about the photo made her uneasy. She stared at it and ran her fingertip along the edges of the image. It showed the boy holding up some kind of certificate. Where did Pinkerton get these things? The little article said something about a science award.

She set it down again, carefully folded back her checkbook, and picked up her pen. Something . . . she started to write *Allison Jennings* on the first line. Something was . . . Naomi lifted her gaze up and stared straight ahead to her bookshelf. She stared a very long time. Then she set her pen down and closed the checkbook.

"Oh my God, it's *you*!"

Dex opened his eyes and instead of a warm female body beside him he saw Allison with the sheet wrapped around her, standing in the corner next to a mahogany Chippendale highboy. She looked odd. His mind was fuzzy from no sleep.

"Allison?"

"That's right, nice of you to remember me at last!"

"What the . . . wait a minute." Dex rubbed his face and pulled the skewed blanket around his waist. He sat up and tried to get some blood flowing to his brain. He grabbed the glass of water beside his bed and took a large gulp. "Now what exactly is going on, Allison, what did I miss after making love all night and falling asleep with you in my arms? Come and sit down over here and talk to me."

"No way. You . . . you . . ."

"What did I do, whisper someone else's name in my sleep? It's probably a cat."

"You actually don't remember me. I don't believe you. How could you go over every inch of a woman's body and not remember you'd been there before?"

Dex stared at her. He was pretty sure the one beer they'd had last night had worn off, yet here she was yammering like a drunk. Damn it. How did he get himself into these situations? Well, that was no secret. He lusted, he acted, and he forgot to think.

"I have no idea what you are talking about. Let's just calm down and have a rational discussion, shall we?" Dex held up a hand to slow her down.

Allison readjusted her sheet wrap and pulled herself up tall. "Let me just refresh your very poor memory, Mr. Needham. It was summer. You and your frat-boy buddies came in to the Bellevue Tasty Freeze just before I was supposed to close up. The rest of them were pretty high, but you seemed different. A little drunk, but not like them.

"I made you all black and whites. Marshmallow cream. Ring a bell? You and I hit it off. I'd just split up with my husband, Rusty, you'd just broken up with some girl. We talked. We had a few beers. Your buddies took off and left you with me. You were in no shape to drive. We ended up back at my place. Wait, you said your name was Skip. *Skippy*, you lying son of a bitch!"

Dex was sitting straight up now. A horrible bolt of recognition was creeping up from his gut to his head.

"You said you'd call me the next day. You said you went to the UW. I never saw you again."

"Allison, that was eleven years ago.

"Oh, so you admit it! Very nice of you, Skip."

"That was an old nickname. They used to call me Skippy because I was so squeaky clean, like the Skippy peanut butter kid. I wasn't lying."

"What did they do, make a bet you could get me in the sack?"

Dexter had a full-blown flashback of Allison's breasts in a uniform, and him unbuttoning it. "Allison, I remember. I do. I remember we were kind of drunk, and that we both talked about how we never did this before, and that you cried over your break-up, and I . . . comforted you."

"How could you make love to a woman and not remember you'd been there before?"

"Did you?" Dex was getting defensive. "It took you till morning."

"That's beside the point, at least I remembered. I knew there was something about you. But I blocked you out. I thought we had a really special connection that day, and then you never called me again. I felt cheap and used. Did you know from that point on I never got involved with anyone again?"

"I left for MIT a week later. I spent the next four years there finishing my master's degree. I tried to find you before I left, I called the Tasty Freeze, and the manager refused to give me your name. I didn't know your last name, and I wasn't too sure on your first. I thought it was Louise."

"Bullshit, Skippy, you never tried to find me. I was just a roll in the hay."

"You'll have to ask the manager. I can't prove anything to you, Allison, I give you my word."

"We've been through four managers since then. Just so you know everything, Dex, I'm still there. I still work there. I have a son I had after Rusty and I split up, and I'm dirt-poor. I've known Bunny since high school because, guess what, even poor girls can attend Bellevue Central."

Dex got up and let the blanket drop. He moved toward her.

"Get away!"

"My pants are in that dresser."

"Oh."

"Allison, I was twenty-two."

"Well, guess what, I was eighteen, a year out of high school. And I liked you, and we had fabulous sex in my apartment, and you took a powder. You skipped out, Skippy. But worst of all, you have no memory of me!"

"That is just not fair, Allison, I felt like I knew you the minute I saw you." Dex was standing very close to her, rummaging in his drawer for boxer shorts and anything he could find for clothes. He pulled things on him until he had enough to feel less vulnerable. "Allison, I'm sorry. I really am." He reached over to touch her hand.

"*Oooooh* don't. Just don't. I'm very confused."

"Come on, be fair here. You didn't remember me either. Did you?"

"What do you think? That I came here to get even with you after all these years?"

Not until she said the words out loud. Then he stopped and thought about it. Stranger things had happened to him. He took a step backward.

"Oh that's *rich*. Yes, I'm just some psycho-bitch that plotted for the last eleven years to come back here and what . . . sleep with you? Meet your family? What . . . kill you?"

Dex took another step back.

"You know what? It's you that's psycho, Dexter Needham. I'm leaving now. I'm going to my room. I was dragged here by Bunny to meet rich men and improve my lot in life. So excuse me if I go mingle with the rest of the loonies because you are just too *whacked* for me." Allison bunched the sheet up around her, took three steps, clicked open the lock, and flung open the door.

"By the way, I poisoned the marshmallow cream, and you should be experiencing a lingering death quite soon. But don't call me, I'll be busy."

With this absurd sentence Dex watched her slam the door behind her.

"Miss Jennings?"

Allison startled to hear her name and turned abruptly. She clutched at the sheet.

"Naomi. Well, that's just perfect." Allison smoothed her hair, but by the feel of it, it was hopeless.

"I'd appreciate a word with you. My office is on the second floor, east side, that end." Naomi pointed. She had on a white double-breasted jacket with brass buttons and navy blue slacks, kind of a quasi-military look. Her face was stone. Kind of a quasi-marble statue deal.

"You'll excuse me if I dress first." Allison just

did not give a shit about Naomi Needham at the moment.

"Please do. I'll be waiting." Naomi turned sharply and marched down the hall.

"*Fuck me.*" Allison mumbled, and dragged herself to the blue room and Bunny. The door was still unlocked, thank God.

Allison stood by the bed and shook her friend. "Bunny, wake up. My life is crap."

Bunny peeked out from under her mask. "Uhhhhh. Go away."

"I did. I'm back. I slept with Dex."

"Well, we all knew that was coming, so good for you." Bunny rolled away from Allison and pulled the covers up around her shoulders.

"Then I remembered it wasn't the first time. And I told him. Actually I screamed at him, and I told him where I work, and that I have no money, and I ran into his mother on the way out the door. She wants to see me in her office. Right now. I think I'm in trouble."

Bunny rolled back over quickly and pulled up her mask. "Now things are getting interesting. Naomi Needham can't do anything to you, Allison; remember that. She's not the principal. She just feels like she is."

"Oh, that's the other thing. I think Dex thinks I came here to kill him."

"Did you?"

Allison sat on the bed next to Bunny. "Yep, I did. I knew all along that he was the cute college boy I had a one-night encounter with who never called me again. I came here to seek my revenge."

"That boy? I even remember. That was your rebound fling from breaking up with Rusty. You were really mad at that guy for never calling you back. Are you telling me that was Dexter Needham himself?" Bunny pulled herself up so they both sat against the headboard of the twin bed.

"In the flesh. I remembered this little birthmark on his ass. When we woke up this morning his extremely sexy behind was exposed—just the way it was back then. Him, in my bed, eleven years ago, same butt."

"So you like had sex all night and never remembered until you saw his ass?"

"Yes. Weird, isn't it? You'd think you'd remember other stuff."

"We've all changed a great deal in eleven years, Allison."

"Apparently."

"Was he good?"

"Unbelievable."

"Wow. Who would have figured?" Bunny giggled.

"I got a little crazy. I yelled at him for not calling me back eleven years ago. Then sort of made a joke and suggested I came here to get even with him. Up until then he was doing pretty well, then he sort of looked like he was going to pass out, and he got dressed really fast. I stalked out the door and ran into Mrs. N."

"Oops. Dragon Lady."

"What shall I wear to see the Dragon Lady in her office? And what the hell does she want anyhow? Do I get detention for not having a hall pass?"

"Wear red, and be sure and sew a scarlet *A* on your chest. She probably wants to dissuade you from having a relationship with her son. You've no doubt been judged unacceptable in her eyes for some reason. Perhaps your hair wasn't quite right." Bunny reached up and fingered Allison's wild locks. "Ehhh sticky. Looks like you two had a hell of a time last night."

"Did you know Dex used to go by *Skippy*?" Allison slid off the bed and went to look in the dresser mirror. Bride of Frankenstein had nothing on her.

"Yep. Skippy. Goody-two-shoes. They all had nicknames like that. It was a frat game."

"I'm getting showered up. See what you come up with for an outfit. I'm not feeling too wallflower-like today. I think the Needhams owe me an apology. Both Dex and his mother."

"You might get one out of Dex, but Naomi would rather eat worms than admit any wrongdoing on her part."

Allison turned on the shower and let the water warm up. Of course she had no right to be mad at Dex all these years later. They were just kids. She knew that, but the rush of remembering how hurt she'd felt back then had caught her by surprise. She'd been hurt and mad. Of course the fact that Rusty had cheated on her and moved out that very week had something to do with all the emotion surrounding that time.

Maybe it was she who should apologize to Dex. That depended on if she believed his story about trying to find her. And what about school vacations, and when he got back from MIT four years later? He could have found her at the Tasty Freeze any time after that.

Who was she kidding? She was a waitress at the time. He probably came back and went right into high-society dating. He'd remembered her all right, years ago he remembered her—a scraggly waitress with a run-down apartment, divorced at eighteen. Just not Needham material.

Allison got into the shower and washed away her night of pleasure. She washed away any silly notions or ideas she might have entertained during the hours she and Dex spent making love. It was the Fourth of July and she was independent again.

Naomi Needham sat behind the orderly Queen Anne desk and actually looked nervous. Allison had to laugh—inside. Here she was with a major case of jumping-bean stomach. That's what she and Ethan called it when either of them got jittery about anything. Suddenly she missed Ethan.

"Please sit down, Miss Jennings. Would you like a cup of coffee?"

She did; she wanted one bad. But she'd be

damned if she'd take one from Naomi. Besides, Allison figured, she'd probably spill it down her own front, she was shaking so badly. This was ridiculous. She sat uncomfortably in the chair offered and pulled at her skirt to cover up more of her thighs. This red suit idea might not have been so good. She sat directly across from Mrs. Needham.

"What is it you want to talk about, Mrs. Needham?"

"I'll get right to the point."

"Please do." What the hell was this all about? There was no way Mrs. Needham knew about her past with Dex. He hadn't run to Mom, for heaven sakes, and when she'd passed his bathroom a few minutes ago she'd distinctly heard the shower running.

Naomi put her elbows on the desk and laced her fingers together. "I'm very protective of my children. You saw the article in the *Bellevue Register*, I assume?"

"Yes. Look, Mrs. Needham, I'm not from the press. I genuinely like Dex. At least I think I do, I've only known him a day." The fact made Allison's cheeks feel hot. How could she have let that man make crazy love to her after one day? She felt sick. And if that wasn't enough, Mrs. Needham was going to rub her nose in it for sure.

"And it seems you've become quite intimate in that short period of time."

"Which is really none of your business, Mrs. Needham, if I might say so." Allison was feeling defensive about her own behavior for obvious reasons. But she also hadn't had much sleep.

"Well, that depends. I've done a pretty thorough investigation of you."

"You what?"

Naomi waved her off. "Don't act so shocked. It's standard procedure in our family. Think about it. Would you want some con artist going after your son?"

"I am not a con artist."

"No, but it says here you are a very underpaid, divorced young lady with a child to support who has managed to get herself invited to our home through an old friend. Your car is broken down, your rent was late, and your son looks to be quite bright. He'll need things. Better schools. Things you can't possibly provide for him. Perhaps you came here with a specific goal in mind." Naomi had been reading from some papers on her desk. Allison saw a pile of photographs beside them.

She felt her cheeks go flaming hot. She was getting very, *very* angry. But like most times when something hit her in the jaw, she got deadly calm. Nope, Allison was not a woman prone to panic.

"Perhaps you should know that Dex is perfectly aware of these things. I told him myself." Allison's voice went steely.

"Dexter has a tendency to overlook people's flaws." Naomi's voice went even more metallic.

"Exactly what is it you want from me, Mrs. Needham?"

"Actually, I was going to ask you that question. What is it you want from Dex?"

"At the moment, sex." Allison cocked her head and stared straight at Naomi.

"Am I supposed to think more of you for your outburst of supposed honesty?"

"I don't care what you think, Mrs. Needham. But you might want to start considering what others think of you. It's none of your business who Dex dallies with. He is a grown man. As far as I am concerned, this little 'interview' is not only rude, but completely ridiculous."

"In a family such as ours every member's actions have consequences. We need to protect our assets."

"Protect your *assets*? You know, I'm not sure what I feel about Dex, except for one thing. I do pity him having you for a mother."

Naomi's face went one shade cooler, but she didn't seem fazed. She unlaced her fingers and picked up a pen from the desk. With very careful deliberation, Naomi fingered the handle end of the pen and spoke. "Have you and Dex met before?"

"How the hell would you know that? Unless he told you?" Now Allison was *really* mad. She jumped out of the damn uncomfortable chair and paced one end of the office. This family really was too much. She should have known better. It was unbelievable to think that Dex just ran on up here to Mommy and told her his troubles. He probably really believed she'd known all along and was back to get revenge.

How could these people think she wanted her own name smeared in some paper? She didn't even know how to think along the lines these crazy-ass people's minds traveled. Well, she had her own son to protect, and she'd had just about enough of the Needham family. The room started to spin so Allison braced herself against the back wall bookcase.

"So it's true."

Allison closed her eyes and didn't turn to speak to Naomi. "Frankly, Mrs. Needham, I don't give a damn about your opinions, or your son at the moment. I'm not very impressed with the Needham family hospitality."

"How much? What's your price? I can't have this business left unfinished, under the circumstances." Naomi opened a checkbook.

Allison would have answered her with some very crude words about where to stick her money, but she wasn't listening anymore. She was staring at an old photograph in a silver filigree frame. She picked it up and stared hard.

A strange, horrible rush of fear shot through her fingertips, down her arms, and into her legs. She could hardly stand up. She slowly turned and looked straight at Naomi. Naomi was staring back at her, having risen from behind the desk. The picture fell from her hands and clattered onto the dark wood floor. Glass shattered.

Allison ran. She ran from the room, she ran down the hallways, up the stairs, and burst into the room where Bunny stood.

"What the hell happened?" Bunny rushed to her.

Allison started to cry. "Bunny, I can't talk. Just lend me all the money you have on you. I have to leave. Right now."

For once, Bunny didn't question her. She went to her bed and emptied out her handbag, pulled bills from her wallet, and put them in Allison's hand, holding on to her for a moment.

"I'll call you a cab."

"Have him meet me at the end of the driveway." Allison stuffed the bills in her jacket pocket and kicked off the high heels she'd put on. She pulled on her tennis shoes and grabbed her wallet, her big straw bag, her dark glasses, and a hat. "I'll get the rest of my stuff from you later."

"I love you, Alli."

"I know, Bunny. I'll call you." Allison took one look out the door and down the hall. She had a clear shot and she made it to the servants' stairs, down to the first floor, and out to the kitchen. Several staff members turned when she entered the room.

She paused for only a second to look around the kitchen at the stunned catering staff. In the stark daylight she felt as if she must have dreamed last night.

Then she turned and went out the outside door. She knew the way from here. She ran as far as she could until she had to slow down to catch her breath. No one was looking for her. When she slowed up the impact hit her. Tears streamed down her face. She tried to stop, but a pain rushed through her and made her sob out loud.

She reached the end of the drive, with its tall, stately poplars on each side reaching out to each other, forming a natural arch.

In her purse she found a tissue. The day was already starting to heat up, but the shade from the trees made her shiver. Or something made her shiver. Maybe the fact that her whole world had just shattered into pieces made her shiver.

The taxi came sooner than she expected. Within twenty minutes she was at the ferry terminal. In the ladies' room she splashed water on her face and took out a small comb. Combing your hair when you've fallen apart has such a strange, comforting feeling.

She started to cry again but stopped herself by splashing on more water and putting a damp paper towel across her eyes. "*Take a deep breath, honey. Breathe it out.*" That's what her mother would say when Allison would cry over some crisis or another. Like the fact her mother was dying of cancer and leaving her alone to raise her little brother.

She knew this feeling. Despair. Pain. Like an old wool coat you have to keep wearing even though it's heavy and scratches at your skin because you can't get a new one.

On the ferry Allison sipped at the tea she'd bought. Peppermint. It was too hot to drink and it burned her lips. She stared out at the waves. Gulls chased the ferry and danced beside them in the air.

How could this be true? How could she not see? It had been the same week—the very same week she'd been with Rusty—it had been their last days together. And then in a moment of weakness after she and Rusty had broken up, she'd flung herself into another man's arms for comfort.

How could she go all these years and not see that Rusty wasn't Ethan's father? How could she not see the lack of resemblance? Sure, Ethan looked like her side of the family, so much like her brother Ben, but even so.

How could Dexter Needham be the father of her child?

13

It Had To Be You

Dex Needham picked up the coffee Mrs. Fisk had brought him and took a very long sip. He stared out the window of his mother's office to the gray morning fog. He sure as hell wasn't in the mood for one of her lectures, so she'd better make it quick.

After Allison had left he'd showered and thought and gone over the details of her story with his usual fine-tooth comb. He remembered that night very well. She was pretty then, but she wasn't stunning like she was now. They'd talked about the music on the jukebox, made some jokes, and hit it off. She'd told him about her break-up with her husband. He remembered being shocked she'd been married so early. He'd been extremely attracted to her, and somewhat drunk.

If he remembered right he himself had recently ended a nowhere relationship at the time. One of those social connection type relationships that was convenient for both him and the girl—college functions, charity balls, she needed a date and he was pressured into it. Carol Stottlemeyer, daughter of a family friend.

When he'd told her he was leaving for MIT, Carol had acted like they'd been engaged. He'd disappointed her. He remembered talking all that over with Allison that long-ago night.

He also remembered her fifth-floor walk-up apartment and what a bad part of town it was in. To him she was a woman of the world. She'd gotten married in high school, her mother had died if he recalled right, and she was taking care of her teenage brother, who was staying with friends that weekend.

He'd felt sorry for her, and she'd comforted him as well. In some ways he'd remembered her forever, because he had never felt anything as real before or after. Ever. That night was like a secret he'd carried through empty relationships—like Mimi. Like all of them.

Had she known all along? Was she some crazy woman back to get her revenge? Dex took another drag of coffee and put the cup and saucer down on his mother's desk. He really didn't believe that was true. Every fiber of his being knew that wasn't true. He just needed time to sort it all out. Time to get his head cleared.

Where was his mother? He was going to find Allison and have it out with her. They'd gotten tangled up in the past, and the present had been brushed aside. So what if they'd been together once before?

Why *didn't* he find her when he got back? Dex knew he had tried to find her before he left, but since he was leaving, he didn't try hard enough. Then when he returned he remembered getting caught up in his graduate work back at the UW and throwing himself into studies to escape from everything. He'd probably just given up. Dex looked at the floor and saw a tiny glimmering shard of glass. He bent to pick it up. His mother must have broken something.

"Sorry to keep you waiting, dear."

Dex straightened up. His mother looked flushed.

"Mrs. Fisk left you a cup of coffee," Dex said. He put the glass shard on the desk. "Look, Mother, whatever this is, can it wait? I'm not in the mood for much today."

"I'm afraid it can't wait, Dex." Naomi shut the door behind her.

Allison set her pencil down on her desk. The phone recording had given so much information it took her three times through to write it all down. She'd have to read it to believe it. DNA testing through the mail. She scanned her notes again:

> *Samples are obtained of the child and alleged father by rubbing a cheek cell swab on the inside of the mouth. DNA can also be taken from hair, tissue, or dried biological fluids such as blood or saliva.*

Biological fluid. Damn it! She should have grabbed that condom out of the kitchen trash. Ecchh. Maybe not. Allison read the information carefully. *Complete test kit, results in five to seven days, two hundred five dollars*. Now where the hell was she going to get that? How ironic. She didn't have the funds to find out if her son was the biological offspring of the richest man on the West Coast.

This just had to be a mistake. Ethan walked like Rusty. He had a Rusty way about him. He just had to be Rusty's son.

Allison felt herself getting extremely upset again. She stood up and went to look out the window.

Just that moment, huge fireworks splashed the night sky with brilliant color. Like lightning gone artsy. The east windows in the living area had a peek-a-boo view of Seattle Center, and this was the time of year she felt it paid off.

Most years she and Ethan had stayed up late, made popcorn, and watched grown men burn up thousands of dollars to make sparkles in the sky. She loved it, though, the little traditions they had developed. They did have traditions.

She blew her nose again and pitched the hundredth Kleenex toward the trash basket. It bounced off and rolled on the floor. At least there was Kleenex in the house for once.

Allison missed Ethan so badly. She'd called and left a message for him but probably the science camp crew had devised some rocket display and he'd forgotten all about her. Well, he'd be flying back tomorrow in the care of Mr. Kerns, so there wasn't much she could do but get ready for his return.

His return—to a completely altered life. She sniffed. She felt like complete hell. Pathetic mommy. Things were such a mess. Allison got up, tightened her oversized chenille robe belt, and shuffled toward the kitchen, one fuzzy Bugs Bunny slipper at a time, dropping tissues as she blotted tears away again.

She needed a good warm carbohydrate moment. A day of strange eating had made her want her own comfort food. The fridge light was burned out but she could see leftover macaroni and cheese in a Chinese bowl. *Now we're talking*. She'd bake that back to life with some potato chips on top and a little ketchup on the side. There was one last generic root beer in there, too. Boy, she'd better go shopping before Ethan got back.

The phone rang and made her jump. She smacked her head on the fridge. Rubbing the spot on her head, she grabbed the wall-mounted kitchen extension and pulled the spiral cord long so she could reach the macaroni project again.

"Hello?"

"Alli, it's me, Bunny. What the hell happened? Dex left, he looked like a ghost. Naomi's as jumpy as a cat on a hot tin roof. What did you do, read the old girl the riot act? Throw a pie in her face?"

Allison laughed. "Bunny, you always know what to say to make me feel better." She wished that were really true. With her Bugs Bunny–slippered foot she slammed the fridge door shut. She set the macaroni bowl on the stove and turned on the oven. The tea kettle was cold. She stretched to the sink and refilled it, popped it back on the burner, and cranked up the dial. Tea always helped.

"What's all the racket?"

"I'm making myself a cup of tea—and reheating macaroni and cheese."

"Man, things must be bad. Are you putting chips on it?"

"If I can reach them. Hold on." Allison let the receiver drop on the ugly plaid kitchen carpet, ran for the junk food drawer and lucked out with one lunchbox-sized bag of Ruffles. Hiking the phone back under her chin, she scrunched up the chips before she opened them.

"Got 'em. I'm sprinkling chips now." Allison popped open the bag and flung the contents on the top of the macaroni. "How many times have we talked for like four hours straight on the phone while we cooked or whatever, Bunny?"

"So many times. I think we did ten hours when I got pregnant with Patricia."

"And when I got pregnant with Ethan. Oh, Bunny," Allison was flooded with the memory of that time. She dropped the chip bag on the floor and went to the wall where the phone hung. She slumped to the ground, digging for a tissue that hadn't been used in her big robe pocket.

"Just tell me Ethan is okay. You're starting to scare me."

"Ethan is fine. It's really complicated."

"How complicated can it be? We can fix it. Do you want me to come over?"

"No, you should enjoy the rest of the weekend. Trish needs you there. Family comes first."

"You are family, Alli; you are my stubborn friend. Well, I'm not going to listen to you anymore, sweetie. We are going to work together and get your life to a better place. It's been too long since we solved each other's problems."

"Honestly, Bunny, there is nothing you can do in person at the moment. When you come back I'll bring Ethan over and we'll get in the hot tub."

"You're crying."

"Am not." Allison blew her nose again.

"If you don't tell me right this minute I'm coming over."

"There's a good chance Dexter Needham is Ethan's biological f-a-a-a-ther," Allison broke down and wailed into the phone.

"*What?* Are you kidding?"

"N-n-n-o. I'm not." She mopped her face with her sleeve, out of tissues, and took several deep breaths. "Remember what I said about Dex being the college boy I spent one night with the week after Rusty and I broke up?"

"Oh my God," Bunny gasped. Then there was silence on the phone line.

Allison could hear Bunny's mind catching up with the story. The memory of how they couldn't believe she'd gotten pregnant from just one slip-up with Rusty. It just had to have been Rusty. She'd used nothing with Rusty. They'd gone all teenage and crazy. But with Skippy-Dex she'd been super careful and used her diaphragm that one night . . . one night with Dexter Needham.

"It can't be true, Bunny, it just can't. But I saw a picture of Dex in Naomi's office—from when he was little. He looked just like Ethan. And I looked in Naomi's eyes and I don't know . . . it was like she *knew*. Now I'm so confused."

"Alli, listen. Dexter left. Do you get what I'm saying? I think he might be coming there. It sure looks like the shit hit the fan from this side. Like I said, Naomi is . . . upset." Bunny's voice had real concern in it.

"He wouldn't. He'd never believe it just like that. What the hell am I going to do? This would just kill Rusty. He's been Ethan's dad for ten years." Allison sobbed again.

"Honey, lay low. Don't say anything until you know for sure."

"The stupid test costs two hundred dollars."

"Methinks the Needham clan will be picking up this tab, hon, don't worry. We'll get my lawyer on it. But first we need facts. There's no use going on spinning out until you've got facts. Do you hear me?"

"Yes, you're right, but no lawyers, Bunny. I need to get the facts, that's all. I can do that without anyone knowing. I just need a little piece of Dexter. His blood will do at this point. Can I just stick him with a pin? It would make me feel better."

Bunny laughed a trying-too-hard laugh. "Sure, stick it to him. All men deserve a prick now and then. Or is that all men *are* pricks now and then?"

Allison smelled an odd smell and she looked up to see the burner with the macaroni bowl on it glowing red-hot. "Oh shit Bunny, I turned on the wrong burner. Call me when you get back. Thank you for being a good friend."

"Okay, don't worry—one step at a time. Go turn off the stove, you dope."

"Bye." Allison flung the phone back on the hook, turned off the burner, and grabbed two oven mitts.

She carefully picked up the bowl.

"*Owwww*!" Searing heat shot through the mitts in all their worn out thin spots and burned into her hands. She dropped the bowl on the carpet, threw off the mitts, and stuck her hands under the faucet, turning on the cold water with her upper arm.

The doorbell rang.

No. Just no.

She turned her head toward the sound of the door and saw a circle of smoke and flames coming up from the floor. The bowl had cracked in half and caught the carpet on fire!

"Allison?" Now there was pounding. "Allison, I smell smoke. Open this door!" The commanding, deep, formerly very sexy voice of Dexter Needham boomed from the hallway.

She froze. Her mind couldn't grasp what to do. Then she turned and grabbed a dishtowel, soaked it with water, and flung it at the fire. The smoke alarm went off. Dex broke through the door. She heard the splinter of the chain lock breaking off the wood.

Dex bypassed the smoldering mess on the floor and ran straight toward her. She heard a scream come out of her mouth. He ripped at her robe and tore it off her.

"Let me go!" she screamed again.

"*You're on fire!*" By this time he had thrown the robe on the floor and stomped out the burning fabric. She looked down to see the edge of her hem singed along at least six inches. Damn, that was her favorite robe. Now she was standing in her smoky kitchen in a ratty faded blue flannel nightgown with a horrible beeping alarm giving her a really, really bad headache.

He grabbed her kitchen stool and reached the smoke alarm, removing the battery. Thank God.

"Let's get some air in here." Dex stepped around her and forced open the difficult kitchen window. It only opened in July when the wood dried out. During the rainy season it was impossible. She watched him muscle the thing into a good two-foot gap. Then he went around and opened every other window he could find.

Allison bent over the stinking carpet and picked up the wet dishtowel with her fingertips. Underneath, the bowl had split clean in half and her macaroni was all over the floor. Each bowl half had started its own little fire—an hourglass-shaped burn revealed itself as she cleaned up. The damn bowl was still hot. She flung it into the sink fast. The pain of the burns on her hands came to life and she ran some cold water on them again.

"Let me see those." Dex was suddenly right next to her at the sink.

"It's not bad," she said.

He held her hands, palm up, and examined them. "Have you got a first aid kit?"

"We've got some stuff. In the bathroom, under the sink." She couldn't believe she'd just said that. Who knew what shape her bathroom was in? But at this moment she didn't feel so hot and she obeyed him when he pointed her to the kitchen nook and told her to sit. A chill came over her without her robe.

Dex followed a very interesting trail of used Kleenexes to her tiny bathroom. It had maroon and pink tile work that had seen better days. He noticed her tufted chenille toilet cover with a rose design on it.

He creaked open the small under-sink cabinet and rummaged to find something he could use for a burn. She had a shoebox marked FIRST AID, and inside was an old Ace bandage, a few cartoon Band-Aids, and a couple of tubes of antibiotic ointment. He brought it up in the light and found some burn cream—a sample size. That would have to do. She did have gauze and tape, thank goodness.

This was it, he remembered with a little jolt. If he

was going to get DNA samples, he was in the place to find them. Toothbrushes. He had the glass sample slides in his pocket. He opened the medicine cabinet and saw one pink adult-sized toothbrush and one that looked like Anakin from the newest *Star Wars* movie. Dex chuckled to himself. He shut the mirror without taking them out. He better get her hands taken care of first. Then he'd deal with the DNA sample mess.

She was pale, sitting in the dim light of the kitchen nook; too pale. He searched the living room and found an old quilt on the sofa. Dex came over to her and wrapped it around her shoulders. "Here, pull this tight around you." He sat down next to her and laid out all the medical supplies.

"Give me your hand." He took her hand when she didn't move.

He got the medicine on her palm and did a simple gauze wrap. She had a very zoned-out look on her face. She must be in mild shock.

"Do you have any bourbon?"

She shook her head no and kept staring at him.

He did her other hand carefully, then got up to look in the fridge: generic root beer, generic yogurt, and generic raspberry jam. All arranged very neatly, which rather emphasized the emptiness. Root beer would have to do. He took it out and went to her cupboard for a glass. He found Coca-Cola glasses from Tasty Freeze.

As he began pouring two glasses a loud knock

came at the door. He automatically went to answer it.

"I'm Mrs. Reed, the landlady. A neighbor called me and said she smelled smoke. Everything okay?" The older woman in her flowered robe, blue leather slippers, and pink sponge curlers tried to peer around Dex.

"It's fine. It was a minor mishap. I'm a friend of Allison's and I'll take care of things here. Not to worry."

"Well, fine." She gave him an odd smile. "Nice to see a man around here for a change. You'll have to repair this door."

"Yes, we will." Dex smiled and gave her a little goodbye wave as he closed the splintered door.

"There goes my damage deposit." Allison's voice came from the corner.

"I've got to make a call. I want you to drink this. The sugar will perk you up." Dex brought the root beer glass with no ice over to the table.

"Don't you know sugar is bad for you?"

At least she was talking now. He tucked the blanket around her a little tighter. "Yep. Bad. Drink it up."

"Okay."

She took a few sips. Dex wished she had something stronger in the house—maybe for himself. He could use a stiff drink right now. "I'm going to make my call. Stay put, drink all of that."

He stepped into the living room, sat down on the

blue plaid slipcovered sofa, and pulled out his cell phone. He wasn't rich for nothing and she could use a few things at the moment. From what he'd observed, and he was nothing but observant, she hadn't eaten dinner, she was out of Kleenex, and her medical supplies were less than adequate.

In a few minutes he'd accomplished what he wanted. He stood up and looked around at the apartment living room.

She had made the best of it, from what he could see. Sure, the furniture was old and she didn't have much, but it seemed homey, and evidence of her love for her son was everywhere—like the framed picture on the desk of the two of them hugging. The small apartment space was extremely organized and clutter-free. Everything had a place. He was impressed at the order she'd put into her life.

Dex went back toward the bathroom to accomplish the other thing he had come for. If what his mother suspected was true, he needed hard evidence to prove it. He could run a DNA test in his own lab.

Of course, his idea of what to do with that evidence and his mother's idea were two worlds apart.

This time he slowed down and noticed the hallway. He'd blurred past it last time.

"Hall of Fame"—she'd cut out construction paper letters and stuck them on the wall. Baby pictures, school pictures done by bad photographers, certificates, unframed, push-pinned into the drywall—she'd lost her damage deposit long ago on this place, he smiled to himself—and row after row of blue science fair ribbons. Ten years' worth of Ethan . . . Ethan Jennings's life.

Each photograph told the truth he was looking for. The angle of his chin, the way Ethan stood in a picture holding a Little League trophy, the boy's smile—Dex was looking in a mirror.

In one picture Ethan was two, maybe. Allison held him in her arms as he stretched to hang an ornament on a Christmas tree. He must have made the ornament himself—green paper cut into the shape of a star with globs of glitter. The tree had paper chains and homemade decorations on it.

Dex touched that picture with his fingertips. He thought of the lush Christmases he'd always had as a child. His family, rich as they were, had a warmth that came from many angles—Grandma Needham; Dex's stable, calm father; even his mother in the early years; and his sister and brother. They were close and their life was so different from what Ethan had experienced—up to this point.

Dex's hand was shaking. No DNA test was going to change the fact that this child was his. He unpinned the picture from the wall and put the pins back in their same holes.

Nothing would keep this truth from him. No one could take it away, not his mother, not Allison, not anyone.

Dex sat down across the table from Allison, with her bandaged hands, her tearstained eyes, and her empty glass of root beer.

"We've got something to talk about." He laid the picture of Ethan on the table.

Allison *was* in shock. All kinds of shock. Dexter Needham had barged into her house, into her life, and she hadn't been able to think it all through. She'd spent the last twenty minutes trying to figure out a way to get his bodily fluids for a DNA sample. What, swap some spit and run to the bathroom for an empty jar? Break his root beer glass and hope he bled on the table? Maybe pull out a hank of his hair?

What she didn't expect was him to come here knowing. Or suspecting. She wasn't ready.

"It's not true."

"He looks just like me. You see that."

"I don't. He looks like my brother, and me. He's my son."

"He might be my son, too, Allison."

"Just because you are rich and powerful doesn't give you the right to come in here and destroy his life."

"Maybe I can help make his life better."

"There is nothing wrong with it the way it is. He's happy."

Dexter looked at her in a piercing way that hurt so bad. She knew what he was thinking. He was surrounded by the evidence of Ethan's low-income life. Dex could give Ethan the world.

"I love him."

"I know you do. But you need to know something, Allison. If Ethan is my son, and we both know he probably is, I've missed ten years of his life. This child might be the only one I will ever have."

"In case you didn't realize it, Ethan has a father. A father that loves him and has been there for him since he was born. You can't just make that go away." Allison sat up and drew in a breath. She wasn't going to cry. Not this time.

"If I had known, I would have been there, too."

"Would you? From what I've seen your family would have paid me off to keep quiet or even get unpregnant. Did you know your mother tried to write me a very, very big check to get out of your life? She figured it all out before we did. Man, she is one smart, controlling crazy woman."

Dex's face changed and he looked like he genuinely didn't know this fact about his mother, which didn't change anything as far as Allison was concerned.

"I'm not kidding, Dex, she had pictures of me, she had reports. Apparently she found a picture of my son taken at his school that I haven't even seen yet, from this week's *Times*, and since she already *knew* we had a past encounter, she put all the pieces together herself. Which reminds me, where do you get off running to Mommy and telling her we slept together eleven years ago? That's sick."

"I did no such thing. She must have seen the resemblance and based her whole theory on that. When she told me, she showed me the newspaper picture of Ethan, and the other one, the one you dropped. My picture." Dex got up from the table abruptly and paced around the kitchen. "Her behavior doesn't change anything. I came here to get some hard evidence. We should test this out. We need facts."

"Right. I was planning on stabbing you for some blood myself."

"Thanks. I'll watch my back."

"And what were you planning on stealing from me?"

"Saliva. Cheek cells. Toothbrush. Or hair."

"Oh. Less drastic I suppose."

"I can run the test in my lab."

"Saves me the two hundred bucks." Allison picked up her empty glass and threw it at Dexter. She missed. It shattered against the wall behind him.

He turned quickly to glare at her. "Feel better now?"

"You are going to ruin my life, and my son's life." Allison put her head down on the table, braced on her bandaged hands. She would not cry.

"Why did it not occur to you I might be the father?"

"Because I'd been with Rusty just the week before, remember? Just as we were breaking up. And he and I had been rather spontaneous whereas I managed a diaphragm with you.

"This is making me sick. I'm not what this sounds like. You were the only man I ever had this kind of encounter with. You need to know that. As a matter of fact, you are the last man I had sex with. That's right, Dex, it's been eleven years between you, and you again." She lifted her head up for that part.

"Was I that good?" He laughed.

"Very funny. I was busy being pregnant. After that I was busy supporting Ethan and me. You vanished, *Skippy*. I don't know. I don't know why I didn't think it was you. Maybe deep down, Rusty was here, and willing to help me, and you were a ghost. Like a dream I had that I woke up from. And then I was pregnant and trying to make Ethan's life work."

She shook her head admitting this to herself. A pain went through her hand as she pressed it to her temple. There were times—moments—she had wondered where Ethan's brilliant mind had come from. But his smile was hers, and she had put those disturbing thoughts away and trudged through her life.

"You have no concept of what it's like to be a single parent, to make a life for a child and the only choice you have is to work very, very hard every day. You have no idea. There is no time to think about things that have no meaning. What could I have done about it if I *had* figured it out? Hired your mother's private detective to track down a guy with a strawberry birthmark on his butt? Sorry, it wasn't in my budget."

"Good point." Dex leaned against the counter and crossed his arms. "I want you to know something. I remember that night we spent together eleven years ago. I've been holding this thought about that night—that I'd never find that kind of free, amazing passion again. Because as soon as anyone knows who I am it's all about the money and the society games. When I saw you at the party I felt like there might be a chance—that someone like you could be outside that realm and reach in and pull me out. You did that. And that was the second time."

"Someone like me?" Her tone was sarcastic.

Dex looked at her and felt a dull aching pain inside him. She didn't get what he was saying. He'd hoped for a moment she might understand. To hell with it. "Look, Allison, let's get practical about this. First, we need to do the test. No, first don't throw anything more at me. I'll gladly give you my blood."

"Leave Ethan out of this until the test is done."

"We need to move past blaming each other for what should have happened or what might have been and focus on now."

"And if Ethan is yours?" Allison's voice cracked. She covered up her mouth with her hand.

The doorbell rang. Dex once again turned and answered her door—he was just steps away, but Allison was starting to get annoyed with that. Although she did have just a quilt and a very ugly nightgown on, so it was nice of him to shield her. She looked at the clock. Midnight.

A man handed Dex three bags from Larry's

Market—upscale grocery. Dex balanced two and put the other on the ground. He thanked the man, who was wearing a chauffeur's uniform. Allison figured he didn't tip the guy because he was already on the Needham staff. Twenty-four-hour-a-day servants. Yep.

"What is all that? I don't need your charity."

"No, you needed some more gauze, and I'm hungry. Also I need a drink. Would you care to join me?"

"Sure. What the hell? Mind if I go freshen up? I promise not to hide the toothbrushes."

"I'll put this stuff away. I got you some dinner. Table for two in the corner nook, ten minutes."

"Fine." Allison slipped out of the built-in and had to take a moment to get her shaking legs back on track. "Make mine a double." Maybe it would help her behave. She was in pain, she was upset, and Dexter Needham was taking the brunt of it. For a moment she felt guilty. He was just as shocked as she was. Then her thoughts went to Ethan, and it all just rushed back at her. She'd need some time for this to sink in.

Dex couldn't find a microwave but the food was still hot. He emptied the bags, kept the first aid kit on the counter, and twisted open the bottle of Glenlivet. If ever a man needed a drink, this would be it. He hardly partook on a regular basis. His mother's generation was the cocktail set. He was the carrot juice and wheat grass set.

He took the last four ice cubes out of her plastic trays and transformed two more cola glasses into scotch and water on the rocks. He'd have to do the dishes later.

Allison would be shocked to see he was capable of such domestic feats. Dex went to the corner and picked up the broken glass she'd thrown at him. That's all he needed was for her to step on this. He threw it in the trash under the sink.

Then he emptied the contents of the take-out containers on two plates he found in the upper cupboard. Roast beef, gravy, mashed potatoes, and baby carrots in a ginger glaze. This ought to do her.

Dex didn't need a DNA test to know the truth. He knew it already, in his heart, a part of him that until recently had not been accessible. The pain in it now made that extremely clear to him.

But his family needed that DNA test. He felt his anger at his mother rise out of the back of his mind. If what Allison said was true, his mother just tried to make his *son* vanish out of their life—his life—by writing a check and paying Allison off. She'd done this without consulting him, considering him, or thinking clearly.

She'd also tried to get rid of Allison, even without Ethan in the picture. That checkbook was already out before his mother put the pieces together. He knew *that* in his heart, too.

Allison had been made into something undesirable in his mother's book. But in his book she was an amazing, desirable woman.

He was quite certain finding out where Allison lived, where she worked, that she had a son, that she was poor, had been enough to make his mother attempt to dismiss her from Dex's life. He'd heard rumors. Rumors he'd ignored. About other times, about Mimi. But he was glad to be free of Mimi, so he hadn't cared about the rumors.

This time it wasn't going to be so easy. This time was different. He didn't want to be free; he wanted his son. He wanted more time with Allison, and if his heart was telling him the truth for once, he wanted Allison in his life, too. His mother would have to deal with him this time. And for once, she might have met her match.

Dex took a drink of scotch and let it hit his body like a slap. Time to wake up, Dex. This time is different.

14

You Always Hurt the One You Love

Allison put on lipstick in her bathroom mirror. Then she wondered why. She'd managed to get on a pair of jeans and a decent sweater: Bunny's celery-green cardigan. She buttoned it up almost to the top. She was still chilled—and it was July.

Her hair had been a bit difficult with the bandaged mitts she was stuck with. At least her fingertips were sticking out, and that helped with the lipstick.

She might look better, but her feelings were a mess. She'd prettied up. For what? Their entire beginning, the spark of magic they'd shared last night, was lost in a tangle of complications and emotions. He was going to ruin her life. He was going to change the one thing that was good and decent and wonderful in her life—Ethan.

She should have listened to her inner voice warning her not to get involved with Dex. The inner voice that made her crawl out on a ledge to get away from him.

But she remembered that wasn't the voice that screamed the loudest. It was the one that said, *Go ahead, let him kiss you, let him in.*

They could both just shut up now.

She emerged from the bathroom and marched into the kitchen.

"I'm ready for that drink."

After she'd eaten the great food Dex had his *servant* deliver, Allison directed Dex to the living room. She picked up her own Kleenex trail as they went. There was nothing like unexpected guests to give you that crappy house feeling.

"Wait, I want you to show me the hallway."

"Seems like you've seen it."

"Not through your eyes."

"Aren't you assuming quite a bit? Why go there if the test doesn't turn out?"

"Ignoring for a minute the intense resemblance between Ethan and myself, let's say I'd like to get to know you, and your son is part of your life, so share it with me."

"I've got albums in the living room. I'll show you those."

"That sounds good. Where is Ethan, anyhow?"

Allison took a long sip of her drink before she answered.

"He won a scholarship to science camp at MIT."

She watched Dex's face. His eyes. Things were

happening. Now she knew why his eyes made her feel strange. They were the same expressive, deeply intelligent eyes as Ethan's. She felt sick.

"Let's go in here. I'll get the albums for you."

"When will he be back?"

"Tomorrow afternoon. You will not talk to him until we know for sure, are we clear about that?"

"Yes."

Allison's heart ached. What would Rusty do? How would Ethan react? Where was the strength she needed to deal with this?

The pictures told the story, all right; they told the story of a boy with a brilliant mind, and Dex knew that mind. Each page she turned was like another shock wave for him.

In between the Spiderman Halloween costumes and the Easter baskets and first-day-of-school pictures, Dex saw Ethan's talents blossom. More certificates, more ribbons were tucked between the picture pages.

Then she showed him Ethan's prize-winning science project. She admitted she didn't know what it was all about. But he did. He was looking at a ten-year-old boy's experiments in *direct methanol fuel cell research*. No wonder MIT grabbed him.

"Allison." He looked at her, pointing to the award.

"Just shut up, Dex. Don't say it. I don't want to hear the words right now." She sat back hard against the sofa and took a drink of the refill Dex had given her.

He could feel her pain. He felt it, too. They both knew the truth.

"You've done a good job with him."

"Thanks. Rusty has been a good father, too."

"None of that has to change. I don't want to hurt Ethan, or you. But I can offer him opportunities. He deserves that."

She twisted away from him and curled up in her corner of the sofa. "I told you I didn't want to hear this right now. I'm tired. My son will be back tomorrow. I want you to go now, Dex. Take what you need and go."

"Allison, don't push me away. We have other things besides what Ethan means to both of us. We have something to explore."

"I'm very confused. It's going to take some time for me to get my head on straight."

Dex moved over close to her and uncurled her body, taking her in his arms slowly. She reluctantly let him. He felt tears on her cheek again, as much as she tried to hide them. He brushed them away and kissed her there, and on her temples, and then on her lips. Her lips felt soft—and sad.

"Allison, this isn't going to be easy, but it doesn't have to be as bad as you are thinking." He ran his hand across her cheek and down her neck, trying to smooth out her pain.

"Just go now, Dex. I can't think when you kiss me. But thank you." She didn't move out of his arms, and he was glad for that. He kissed her once more.

"Now listen, this is very important. Do not listen to anyone from my family but me. Do you understand?"

"Sure. Don't listen."

"I bought you new toothbrushes. Ethan's is the *Star Wars* figure." Dex smiled.

"Oh thanks. I guess this means you're taking the old ones?"

"It would help if you ran it around inside your mouth once."

"Won't the booze spoil the sample?"

"Rinse and spit."

Allison got up and headed for the bathroom. Rinse and spit indeed. She should have aimed better with the cola glass.

Dex had a son. Even the twelve-marker test showed paternal relationship. The twenty-five-marker test confirmed it without a shadow of a doubt. It was really the three-way match indicator that convinced him, though. That test had a one percent error factor. Even using the polymerase chain test, which took him only half the day, it was a perfect match.

He leaned back in his swivel chair and felt a rush of excitement. There were times he thought he would never trust any woman enough to proceed into parenthood with her. Would she be lying to him and trying to trap him by having a child? Then after a few years just toss him aside and take the child, just to get the huge amount of child support that went with that package? Then he'd be denied his child, and . . . His mind just went spinning off. This was why he seriously doubted he would ever have a child. He could never trust enough.

He got up and gathered the readouts he'd produced. Now this, this was different. Allison had no idea who he was when she conceived Ethan. She didn't even try to find him, or, for that matter, entertain in her mind that he was a factor.

Dex went through the clean room airlock and took off his lab coat. He'd had to use his city lab for this, as the Grand Island mini-lab didn't have the equipment he needed. The house was nearly empty with the family off on Grand Island for the remainder of the weekend. Just a few staff members and gardeners.

His first job was to call Allison on the phone. Then he was going to get on the ferry and have a family meeting. It might cause a stir among the guests but he really didn't give a damn.

She'd said Ethan would be back this afternoon. Dex headed into the kitchen to make himself a late lunch. His grandmother was always after him not to get lost in his work and forget to eat. Tutu would be thrilled. A great-grandson. She loved all children, but Dex knew she had a soft spot for little boys.

His father would accept this with his usual calm, warm manner. His mother was another matter. What was eating her these last few years anyway?

When the family was focused on Celia's illness his mother was a rock of strength. Now she seemed to be making all kinds of secretive moves, most involving his love life, as far as he knew. Maybe she'd been like that for longer than he knew. Maybe he was just paying more attention now.

Dex had decided yesterday morning during his mother's brief talk with him that it was time to put a stop to her meddling. The best cure for that was to air it out with the entire family.

Bunny had driven her out to the airport. After all, her hands were still wrapped up, her Nova was still in the shop, her head was hung over, and her heart was just all twisted up.

"Here, drink some coffee. Perk up. This isn't the worst thing that could happen, girlfriend, you've got a rich man's child here. Ethan's life is going to be much better for it. DNA tests don't lie. And from what you've told me Dex said, this one came out very, very positively."

"So you think destroying everything Ethan has known as stable and predictable will improve his life?"

"Destroy, what destroy? Life changes. Shit happens. You can't keep him in a bubble. Look, instead of two great parents, he'll have three. And one of them will pay for private schools, and college, and maybe buy you a new car and get you out of that apartment."

"I like my apartment. It's our home."

"Get over yourself. I should have dragged you out of that dump years ago. I can't believe I've let you waste away this long in that job. I haven't been much of a friend for the last five years."

"Your husband died. You had a daughter to raise. You were busy getting married and unmarried. And most of all, did I ask for help? I've been doing fine on my own. You know, Bunny, I've worked hard and I have some pride in the life I've created for myself and Ethan. It's decent and loving, and we get by just fine." Allison was getting mad. People kept assuming she'd done such a bad job. She took a sip of the coffee and for once it didn't burn her lips.

"I know all about you and your pride. I've watched it for years. I know you've worked hard, Alli, and yes you did make a decent life for you and your son. But here's the flip side. I'm done grieving, I'm done with husbands for the time being, and Trish loves you, too. Why don't you come and live with me? You and Ethan. I have a huge house. It'll be a ball for us, and Ethan and Trish will have great fun. It'd be good for her to have a playmate that's not Britney Spears–driven. If you didn't have to pay rent you could consider some other job options. Maybe go to school."

"What, just sponge off you?"

"Yes. Sponge off me. Get a leg up."

"I've lived in that apartment for seven years."

Bunny took a sip of coffee, crossed her arms, leaned on her elbow, and just stared at Allison. She had on a sweater with feathers at the collar and cuffs. She had orange lipstick and nails and an arched eyebrow that went so far up it vanished in her dark brown wispy bangs. Allison tried to keep a straight face, but Bunny's posture was too funny.

"Like I've been trying to tell you, I have my pride." Allison tried to say that without laughing.

"Screw your pride, and screw your apartment. You need to show Dex something here, and you know it."

"I'll think about it. There he is!" Her Ethan. He came out of the ramp doorway with Mr. Kerns right behind him. He was looking for her, she could tell. He looked so tan, so much older; he had on a white short-sleeve polo shirt that wasn't his. Maybe they gave them out at camp. Maybe someone bought him clothes because he didn't have the right stuff?

"Mom!" He ran like a ten-year-old boy, not a sophisticated genius, right into her arms. She held him close to her for a very long time. Long enough to wipe her eyes with the back of her bandaged hand before he saw her tears.

Dex paced the back of the room. They'd sealed off the dining room from the staff and assorted leftover guests, and all he was waiting on was his mother, of course. His father, grandmother, grandfather, sister, and brother were all there.

"What's up, Dexy?" Tutu bent toward him and whispered, as if his father sitting right next to her couldn't hear. "Are the cops after you?"

He smiled at her. She was such a dear. "Hang on, Tutu, I might as well do it all at once."

His mother came in through the door that the staff was guarding. "Sorry, I had to check on dinner. The caterers arrived. Mrs. Fisk was in the pool. Is this necessary? We have guests departing and they are beginning to talk." Dex's father had risen and pulled out a chair for his wife. She slid in, and he pushed her close to the table.

"Let's give Dex a bit of our time." His father nodded to him.

Show time. He moved the head chair aside and stood at the end of the table.

"It seems I have a son." He'd practiced this line and versions of it several times. "He is ten."

"Hot damn, Dexy, I knew you'd surprise us someday." Tutu slapped the table and grinned. Several teacups sloshed a spot of Earl Grey into their saucers.

Naomi steadied hers. "Really, Mother. You better hear the details. That woman that arrived with Bunny, she is the mother."

"That *woman's* name is Allison Jennings. She did not come here to blackmail me, or trap me. She didn't even know I was the child's father until we had a—"

"Till you got it on and she remembered you!" Tutu added.

"Thank you, Grandmother." Dex smiled.

"Maybe you better explain fully, son." That was his dad. A just-the-facts kind of guy.

"Eleven years ago Allison and I had a brief encounter. We had both broken up with people; we were hurt, and found comfort in each other for a night. I left for MIT that next week, never knowing she had conceived a child. Her ex-husband was the most likely father, and she assumed the baby was his, having had unprotected sex with him the week earlier."

"Did you and she have unprotected sex?" his father asked.

Here they were discussing his sex life like it was a science experiment. "No, she was using a diaphragm. If you'll do the math you'll remember I was barely twenty-two. I know, I should have used a condom, but to be blunt, I was somewhat drunk."

His brother had been grinning at him silently. "And here we always thought it would be me to get some girl in trouble. Dex, old boy, congratulations." Edward rose out of his chair and slugged Dex in the arm, then sat back down.

"So her diaphragm failed. And is this conclusive?" Dad the scientist asked.

"Yes, I ran the tests myself, back in town. There is no doubt. And, as Mother can tell you, the boy is a dead ringer for me as a child. Right, Mother?"

His sister, Celia, started to cry. Edward handed her his handkerchief.

"Celia, please. It's not that bad," Dex said. "Allison is a good woman."

Celia mopped her eyes. "I'm actually thrilled,

Dex; I'm very touched. I know how important children are. I wish Warren and I—well I'm sure very soon I'll be giving you all good news, too. I guess I'm a little jealous. But I did like her, Dex. She's a peach."

Grandfather thumped his knee enthusiastically. "It is good news. We've got a great-grandson! The more men in this family the better. Sorry there, Celia, we love you, too. I'm sure you'll give us a boy very soon." Grandfather Needham was a bit of a chauvinist pig. Celia cried again, probably from exasperation this time.

"Like hell it's good news. I don't see why you're all so jolly. You left a few parts out, Dex, like how Miss Jennings is nearly destitute and suddenly she shows up at our house? Surely she knew the child was yours but just didn't have the nerve to play out her game until now."

"Why would she wait ten years, Naomi?" Dex's father picked up his cup and saucer and calmly sipped his tea. Good old dad.

"Yes, woman." Grandfather Needham did that thing where he called Dex's mom "woman," which Dex knew she hated. "Not every girl that gets herself pregnant is out for our money."

"I've chased off more gold diggers from this family than any of you can imagine. You're all *grossly* naive."

"And about that, Mother. From now on you will keep your checkbook closed when it comes to my life. I don't even want to know what you've done in the past. My son is my affair, and I'll deal with it my own way. All I expect from you, my family, is support. This is my son we are talking about. I intend to know him, provide him with a good education and all the privilege being a Needham entails. I expect you all to welcome him into our family."

Naomi stood up abruptly. "Are you crazy? Just pay her off and set up some kind of trust fund for the boy."

"Sit down, Naomi." Dex's father didn't use that tone with his mother too often. Dex watched her head snap in Dad's direction, then she sat down with a thump. Bravo, Father!

"Which reminds me, Mother, part of the reason I had the family in here is to have a sort of . . . intervention. I can't begin to understand what has been going through your mind lately, but let's assume you are being overprotective of the family.

"Whatever it is, it's got to stop. You must accept that we are adults. I will not pay Allison off, and I intend to get to know my son. He is also going to get to know all of you. I need for you to promise you will stop interfering. Promise me this in front of the family."

His mother looked unfazed "Someone has to keep our family name out of the mud. I'm your mother. It's my job to make sure you and Edward and Celia are happy. What will people say? What's my bridge group going to say when they find out you've got an illegitimate child?"

"Would that be Lavinia Thurman's bridge

group, Mother? Lavinia, whose husband ran off with his massage therapist, who happened to be a man?" Celia chimed in, handing Edward back his handkerchief.

"Yes, that bridge group, thank you, Celia," Naomi gave her a nasty look.

"You see, Mother? Life is just full of surprises. So you must promise to let us live our own lives, as misguided as we may appear to you. Now promise."

"I obviously have no choice."

"That is correct," Dex answered her.

"Naomi, this is our grandson you are talking about, our own blood relative. I won't allow you to shut him out of the family. Frankly, I'm surprised at you." Dex's father had his arms crossed now and spoke sternly.

"Do what you like. I have no say."

"I know you still have a good heart, Mother. Try and access it more often," Dex said.

"I'm not going to stay and be insulted." Naomi Needham got up and stalked out the door, flattening a maid against the other side, who obviously had her ear plastered to the door. Edward let out a quick laugh, but obviously thought better of it and silenced himself.

"When do we meet Master Needham anyhow, Dex?" his father asked.

"He is just getting back from his science scholarship program at MIT today."

Celia gasped. "My gosh, Dex, he's a chip off the old Needham block!"

"You don't know the half of it. His name is Ethan Jennings—for now anyway." Dex picked up his tea and took a long-awaited gulp.

Look at that. Even the household staff would know now. She would fire the girl, but then she'd run off to the papers for sure. Instead Naomi gave her a wink. She'd better put a bonus in this girl's envelope. The staff around here knew perfectly well what would happen to them if they ran with tales of the family to the press. She'd sued one maid into the poorhouse just to serve as an example when the little snitch went on about Celia's illness to some society columnist.

Dex was wrong. This Jennings woman was trouble. Dexter wasn't acquainted with the fine workings of a large family. Her own father had taught her a few harsh lessons about behaving in ways that dishonored the family. He was a hard man, Oliver Schmidt. But he'd been through so much—poverty, war.

Naomi kept moving toward her office. Her sanctuary. It was an exact duplicate of her office in the Bellevue house, just not as many books and such. That way she knew where everything was no matter which house they were in at the time.

She had obligations. She was a community leader. She was well respected. People valued her opinion. Except, apparently, her own family. Just like Pop.

She stopped on the stairs and steadied herself

against the wall. Her thought surprised her. It was true, though, she could never get her father to approve of her, or compliment her, or even accept her in any way. She remembered when she met her husband how wonderful it was to have someone tell her she was pretty and smart.

And her family had enough money, but her father made them live like they were poor. Naomi knew firsthand what it was like to want to be rich so bad your teeth hurt. She knew. *She'd married her husband partly for his money.* Money he was willing to spend lavishly. Money he had a knack for doubling and tripling. She saw that in him and knew that was what she wanted. It took some womanly wiles on her part to finally get him to the altar.

So don't talk to her about this woman not being after Dex's money. She knew Allison Jennings could just taste the rich life, just as she had before she married into the Needham family.

Of course she loved her husband. She'd grown to appreciate and love him over the years. But that was a rare thing.

She continued climbing the stairs. She really did want Dex to be happy. They were all being too hard on her. She had only his best interests at heart. And yes, she had a heart, damn it.

15

Five O'Clock Whistle

She'd had only two days with Ethan. One and a half, really. There was no way she could tell him. They spent the entire day Sunday talking about his adventures in science camp.

He'd been all worried about her hands so she'd unwrapped them even though Dex had said to wait two full days. There were a few blisters, and they hurt like hell, but she didn't let Ethan know that.

She would have had to unwrap them today anyway, because she was back at work. Back standing behind a counter. She felt like a different person. Like she'd been beamed down from her hovering mother ship. The woman who had left here two weeks ago had been body-snatched, and instead *she* was here. Making coffee as usual.

Rusty had generously offered to pick up her and Ethan this morning, after Allison had told Rusty she needed to have a serious talk with him. They'd dropped Ethan off with Pamela together. He was going to have to hang with the girls today and be stuck playing Barbies. Poor Ethan.

One of the things they needed to talk about was what to do with Ethan for the rest of the summer while she worked. Pamela was getting big as a house, and Allison knew she was pressing it even having him there today. Ethan would probably end up back with Grandma Trask if they didn't come up with some day program money.

Worse than all of that, now she was going to have to have that talk with Rusty and tell him that Ethan wasn't his.

She knew the place would be empty. Terrible Tim was taking the day off. Rusty sat reading the paper. She might have done it in the car, but he was driving, for heaven's sakes. This way was better. Here she was going to change his life forever. She poured the coffee into a thick white cup, set it on a saucer, and put a thin chocolate sugar wafer on the side. Old habits die hard.

"Here you go."

"Thanks, Alli." He took a slurp. "Oh look, my favorite cookie. What's up, Alli, you've got that fidgety thing going on."

She slid into the booth with him. Her own coffee had gone a little cold but she sipped one sip for strength anyhow. "You know me so well."

"Duh. What, fifteen years?"

"This is way hard, Rusty."

"Say it now because you're starting to wig me out. Ethan isn't sick, is he? He looked fine this morning."

"No, he's fine. He had a great time." She swallowed hard. "Rusty, Ethan is not yours. I thought he was, but it turns out he's not. You are not his biological father."

Rusty looked at her blankly. Then he looked into his coffee cup. "Holy shit."

"Exactly."

"Are you sure?"

"Totally."

"Man, I should have known. A couple of times I did know, but you know, you raise a kid up and he kind of acts like you and you just push it away in your mind."

Allison reached out and put her hand on Rusty's arm.

"I should have known it was impossible for me to have a boy." He sort of chuckled.

"How do you figure?"

"I've got a low motility on my sperm count—which leaves more girl sperms than boy sperms I guess. Pamela and I had me tested one time. Seems we can get pregnant fine but girls are my specialty." He looked up at her. "Who is the father?"

"Dexter Needham."

"*What?* Dex Needham as in the rich guy Needham?"

"That would be the one." She took her hand

away and picked up her coffee cup, sucking up as much of its warmth as she could through her fingertips without pressing her burned palms against it. She felt so very odd.

"Holy shit."

"Again, exactly."

Rusty ran his hand over his face and rubbed his forehead. He looked like the impact was finally getting to him.

"How did that happen?"

"It's a long story. Right now I want to talk about Ethan and you and me."

"Man. This stinks."

"Look, you've been a father to Ethan his whole life. He needs you to stick around no matter what happens now."

"Of course I will. He's my buddy." Rusty looked bad. He looked like he might cry. "You like . . . slept with this guy the week after we broke up?"

"Damn it, Rusty, I didn't know. I'm really sorry."

"Hey, it's okay. If you recall, I was already messing around with Pamela. So, that night we had that little wild moment—where we did the deed—that wasn't when you got pregnant after all?"

"Nope."

"Man. To think I've taken heat for that night for years." He laughed. "So this Dex guy, what's going to happen there?"

"Obviously, I have a bunch of stuff to tell you

about that, but the most important is that he's a very nice man, he wants to know Ethan, and he promised me that we'd all work together."

"Sure. We can do that. Hey, at least Ethan will have a college fund and all that. He's a smart kid. Smarter than either of us. I'm betting he's got the sperm donor's smart genes?"

"It would seem so."

"So you haven't told Ethan yet?"

"I wanted to talk to you first."

"I want to be there. I'll pick him up from my house and we can tell him together."

"You may not be a genius, Rusty, but you're pretty swell in all the ways that count. Pamela's a lucky woman."

"Thanks, Alli. Can you get out of here by four? We'll come here and get you."

"Sure. I've got Heather coming in. She's smart enough to lock up."

Rusty finished his coffee and shoved out of the booth. He rolled up the rest of his paper and gave her a kiss on the cheek. "Don't worry, Alli, we'll get it all figured out. And by the way, you look great."

"Thanks. I'll see you when you get here." She watched him go out the door. Grabbing her wipe rag, she cleared the cups and cleaned up the table they'd used. She pushed back her hair with her forearm so the wet rag wouldn't slime her new cute do. She wasn't used to the shorter style. Ethan had loved it. He said she looked like a movie star with her reddish-blond hair and peach-colored lipstick. He was her biggest fan, no doubt about it.

They would get this all worked out. Dex could just visit with Ethan. Rusty could do some weekends. Maybe they could just both take every other weekend. She'd have to ease Ethan into this new arrangement. It could work. Hopefully.

Bunny Barnes Winchester Parker came sweeping through the door. She had on red.

"Good morning, Alli!"

"It's two-thirty, Bunny."

"Whatever. Are you ready to move in with me today?" She perched on a red leatherette barstool by the counter.

"No. I appreciate the offer, but this is not the time to change Ethan's home along with everything else."

"Look at yourself. You look wonderful. You don't belong here."

"I sort of felt like that today. But then those pesky bills have another idea. They all told me they wanted to be paid, can you imagine? They actually screamed at me."

"Don't listen to them. Put them in a box in the closet. You won't be able to hear them in there."

"At night they come out and haunt me."

"Monsters in the closet. Speaking of monsters in the closet, what's the update on the *situation*?"

"Rusty took it pretty well. He's bringing Ethan here in about an hour. We're going to talk to him together."

"Poor Rusty."

"Ouch."

"Sorry, hon, I'm glad he's rising to the occasion. So to speak."

"Very funny."

"And what about Dex?"

As if on cue, Dex Needham strode through the door of the Tasty Freeze. Something told Allison he wasn't there for a milkshake.

"Bunny."

"Dex, darling." Bunny twisted around on the barstool as if she was getting ready for the show.

"Allison, I wonder if we could have a minute."

Bunny got up. "You go ahead. I'll mind the counter."

"Are you kidding?" Allison blurted.

"No, I'm not kidding." She looked cross-eyed at Allison. "Now, give me that apron." Bunny, shockingly, grabbed the apron from Allison, tied it on, and went behind the counter humming. "Look, it matches me. Red stripes. Heather will be here in a minute anyhow. I'll whip you up something."

Allison turned and walked to an empty booth. Dex followed. Her whole life was taking place in the booths of the Tasty Freeze. Not to mention Dex Needham was now seeing her in her nurse-white shoes and her Tasty Freeze uniform. Hardly the picture of the girl he'd *done* in the kitchen at the Grand Island estate.

"Wait. Before you sit down, there's something I'd like to give you."

"What, a summons?" Allison turned to face Dex. He gathered her in his arms, and she didn't have time to even close her eyes. Her arms went out straight, she almost lost her balance, but his kiss hit the mark. In ten seconds she'd forgotten where she was and melted into his arms.

"Wooo hoo!" Bunny hollered from the counter.

A flash of light made Allison blink. She looked behind Dex's shoulder to see Tim the Idiot—with a camera.

"Boy, I knew this would come in handy today, but this is better than bird-watching."

"What the hell are you doing, Tim?"

"Getting an exclusive! I had a feeling I should drop into work today, just to see what you were up to. And look—a follow-up on the *Register* article! I'm gonna make me some money."

"Oh no, you don't." She couldn't take him anymore. Her cerebral ability to control her urge to kill him snapped somewhere in the rage quadrant. She pushed Dex away and went three strides in for Tim and his camera. He kept playing keep-away with her and she was about to pop him one. That *bastard!*

Dex came from behind her and pulled her off him, her fists flailing. "I'll take care of this guy, Allison, get off him."

Bunny came from the side with a loaded can of Reddi-wip. She filled Tim's sputtering mouth with a well-aimed squirt. Lots fell on the floor, and Tim did a slip-and-slide move that ended him on his ass.

Bunny put one smartly done blob on his head and finished him with a nice maraschino cherry, stem and all.

"Wow, Bunny, you've got talent," Allison said. She'd been subdued by Dex long enough to watch the Bunny show.

"Allison Jennings, you are fired—*fired*!" Tim sputtered. "Get out now. Clear out your locker. I want you out of here in five minutes."

"I quit, too!" Bunny took off the striped apron, threw it on the ground, and stomped her high-heeled feet.

Allison laughed. "Bunny, honey, you don't work here."

Dex handed Tim a counter towel. Allison had no idea why he'd extend any kindness to the guy, and she resented it. Really bad.

"Don't be nice to him, he's a jerk. He tried to grope me a few weeks ago."

"Well, in that case . . ." Dex picked Tim up off the floor by the front of his collar and set him upright. He then deftly removed the camera from Tim's grasp and looked like he was about to punch his lights out.

"I'm sorry. I'll never touch her again." Tim cowered.

Dex lowered his stance and gave Tim a very stern look. He turned to Bunny and Allison and held up the prize camera. "You see, girls, no violence is necessary."

Just then Tim lunged at Dex and the camera. Allison took a step back. Dex decked him, purely in self-defense. Tim flew backward onto the floor. Allison started laughing again. She looked up. Rusty and Ethan stood in the doorway. Oh God.

"Mom?"

Heather was right behind them, practically in hysterics herself. Bunny had her hand over her mouth, stifling herself, but it wasn't doing much good. She screamed with laughter and doubled over.

Allison noticed Tim was out cold. He'd smacked his head on the floor the second time around. "I think we better leave, Rusty," Allison said, giving Rusty the old you-know-what-to-do look.

Rusty nodded and backed Ethan out the door. Dex looked like a stun gun had zapped him. "The first thing my son saw me do is hit someone."

"Don't worry, it will make a good story later. If you came her to ask me how that was going, I haven't told him yet. Now I'm going to. Rusty knows. Bunny knows. Hell, the lady in the corner booth knows *something* anyhow. Call me later for the rest. Why did you kiss me?"

"Before our lives went *As the World Turns* I had a thing for you, remember?"

"Yeah. I do. The whipped cream brought it all back."

"*Run!*" Bunny screamed again. This time she was pointing to Tim, who was groaning on the floor.

"Dex, you better get out of here before—*I don't*

know-the *Tattletale* drops a guy in by parachute?"
Allison nodded toward Tim. "Bunny, gather up my stuff, will you? I'll get it from you later. I think I better go."

"Don't worry, Bunny and I will duck out the back," Dex said.

"Don't worry, Miss Jennings, I've got it covered." Heather gave her a thumbs-up from behind the counter.

Allison ran out the front door. Rusty was in the truck with the engine on. She jumped in beside Ethan, breathless. "Hey guys, shall we go out for a burger?"

"I take it we won't be back to the Tasty Freeze any time soon?" Rusty said calmly.

"Nope."

"Mom, did you quit?" Ethan looked at her.

"It would seem so."

"Good. Now we can have some fun."

Allison leaned back and took a deep breath. That was one way to look at it.

Harry Pinkerton got up from the corner booth and straightened his curly gray wig. The lady in the corner table did indeed know everything, and that lady was *him*. This was worth a cool half-mill for sure.

They didn't have to drop a reporter from the *Tattletale* out of the sky; he'd just give them a ring from his office later. He had plenty for them. He might consider offering it up to Naomi Needham, but her cases had been few and far between lately, and it might be time to go for bigger stakes. Also, she'd been sort of snotty to him on the last job, after all his hard work. It hadn't been easy digging up all that information on Allison Jennings so quickly.

He'd also had some pretty bad days at the track lately. The ponies just weren't running his way.

BILLIONAIRE HAS LOVE CHILD WITH WAITRESS—KOS HER BOSS. Well, he'd leave the writing up to the writers. Pictures were his thing. He still had negatives from the window ledge caper on Grand Island, and now this new stuff. These mini cameras were the best.

Harry made a cool exit from the Tasty Freeze, his last pictures being the manager out cold, the counter girl calmly cleaning up the floor around him, and Dex Needham putting on his dark glasses and climbing into his Benz.

Dex felt alive, upset, confused, and sick all at once. But at least he *felt*.

He was also worried. In the last few hours he'd started to realize that the fact that Ethan was his son might become public. One thing he was starting to understand about his mother since he'd found out about Ethan was the deep need to protect your child.

But how could he do that with Ethan so vulnerable, so accessible? It was a sad fact that there were evil people out there. Greedy, evil people. Just ask the Lindbergh family.

Maybe he could hire Ethan a bodyguard. He

could just hear Allison's reaction to that. But she was going to have to face some facts.

His family had never gone that far with him or Celia and Edward, but they were extremely sheltered, nevertheless. They went to private schools that knew how to keep an eye on rich children. They attended very controlled events, when he thought about it. Tennis matches, plays, concerts, and many of their activities were brought to them in their own home.

But times were different now and safety was more of an issue than ever.

What he really wanted was to sweep Ethan and Allison up into his life and keep them both safe. He longed to spend time with Allison, to have a dinner date, or go to a movie, or hold her in his arms again and make love to her. He wanted to just *know* Allison more. But now she wouldn't see it as clearly as she might have before. She might think he only wanted her because of Ethan.

Dex turned down their drive and flipped the gate remote. This was quite the turn of tables. Instead of some girl having to prove to him she wasn't after his money, he was going to have to make Allison understand his attraction to her was genuine, whatever that led to.

Dex smiled to himself. She was quite the wildcat, going for that camera. She'd also just lost her job, which from what he heard was a blessing in many ways.

This put even another wrench in the gears. He'd

planned on stepping in on as many levels as possible financially, but letting her keep her sense of independence. That was going to be very hard now. He couldn't have his son go without decent food and shelter. But she sure as hell wasn't going to let him step in at this point and pay everything for her.

The family was still on Grand Island. He was going to cook himself dinner and think all this over. Then he'd call Allison later tonight, after she'd had plenty of time with Ethan. One thing was for sure. He was going to meet his son tomorrow.

"That guy in the Tasty Freeze? The one that hit your boss? He is my—my . . . father?" Ethan had cried, and questioned, and cried again. She thought she would die. Her insides were raw with pain. Rusty put his arm around Ethan again.

"That's the guy," Rusty answered. "We're just gonna keep it simple for now, champ. A mistake was made, but this doesn't change anything. We love you. I love you. Dex will love you, too. You're a lovable guy. It's just more love to go around."

"He doesn't even know me."

"He'd like to, if it's okay with you." Allison said quietly.

"I guess so. I'd like to see what he looks like. Do we look alike?"

"You've got similar features," Allison said.

"And how did you figure all this out, Mom?"

That was the question she just didn't want to do. "I remembered him when I went to the party with Bunny. We got to talking and realized that we'd met—dated—before. Then I saw his picture from when he was a boy." Allison gave Ethan the PG version. The one that left out all the sex, scandal, and crazy stuff, for now. Allison hoped her brilliant son wasn't going to probe too much further, at least for now.

"He's a scientist?"

"Yes."

This odd fact seemed to make Ethan calmer. He heaved a big sigh. "Well, I guess we'll take it one step at a time," he said.

The kid really was a genius. The phone rang, and Allison got up off the sofa to answer it in the kitchen.

It was Dex. When she heard his voice she wished, for the first time ever, that he were here with her. That he was right here to put his arms around her and comfort her in a way Rusty couldn't, because she and Rusty were just pals, and he was happily married to Pamela with their passel of cute little girls.

"It's been a tough evening. But he's agreed to see you tomorrow. Just go very slow with this, Dex."

"I'll come over early and we'll talk, then we can go meet the rest of the family." Dex's voice sounded very pushy.

She didn't like the pressing tone in his voice. "Yes, pick him up, but Dex, just you, okay?" She hung up the phone and looked at the burned spot in the carpet and its funny butterfly scorch from the two sides of the split-in-half bowl shape. She could cut that square out and try and replace it; Mrs. Reed probably had a remnant in her storage area.

What the hell was she going to do without a job? Maybe she could get unemployment for a while. Maybe food stamps? She felt sick and backed up against the refrigerator. What had she done? Why did she have to go off and try to kill Ratty Tim?

She walked back to the living room and Ethan. It was going to be a long night.

16

Pistol-Packin' Mama

Naomi Needham tapped on the window and signaled the driver to stop. The neighborhood wasn't quite as bad as she'd envisioned. Unfortunately, her son's Mercedes was parked on the street in front of the apartment building that contained Allison Jennings.

She hit the intercom button. "Simons, drive around the block and park one up from here."

Simons touched his hat and nodded. One block up would give her a good vantage point. She intended to speak to Miss Jennings, and Dex didn't need to know about that.

She felt a bit nervous, which wasn't like her. She wished she'd timed this better. Naomi picked up the sherry decanter from the center bar and poured herself a small glass. Even if it was nine-thirty in the morning, she needed something to steady her nerves.

Finally Dex emerged from the walkway. He had

the child with him, which surprised her. The boy was wearing a cartoon T-shirt and shorts, and, she noted, they looked like father and son. They climbed in and eventually drove away. She prepared herself for exiting the limo. This was better, without Ethan.

Inside the hallway of the apartment complex Naomi searched for 2B and found it. The building was very old and looked to be built in the forties, with sturdy brick construction. It had some charm to it, but not much. She pushed the doorbell with her gloved finger. It didn't seem to work so she took off her gloves and rapped on the door.

There was a pause while, she assumed, she was observed through the view hole. The door opened and Allison stood before her.

"Why, Naomi Needham, as I live and breathe. What brings you to my end of the world?" Allison could hardly believe Naomi would venture out of her territory. But maybe Allison had threatened her territory too much, and she was here to push the boundaries back again. Allison held the door firmly.

She had on an ice-blue suit. Very tailored in that sort of Chanel look Allison had seen in a few magazines. Very striking on Naomi really, with her dark hair and ice-blue eyes. Her high heels matched perfectly.

"I wonder if I might come in and have a woman-to-woman chat with you."

"Be my guest." Allison opened the door wider and gestured for Naomi to enter.

She took a few steps in the door and seemed surprised to find herself in the kitchen. In this room, the odor of burned carpet was pretty strong. Naomi put her gloves up to her nose.

Allison tried not to smirk at the disgusted gesture Naomi made. Woman-to-woman chat, aye? Naomi came to check her out, or worse, get rid of her.

"We had a small fire," Allison said.

Naomi stared at the burn marks on the faded kitchen carpet.

"Why don't we go into the living room and have that chat. Can I get you anything to drink? I've got root beer, Sprite, orange juice, coffee, scotch?" Allison was kidding about the last one.

"Scotch," Naomi answered, much to Allison's shock. Obviously, Naomi missed the joke. Scotch at nine-thirty. This should be interesting. Naomi seemed unaware of her own odd behavior. Wow, Naomi Needham was full of surprises. She also ordered everyone around like they were on staff.

Allison really shouldn't toy with the woman so much. But it was just too tempting. She'd lost whatever fear she had of Naomi somewhere around the time Dex had made it clear he was in charge of the situation.

"Coming right up. Make yourself at home." Allison pointed to the living room archway. Naomi started to walk toward the larger room, then saw the wall of Ethan's pictures and awards and veered off. Allison knew that would catch her eye.

She poured Naomi's Scotch and added a few ice cubes. Maybe a little Drano or just straight-up rat poison might be a good addition. She poured herself a glass of orange juice and considered the addition of a shot of Dex's great scotch, but decided she'd better stay on her toes for this. Allison took her time, letting Naomi get the full "Hall of Fame" experience. She was proud of her son.

Naomi was still standing looking at pictures. "Here's your drink. Good-looking boy, isn't he?" Allison said.

Good-looking indeed. Naomi could see the striking resemblance Ethan had to Dex. He was also a brilliant child, as evidenced by the numerous awards, which was clearly a result of genetics, the Needham side. "Thank you. Your son . . . Ethan, is quite an accomplished young man."

"Yes, he is. Let's go sit down, Mrs. Needham."

"Please, call me Naomi."

What a hard edge on the girl. Naomi stepped into the living area. The bones of the apartment were good: wide moldings and window trims on double-hung windows with even a bit of leaded detailed top trim, built-in bookshelves, but the obvious lack of funds for decent furniture and lighting gave it a shabby air. It was also clear Allison wasn't much of a decorator, but at least there was order.

They both sat on the poorly slipcovered sofa.

She'd evidently been going for a country look but didn't carry through. Naomi took a small sip of the scotch. It tasted like top-brand. She was oddly surprised since everything else was so . . . bargain basement. The glass she'd been served in said "Tasty Freeze" across the side. How could Dex ever have gotten mixed up with this girl?

"Let's just cut the bull, shall we, Naomi? Why are you here? It's early in the morning, and I have quite a bit to do."

"I'm afraid we've gotten off on the wrong foot. Under the circumstances I think it's important we try and find some common ground." Common was right, Naomi added to herself. This woman was as common as they came.

"Since you are apparently my son's grandmother, I guess you're right," Allison said.

Naomi gave a start. She put down her glass on the table next to a neat stack of inexpensive photo albums. It was the first time she'd heard the words out loud. "Is your own mother living?" Naomi watched Allison cross her arms in a protective stance.

"No, she died when I was sixteen. I raised my younger brother. He's my only living relative—that I know of."

Which obviously meant there was no father in the picture for Allison and her brother. She'd been raised in poverty. Of course. "How sad for you. I'm sorry."

"So am I, she was a wonderful woman."

Naomi shifted back slightly. "As a mother I'm sure you understand, I only want Dex to be happy."

"I do understand. Probably more than you expect I do. I also want what's best for my son. I'd appreciate it if you'd keep that in mind."

Naomi could just imagine what that meant. Money. She folded her hands and thought about that carefully. Allison remained in her protective posture, she noticed. "And what would be best for your son?" she asked carefully.

"Basically, Mrs. Needham, I'm not going to let you treat Ethan as badly as you've treated me. You've been cold and judgmental toward me since we first met. Ethan deserves better than that."

Naomi got up off the sofa and picked up her drink glass. "I'm sorry you feel that way. I'll be sure and treat you with the respect you deserve from now on, Miss Jennings." She took a good swallow. The alcohol burned her throat on the way down. She set the glass back down hard, and it clinked loudly.

"And I'll do the same for you, Naomi."

The chill in the room was palpable. She set down the cup and picked up her gloves "Thank you for your time, Allison," Naomi had gotten all the information she needed for now. It was time to move on.

"Please do me the courtesy of calling before you drop by in the future, won't you?"

"That won't be necessary. I'm sure Dex will introduce me to your son in a more appropriate setting."

"You mean *his* son, don't you?"

"Yes, his son." Naomi picked up her purse and walked to the door. Allison was on her heels.

"Goodbye, Miss Jennings."

Allison held the door open for her and didn't say another word. When she saw Naomi head down the stairs she slammed the door hard and locked it with the new dead bolt Dex's handyman had installed when he fixed the broken door.

Naomi Needham had better watch her back because as far as Allison was concerned, Naomi had met her match. If she thought that all her power and money gave her the right to hurt Ethan in any way, she was underestimating the extremes Allison would resort to, to protect her son.

Maybe it was better that she wasn't burdened with work right now. This wasn't going to be as easy to deal with as she thought. This whole situation might need closer attention. And Allison needed some advice. Bunny had been through all sorts of divorces and domestic legal scrapes before. It was time to call in the big guns. Bunny's lawyer.

Back in the limo Naomi autodialed her attorney, Jeffrey Tilden. Miss Jennings was about to get a few surprises. First Naomi would make sure paternal rights were established legally. Then she'd work on custody issues. Visitation. After all, this child was a Needham.

She tapped her fingernails on the limo armrest waiting for Tilden's secretary to pick up.

It suddenly occurred to Naomi that she'd drunk an entire glass of scotch in Allison's house. What *was* she thinking?

Dex flicked on the lights to the lab and let Ethan have a look around. "This is where I work."

"Wow, this is awesome. What's your current project?" Ethan said as he read a chart Dex had created on his recent results.

"I'm trying to isolate a fungus that's used in a particular medical treatment. It's very expensive, and not available in this country. I'm trying to find a way to produce it for less money, and get the Federal Drug Administration to accept its use."

Dex watched Ethan move from table to table, not touching, but examining the glimmering rows of glass tubes and beakers. They obviously fascinated him.

"What kind of results are you seeing?"

Dex couldn't believe the questions Ethan asked. He was truly a scientist. It was rather startling. "This one here." He came closer and pointed to a row of petri dishes in a long glass incubator. "Seems to be responding very well. It's a tropical environment, but it could be duplicated for optimal growth easily. The trick is to add saline mist because the fungus thrives by the shorelines of Brazil on a particular tree. If we could just reproduce the environment, it wouldn't have to be harvested at such great expense in Brazil. The catch is, of course, is the quality as good, and does it effect the same results as a medicine that the original does?"

"Have you done human trials?" Ethan stared at the various rows one at a time.

"No, that's a problem. Shimner's disease doesn't appear in the animal realm. I'm passing my research over to the clinical trial department at the university. They've determined it has no adverse affects on rats. This is always the risky stage.

"We've got a few people willing to give it a try at this point. At least this gives them something to try here in the States, and the trial is fully funded by . . . us."

"Your family?" Ethan asked, turning to look at Dex.

"Yes, my father and I. It's our project. You see, my sister had Shimner's. We found out about the drugs used in Europe and sent her over there for a year of treatment. She came back completely cured, or at least in long-term remission as far as we can tell. It's a disease like lupus. I'll have to show you some descriptions for you to understand it fully."

"Is it hereditary?"

"Not that we know of. It's rare. We don't know the cause. Probably a genetic flaw." Dex directed Ethan over to the greenhouse area.

"I grow orchids on the side. They have amazing properties."

"Wow, they look like alien life forms. I thought orchids were all really pretty."

Dex chuckled. "Some are more like alien life forms. Hey, let's dip a few in liquid nitrogen and see what happens."

"Awesome. I've always wanted to do that."

"And maybe a tennis ball. Let's see, what else do we have kicking around?" Dex said.

Dex had so much fun with Ethan freezing and shattering whatever they could find to dip in the nitrogen they lost track of time. Finally his stomach growled.

"I think it's about lunchtime. Shall we see what Mrs. Fisk has for us? You can tell me all about your trip to MIT. I went there for four years of my college."

"No kidding?" Ethan looked up into Dex's face.

He seemed to be searching for something in Dex's features. Dex smiled. "Come on, I'll tell you about my experiences there, but I want to hear yours, too." They walked toward the exit together. "Where'd they put you up?"

"Bexley Hall. It was cool. I roomed with a guy from Japan. He spoke English better than me. Where did you stay?"

Dex opened the airlock door and held it for Ethan. "I was a Phi Beta Epsilon member. That was my father's fraternity. It was pretty formal—we had to dress for dinner and it was very academically focused."

"Was the food good where you were?" Ethan slipped off his cap and shoe coverings. Dex had loaned him a lab coat—too big, but serviceable—and he helped him out of it.

"Not as good as our cook now, but passable. What's it like on campus now?"

"Awesome. Best stuff I ever ate. We had roast beef, gravy, and mashed potatoes. I even ate parsnips. Have you ever had parsnips?"

They walked through the clean-room door and climbed the stairs together. "Yes, I've had parsnips. My grandmother grows all sorts of things at our country place. She lives out there most of the year and comes back here to Bellevue for the winter months, or sometimes to Scottsdale, Arizona. She has a house there."

"Your family is so big," Ethan said. "I'm glad you came to meet me. I know this is way weird, my mom and I talked about it a lot."

"I'm glad I came to meet you, too. We'll talk more. Right now, I'm starved."

"Me, too. Let's eat."

Naomi came in the front door just in time to watch Dex and Ethan walk down the hall toward the kitchen. Their hair was exactly the same color. Their build was similar. She saw tiny nuances of physical similarities that actually shocked her.

She removed her gloves and hat and placed them on the hall table. Where was everyone anyhow? Some good fragrance was drifting down the passages. Her stomach growled. She hadn't eaten breakfast, and she was feeling more than a little tipsy.

As she approached the kitchen she heard laughter. Dex's laughter, Ethan, and . . . She pushed the swinging door open to see what was going on.

"Naomi, come and join us." It was her husband, sitting with Prescott, the main house butler; Mrs. Fisk, the housekeeper; and Dex and Ethan. They were all around the big kitchen table. It was uncommon for them to lunch in here. Well, in the last five years, anyway. Before that they did it all the time. But considering Ethan's presence, you'd think they'd set up the dining room.

"Ethan, this is my mother, Naomi Needham." Dex stood up as Naomi approached the table.

"How do you do, Ethan?" Naomi offered her hand.

Ethan shook it with a strong grip. "I'm fine. It's nice to meet you. So you're my grandmother?"

A stab of pain hit Naomi somewhere around her left temple. Her eye twitched. "Yes, that would be correct," she slid into a chair next to her husband, seeking some stable surface.

"You've got a keen house here."

"Thank you." Naomi reached for her water glass. At least they had set a decent table.

"Here, ma'am. Let me serve you up some lunch. Margaret made macaroni and cheese." Mrs. Fisk rose and bustled around Naomi's chair. For some reason it became clear to Naomi that Mrs. Fisk knew she'd been drinking.

"Macaroni and cheese?" Naomi stared at Mrs. Fisk, who winked at her and nodded her head toward Ethan. "It was a special request. We've also got some pesto pasta salad with langostino here, and can I get you a nice strong cup of tea?"

"That would be lovely. I'll have the pasta salad, also." That seemed to come out clearly, but Dex stared at her hard. "And bring the tea first, will you Mrs. Fisk?"

"Ethan here has been telling us about his visit to MIT," Dex said. His mother was acting completely odd, and, if he could believe his nose, she had the faint smell of scotch on her breath. A charming image to present to Ethan. Perhaps Ethan didn't notice as clearly as Dex himself. Hopefully.

"Yes, you went to science camp for several weeks, I hear?" Naomi asked. Dex saw her smile at Ethan stiffly.

"Two whole weeks. It was a huge campus. Dex told me how he went there for college," Ethan answered.

Mr. Needham perked up. "It's been a Needham tradition. My father went, then me, then Dex. Dex's brother went elsewhere. He was more interested in business."

"You have a brother?" Ethan was poking large bites of macaroni and, Dex noticed, doing a pretty good job of devouring the stuff without talking with his mouth full.

"Yes, Edward. And my sister I was telling you about, her name is Celia."

"My dad has two girls with his second wife, Pamela. They're okay but they just want to play Barbies all the time." Ethan paused and glugged down half of the apple cider Mrs. Fisk had poured him.

"You have friends your own age though, right?" Naomi, for some reason, chimed in.

"At school. I don't have friends over too much because my mom's usually at work." Ethan started to talk, then Dex watched as he became guarded about what he was saying. "Until I get back from school, that is, she never leaves me alone."

He could see Ethan's caution was from his understanding of the odd situation they all found themselves in. Most likely he could sense Dex's mother's tension, too. Damn her, couldn't she just lighten up for once? Dex's father was doing so well.

Ethan was obviously more than just extremely bright. Dex had been amazed at Ethan's ability to grasp complicated scientific concepts even in these few hours they had spent together. Basically, Dex was astounded with Ethan's overall intelligence. It made his mind go in a thousand directions.

Ethan should be given every opportunity to develop that mind. Dex took a drink of water and tried to stop thinking about what his son hadn't had for the last ten years.

"Who's up for dessert? We've got chocolate cake." Saved by Mrs. Fisk.

"Yes, please!" Ethan answered.

* * *

At least she'd taught the boy some manners. Naomi watched every little move Ethan made. She studied him like she sometimes studied artwork before an auction to see if it was genuine. There was no doubt about it; Ethan was a genuine Needham. Naomi drained her tea down to the last drop, which Mrs. Fisk had brewed strong enough to raise the dead, thank God.

17

Don't Fence Me In

Ethan used his own key to open the apartment door. He flew through the door and went straight for his mother, wrapping his arms around her.

"Mom, you wouldn't believe the lab Dex has in his house. We had so much fun. He showed me what happens when you dip an orchid into liquid nitrogen."

"What did you do, stink up the place?"

"Nah, it makes it totally frozen and it shatters like glass. We stuck a bunch of stuff in there. You should have seen the tennis ball. And Dex gave me a new microscope."

"Oh, really."

Dex knocked on the open door. "Hello, we're back." He stepped in the kitchen.

At least this time she had clothes on, and her hair combed, even if it was just her jeans and a Tasmanian Devil T-shirt. Allison was struck by how tall

Dex was. Probably six foot three. That's where Ethan got his tendency to height, for sure. She was only five foot six and Ethan was in the ninety-eighth percentile of height according to their family doctor. Rusty came in at about five foot nine. They had both figured it was from Allison's absentee father. The invisible father she hardly remembered. And here Ethan had two now.

"Here's the microscope; it's one I don't use anymore. I showed him how to use it. Every microscope has its quirks."

"Of course. That's very generous of you, Dex." Allison eyed him carefully to see how the day really went.

Dex seemed to sense her probing. "We had a great time. He had a good lunch." He set the microscope down on the kitchen counter. "Would you both like to go out for dinner?"

Allison turned to Ethan, who had a very odd look on his face.

"Do you like Chinese?" Ethan said, smiling his odd little knowing smile. "My mom loves Chinese."

He was making Allison squirmy.

"Ethan, why don't you go put that microscope in your room and let Dex and me talk for a minute."

"Sure. I'll set it up. It's going to take me a while, you know."

"Holler if you have any problems," Dex said.

Ethan gave Dex a thumbs-up and marched to his room.

"How did things go, Dex?"

"We kept it light. He didn't ask too many questions, only scientific questions. Those kind are easy to answer. We had a very nice time. How about you agree to dinner tonight? I think Ethan would like that."

"I guess that would be okay. I'd go in half with you but as you know, I currently have no job."

"I feel responsible for that."

Allison laughed. "I think it was me that went for him, if you recall. You tried to pull me off of him."

"But after that I lost my head. I explained to Ethan that violence is not a good alternative, and that I regretted my actions. He said something like Tim deserved it. Ethan is quite a character. You've done a wonderful job with him."

"So has Rusty."

Dex leaned up against the counter close to Allison. Very close. "I know how hard it is growing up as a very bright child. Sometimes you lose your childhood in the process. Ethan has a good heart, and a good sense of right and wrong. That comes from parents who care."

"Thanks. I haven't been a perfect parent, you know."

"What parent is?" Dex put his arm around her. "Which reminds me, your mother dropped by."

"What? I specifically told her to keep her nose out of my affairs." Dex took his arm away, and the tension meter between them went back up to ten.

Just when it had dropped back to a decent eight a second earlier.

"I think she was just checking me out. It must have dawned on her that Ethan is her grandson now."

"Was she horrid?" Dex asked.

"Semi. It helped that she had a shot of your scotch on the rocks. Does your mother always drink that early in the morning?" Allison asked. She felt a little thrill ratting out Naomi.

"Never before five in the evening, and only on weekends. You must have given the old girl a fright." Dex relaxed a little, and back went his arm. This time he pulled her a little closer. "We've gotten derailed, Allison."

"That's the word all right, Dex. Derailed. I don't even know what station we are headed for, and I sure don't know how to get it back on track. There is so much to sort out. There are things I need to do. Now that you know who I really am, I'm about to turn into someone else."

"Maybe I'll like her, too." Dex turned her toward him and lifted her chin with his finger.

She could feel the warmth . . . heat, really, of his body next to hers. She looked in his eyes. She wasn't sure if she should let him kiss her or not.

"Dex, don't get Ethan's hopes up. If we are going to get back on those tracks we have to go very, very slowly this time. And don't let on to him what you are feeling. I don't want him to get the wrong idea, then be disappointed if things just don't work out.

And you know the possibilities are very high things between us just won't pan out."

"We've gone from trains to pans. I hear what you are saying, Allison, and I respect that. But don't shut the door on this thing between us yet." He leaned down and kissed her very gently. "Besides, the sex is great," he whispered.

"Mmm. Good memory." She felt her heart ache at the touch of his lips on hers. "But for now, that's all it's going to be—a memory." She took a step back from him and resumed her spot beside him, leaning on the counter, slightly less close than before. Out of the corner of her eye she saw a movement that could only mean Ethan had just spied and fled. Damn it!

"I can do slow, but let's do some things together, Ethan and you and me. Like dinner tonight. That will give him a sense we aren't on opposing sides. We'll keep it simple. Oh, and at some point I'd like to sit down and discuss the not-so-simple stuff, like the paternity petition that's been drawn up to confirm Ethan's legal status as my heir, and some educational funds I've set up for Ethan. Not to mention I can't have you losing your apartment. We need to have a serious talk about what to do about that."

"We'll have to try and find some alone time for that. We're, um . . . being observed." Alli nodded toward the hallway.

"Oh, gotcha. But we need to talk soon, because the attorneys are probably going to send that over fairly quickly. You know, Allison, I'd be happy to take Ethan for the rest of the week. I know you have things to put in order and decisions to make."

Allison felt a chill run through her. She took another step away from Dex. "I suppose I do, but Ethan has been gone for two weeks. We need to spend some time together, just the two of us."

"Look, let's talk about it more. I could take him Wednesday night overnight, and all day Thursday. I've got tickets to a play at the Fifth Avenue Theater Wednesday, and it goes pretty late. He might as well spend the night. It's the touring company of *Guys and Dolls*. Then we'll get him back to you Thursday."

Allison went from chilled to hot around the collar. She'd always wanted to get tickets to that theater and take Ethan to a musical. Any musical. She could never afford music lessons, or an instrument, or the tickets. It made her unreasonably mad that Dex was doing this. She should be grateful. She should. This is the sort of thing she always wanted for Ethan.

"That's fast."

"Yes. I'm sorry about the late notice. My sister gave us the tickets this afternoon."

"Let's just get to dinner. It's getting late. Ethan?"

Ethan appeared just a little too quickly. *Damn* it, Allison swore to herself once more.

Bunny and Allison sat across from James McGowan in cold leather chairs. He had the air conditioning cranked up too high for Allison's taste. Bunny was all in black and her high-heeled shoes were practically architectural. Allison was so nervous she kept staring at Bunny's shoes. So did Mr. McGowan.

"James, just explain to Allison what it is she had dumped on her by Mrs. Needham's evil attorney. I couldn't even read it myself. I was too upset for my friend."

"Now, Bunny," Mr. McGowan said. "Mr. Tilden is just doing his job. The Needhams, specifically Dex, filed this petition, and it's his duty to carry out their wishes."

"Don't try and convince me of the virtues of lawyers, James, I've seen it all. Of course, you are the craftiest devil of them all, so how can we make this go away?" Bunny rearranged herself on the chair after her speech.

"I just need to know what this all means, Mr. McGowan." Allison tried to redirect the conversation to the point—she needed information.

Her stomach twisted every time the lawyer flipped another page of the lengthy document the Needhams' attorney had drawn up.

After a lovely evening out with Dex and Ethan, and Ethan leaving with Dex the next morning, Allison had been served a petition for paternity rights before the dust had settled on their departure.

Bunny had taken the petition straight to her attorney and was paying for the entire thing. Bunny's attorney, the somewhat slimy Mr. McGowan, had contacted the Needhams' attorney, and a document the size of a *Guide to Microplus Sub-Cultures and All Available Programs for Dummies* had been messengered over within hours. Only on Bunny's dime did a lawyer move this fast.

Now here they were in his office a day later. More like a sleepless night later. He'd skimmed the pertinent parts, he said. He called it an *Agreed Order*. The trick was, she had to agree.

Naomi had beaten her to the punch. She should have met with Dex and drawn this thing up with him. Instead, she was faced with a legalese nightmare. Not only that, but Ethan was, at this minute, still with Dex, having spent the night.

She'd reached an answering service on the cell phone number Dex gave her, and left an icy message about having to meet with Bunny's attorney and saying that she'd expect Ethan back by dinner. She wanted her son back now.

Sharing him with Dex was awkward. Dex wanted more from her and from Ethan than she was prepared to give.

Rusty, she had known most of her high school years. He'd diapered Ethan and been there through colds and chicken pox, and even though they didn't live together, she knew she could trust Rusty to take good care of Ethan. Despite Bunny's reassurance, she still didn't know Dex that well. It made her nuts. Just freakin' crazy nuts, especially with this surprising new legal stuff.

Why hadn't Dex just come to her straight out

and discussed this before it was even drawn up? Having a process server show up at her door was a shock. Yes, he'd told her he was establishing legal paternity. She just didn't know it was this extensive.

If she understood this new document correctly, Dex was taking a very high hand with custody and visitation and the direction of Ethan's education. Dex was asking for joint custody of Ethan. That would mean both Dex and she would have to agree about every decision regarding Ethan's life: schools, living arrangements, and vacations, just *everything*.

Allison wasn't happy about that at all. She had run Ethan's life by herself since he was born. Sure, Rusty had input, but she couldn't remember a time he had objected to any plan she had. Rusty had the wisdom to let her call the major shots. Of course Rusty was like a big kid, and together he and Ethan just played most of the time. She was the one keeping the homework on track and making sure his teachers gave him accelerated learning opportunities.

This whole thing scared the hell out of her. Dex was going to railroad her into Ethan living there. He had money and power, and she had nothing. Nothing but Ethan.

"It's a pretty straightforward draft as far as the paternity goes, but I'd watch myself after that. What we need to do is give their attorney a response that either says we agree with everything Mr. Needham has proposed, or that we don't agree. The court will assign a mediator if we don't agree.

"Either that, or we can arrange mediation at the expense of the Needhams ourselves and speed things along. But from the looks of things I don't see why you wouldn't agree to the entire thing.

"He's asking for a great deal of input here in regard to your son's life. On the other hand, he's also suggesting an astounding amount of support come your way for the care of the boy. Did you read this figure?"

"Yes, I did."

"Private school tuition, college fund, a house in Bellevue for you and the child, monthly support I could retire on, a trust fund that has the word millions in it?"

"And what would that make me, a kept woman?"

"That would make you extremely well-off, and your son fixed for life. It does say here that the house is available to you up until you decide to remarry, so there are some stipulations."

That part hurt particularly badly. Allison closed her eyes for a moment to dull the pain in her head. Was Dex saying there was no hope for them? Was he saying, "*Marry someone else, I'm not interested*"*?* And then if she did, she'd be out on her ear! Why would he put that clause in there?

Anyhow, remarrying was the last thing on her big to-do list right now.

"Believe me, when it comes to giving a house,

that last clause is quite common. It's to protect *you.*" Mr. McGowan added, oddly enough. It still didn't ease the pain in her throbbing temples.

"Let me ask you a few questions." Mr. McGowan took out a legal pad and a pen. He scribbled a few things, then looked Allison in the eye. He had very smarmy eyes.

Allison reached for the soda the receptionist had brought her. She took a quick swallow and held on to it. This wasn't going to be pretty; she just knew it.

"Are you currently employed?"

"No. I lost my job last week."

"I see. And what was your position before you became unemployed?"

"Assistant manager at the Bellevue Tasty Freeze." She just spat it out for him to scribble down and judge her about. So there.

McGowan's right eyebrow rose up in an arch. It was a very bushy eyebrow. A small smirk played at one corner of his mouth. "And what are your plans as far as a new job?"

"I'm not sure."

"What is your average hourly wage?"

"I'd be hoping for thirteen."

"Dollars an hour?"

"Yes, yes, an hour. I was making twelve."

"Do you have job prospects?"

"Not presently."

"Have you paid your rent for August?"

"No. It's not due till the first."

"Do you have the money?"

Allison set down her glass of soda. She couldn't take any more. A strange heat rushed to her face and made her feel sick.

"No, I don't. I'm flat broke. I had to have my car repaired and without the full paycheck I was expecting on the thirtieth of this month, I haven't got enough to go two weeks in my apartment, buy groceries, pay the power bill, or put gas in the car to go find a new job. This has hit me at a particularly bad time, Mr. McGowan."

"Why, Allison Jennings, I had no idea you were this bad off." Bunny took her hand. "Shame on your for not letting me help you all these years. Why didn't you come to me? I thought you had some savings, or something. I though Rusty was keeping an eye on you. I know we lost touch for a while, but you still know my stinking phone number. I'm hurt you didn't ask."

"Rusty was keeping an eye on us, as best as he could. But without my income, it will never be enough. Besides, I can't very well ask him to pay child support for Ethan any more now, can I, since we've established that Ethan isn't his?"

"Did he say he wouldn't?"

"No, he offered to keep paying until I got another job. But it's no use. Time is not on my side."

Mr. McGowan cleared his throat. "Do you have relatives you can go to?" He held out a tissue box to Allison. She wasn't crying, but she took one. She was just mad. Mad at herself, really, for painting her life into a corner. She'd been a fool. She should have gotten a better job years ago. She wadded the tissue up in her hand and leaned her head back against the chair.

"Allison, why not take this offer from Dex, the house and the money? It just makes sense," Bunny said.

"It's much more complicated than that, Bunny. I see the sense in it, but it puts me in an incredibly awkward position. Dex and I were . . . I actually thought we might . . ." Allison unrolled the tissue and wiped at her eyes. They seemed to be leaking tears. Damn it.

"Miss Jennings, in matters of custody and parental rights, it is vitally important that you have a stable household and stable income to provide for the child. From what you've told me, you have neither, and that puts you at an extreme disadvantage in this case. As your attorney, and after hearing your situation, I'd highly advise you to take Mr. Needham's generous offer. You're not in any position to contest his claim, or even fight the terms of the petition from the court's viewpoint. He seems to have the best interest of your son at heart, and frankly, I'd trade places with you in a heartbeat if I was a woman."

"Legal advice, James? You sound envious." Bunny handed Allison another tissue as she spoke.

"Let's just say I'd have Dex Needham's baby anytime if it would net me this amount of support."

Allison waved her tissue at the lawyer, trying to speak. Bunny handed her the soda. She took a sip, which cleared her voice a bit. "I just can't do it. I'll accept the tuition and the college funding and the trust fund for Ethan, but not the house. I guess I accept the child support, and I'll put every dime of it toward Ethan's care. I don't need the maintenance money on top of the child support.

"But the joint custody thing needs fine-tuning. I'm not used to signing a paper that lets someone I barely known take my son to live with him half the year. Or that part about Switzerland for winter school break. He'd be leaving the country with my child!"

"Oh Allison, I know you are upset, but like I said, I've known Dex for years. He is only trying to give Ethan what you've dreamed about giving him for the last ten years. How can you turn that down? You're being so stubborn. Take the house. You need it." Bunny poked her.

"I can't. I can't let Dex Needham keep me like a mistress. I can't explain it to you properly, Bunny, but I just can't."

"Well, then come and live with me. I've asked you a dozen times, now say yes. You can get on your feet and figure out what you want to do."

Allison had always avoided accepting Bunny's invitation before. She'd been determined to make her own way. She thought accepting her charity would permanently damage her friendship with Bunny. After all, a freeloading friend wore thin after a while. A very short while.

And she'd been hiding how bad things really were from Bunny for a very long time. But now things were different. There was too much at stake. She needed help. She'd been thinking about this for some time now, after she'd gotten fired. About what she'd do with the rest of her life, and how she and Ethan would live. She'd gotten very little sleep in the last week. She hadn't wanted to add moving to Ethan's life right now, but very soon, there would be no choice.

"I accept your offer, Bunny. But it's temporary. I'm going to get some training starting in the fall. Then I can get a better job."

Bunny grinned and patted Allison's hand so hard it felt like a slap. "Damn, girl, it's about time. You are one stubborn woman."

"Fine, then we've established that you will accept the trust fund and educational funding that will be set up for your child. You'd be completely insane not to take this child support, which leaves the house and the maintenance support offered. What part of a hundred thousand dollars a month doesn't appeal to you, Miss Jennings?"

"Good grief, Allison, what's the problem?" Bunny sat back, stunned.

"I have to make my own living. I can't take that kind of money from Dex. I just can't."

"Let's look at this a different way, Miss Jennings. Unbeknownst to Mr. Needham, you have suffered hardship partially due to the fact you had a child alone. Being a single parent is very difficult. Now that this fact has become known to Mr. Needham, he is willing to help you regain your life. If you'd had his child and married him, the standard length of time for spousal maintenance for the purpose of the woman reestablishing herself as an employable entity can go as long as six years. Do you follow me there?"

"I do. I'm still just not sure about that part. Now what happens?"

"I'll draw up your wishes, and to save time, we might just schedule a meeting with the Needhams' attorney and Dex. We can work out the items you seem to have some trouble with at that time. Although I believe you might want to schedule in a short trip to a psychiatrist. Take a look at your life, Miss Jennings. You've just won the lottery and you're not willing to cash in the ticket."

Bunny rose up out of her chair. "That's enough, Jim, let her alone. I'll take it from here. Let us know when that meeting is set up. And your bill comes to me. Come on, Alli, I'll treat you to a fabulous lunch. We need to have a long talk. After that we'll start packing you two up."

"Thank you very much, Mr. McGowan. I don't see things exactly the way you do, but I appreciate your viewpoint."

"Yeah, Jimmy, the sentiment is overwhelming," Bunny snapped.

"I'm not paid to be subtle, Bunny. I'll have my secretary set up a meeting time and get back with you."

"Gordon, this is my best friend Allison. Bring her a blended margarita, will you?" Bunny flirted with the waiter in the upscale Southwestern restaurant.

Allison glanced up from the menu. "Extra salt."

"And the usual for you, Mrs. Parker?"

"You bet." Gordon walked off, and Bunny shifted her full attention to Allison.

"Welcome to your new life, girlfriend. We are going to have so much fun."

"I feel like I just bought a very expensive pair of shoes that are killing my feet, but look fantastic."

"Yeah, we'll go shopping later for sure."

"That's not what I mean."

"I know, I know, but get over yourself. You told me just weeks ago how you felt like you were living your mother's life all over again. Well, the universe, in its infinite sense of the insanely whacked, has provided you with the door to freedom."

"I used to want money so badly, but I never could figure a way out of survival. Now I'm just weeks away from having more money than I ever imagined, just because I accidentally had Dex's child. The thing is, I was just on the edge of figuring it out for myself. Now I sort of feel cheated."

"As my wise first husband used to say, *Work it, girl!* Who knows what will happen tomorrow? Do what you've always wanted to do and get yourself in a better place in life. I'll tell you this, Alli, there comes a moment in the life of a woman who has had a bad run of hard luck where she needs to face the fact she needs a little help from her friends. You should have faced that fact a long time ago, and I'm really furious at you for waiting so long." Bunny turned her head sideways and glared at Allison until they both cracked up. "There, that's better. Don't think I've forgotten you sitting by my bed handing me hankies when Race was declared dead. Or making sure Trisha got to school, getting her dressed, feeding her, while I couldn't face the world for three straight months. I let you help me then, now it's my turn."

The drinks arrived and Gordon excused himself. Bunny winked at him and grabbed up her big, tall very groovy glass with its salted rim and lime slice. Allison took a big gulp of hers. It was deee-vine.

"Akkkk, *brain freeze!*" Allison put her free hand up to her face. The rush of cold was painful.

"One does not gulp one's slushy tequila, dear. One sips through this fat straw."

"*Buuuuunny* Barnes, and her pal *whatzername*. Scooch over, will you?"

Only one person Allison knew talked like that. Babs. Babs had on a devastatingly chic red suit. Allison wondered if she'd sell it to her when she was sick of it. It was awesome and reeked of money. She wore fat gold accessories and a big red hat over her perfectly done blond hair. Subtle was not Babs' middle name.

"Babs *darling*, I hear congratulations are in order," Bunny twanged back at her.

Allison knew she was doing it to make fun of Babs's way of drawing out all her syllables in a sort of rich-girl way, but apparently it passed right over

Babs' head. Not a difficult leap. "Hello, Babs, what are we congratulating you for?"

"Reggie finally saw sense and asked me to marry him." She held out her left hand and displayed an engagement ring the size of a small foreign car.

"My goodness, what did he do, buy a diamond mine?"

"DeBeers did that for him. He just gave them a very big check."

"Well, Babs, you finally caught Reg! He's been such a slippery little devil," Bunny said. She sipped her drink and licked salt off the rim. Allison giggled.

"Oh well, it was sort of a surrender on his part. We know all the same people, go to the same parties, we might as well do it together. He'd been through the roster of everyone in our circle, and finally came back to where he belongs. We're just cut from the same cloth."

Yeah, the same cloth, Allison thought. And here she was having this secret fantasy of her and Dex getting together. The truth was that Dex would always defer to his own kind. The well-bred, highly educated ladies of the upper crust. She took a big noisy slurp of her margarita and gave herself another brain freeze. What an idiot she'd been. Babs stared at her.

"So, we're planning a December thirty-first wedding. New Year's Eve. Then we can file a joint tax return for this year *and* we can jet out of the horrid January weather and spend a month in Barbados."

Babs admired her own ring the whole time she was talking, then clunked her hand on the table and turned her attention to Allison. "I hear I'm not the only one that gets a congrats, Bunny, your friend here . . . what *was* your name? I forgot it when you hit me in the face with that tennis ball." Babs smiled slyly.

"Allison."

"Well, Allison, way to *go*!"

"For what?" How could she possibly know? She couldn't. Even Bunny kept her mouth shut. They both paused in mid-slurp waiting to hear what Babs was babbling about.

"Oh come on, everyone knows, for pity sakes. Here, haven't you seen your pictures? By the way, you have fabulous thighs. Do you do Pilates or something?" Babs reached in her oversized red leather tote and pulled out a newspaper. Not just any local newspaper, the *National Tattletale*.

Allison grabbed it away from her. Splashed across the front page was a picture of her inching across the ledge at the Grand Island house in her underwear. The good underwear. Beside that was one of Dex hitting Tim, her old boss, and one big close-up of her and Dex kissing. Worst of all, in the corner was the picture of Ethan that had been in the *Times* for winning the science camp award. Her son was now identified as the child of one of the richest men in the country. "Oh my God, Bunny, No. *No!*"

"Oh yes," Babs waved at Gordon to bring her a

drink from the bar. SEXY DEXY, BILLIONAIRE RECLUSE HAS LOVE CHILD WITH WAITRESS. "Bunny, you forgot to mention Allison here had recently been employed in the food services industry. I'd say your job prospects just improved greatly."

"Let me see that." Bunny grabbed the paper out of Allison's frozen hands and scanned the story. Then she flipped to the center. "Uh-oh, this is really, really bad, Alli. We better get Ethan and hole up at my house."

Allison was already on her feet. Bunny stuffed the paper in her purse and threw a twenty on the table.

"Well, I never," Babs said. Allison looked her in the eye and saw the gleam of delight there. Somehow she bet she had ever.

"Thanks for the heads-up, Babs. Next time I'll aim that tennis ball for your heart. Oh, that's right, you don't have one. Silly me." Allison grabbed her purse and followed Bunny.

"I do so," she heard Babs say in the distance.

They flew out the front doors into the arms of ten reporters. Cameras flashed, blinding Allison. She put her hands up in front of her face. "Is it true you are Dex Needham's mistress?"

"Did you get pregnant on purpose?"

"Why didn't you tell Dex Needham you had his child for ten years?"

"Where's the kid? Is he really Dex Needham's son?"

How the hell did they find her? She could only

figure from Bunny's car. Bunny grabbed her arm and barreled through the aggressive reporters, dragging Allison with her. She pushed her key ring car lock and they dove into the Jag as fast as they could, locking the doors behind them.

Bunny laughed, breathless. "Alli, we're going to have to upgrade your entire wardrobe if you're going to be a celebrity. If they think Dex is keeping you, you'll have to dress the part. Otherwise the Needhams will be blamed and you'll get sent to Naomi's office again. And damn, girl, put on some lipstick. You look like Casper. Where is that new shade I bought you?"

"Just get me to Ethan. Get this car moving, Bunny."

18

Rumors Are Flying

"Open this freakin' gate, Dex! It's Bunny and Allison. We're being followed!" Bunny screamed into the intercom. There were headlights coming up behind them despite Bunny's best efforts to dodge, weave, and distract the paparazzi.

Silently, without reply from the box, a security camera adjusted itself to see them, and then the black iron gate slid open. Bunny's yellow Jag slipped through like greased lightning. Her dainty black high heels were lead boots on the gas pedal. The gate closed behind them, and Bunny peeled out down the Needhams' long driveway.

"Wooo hooo!"

A uniformed guard stuck his head out of the booth by the gate as Bunny whizzed by.

"Bunny, this isn't the time to play speed racer." Allison hung on to the side door handle for dear life. Bunny was nuts.

"*Au contraire*, it's the perfect time. I love a good chase!" The Jag came to an abrupt halt under the Needhams' huge covered entry drive. Bunny cut the engine and stomped on the parking brake.

"Wow."

"Yeah, this is the big house. Grand Island is the *cabin*."

"When I wished to be rich I didn't get this far."

"Welcome to your wildest dreams."

A butler opened the car door and held it for Allison while she grabbed her purse. "Welcome to the Needhams', Miss Jennings."

Bunny popped out the other side of the Jag. "Hey, Mike, it's me, Bunny.

"Nice to see you, Mrs. Parker."

"We're on the run, Mike, the tabloids are hot on our tail."

"I'll buzz Duncan at the gate and let him know to pump up security. You're safe in here, ladies." Mike escorted Bunny and Allison to the front door, opened it for them, and gave a wave to yet another staff member. They were being handed off. Allison heard Mike start Bunny's car outside.

Here she was, fresh from the lawyer's office and having to face Dex, who had vastly understated his legal intentions last time they spoke. She felt her face get hot with anger. But all she really cared about was seeing Ethan right now, Dex be damned.

"Where is everyone, Prescott?"

"In the television room, believe it or not." Prescott winked at Bunny. He had an English accent. "That is, Master Dex and Master Ethan are in the television room. Mr. and Mrs. Needham are in the library having afternoon tea. Shall I announce you?"

"No, please don't. Dex is expecting me—sort of. The TV room it is, then." Allison realized she snapped a little too much on the thought of talking to Naomi just now. She was still fried at Naomi, who she was sure had pushed Dex into the joint custody plan, and probably had even more evil things in mind.

She shuddered as they walked down the long white marble hallway. Prescott led them up a grand staircase and down another hall, this one carpeted. Naomi reminded her of the evil Mrs. Danvers in *Rebecca*, and this house was about as big as the one in that old movie. Let's hope Dex didn't have a crazy wife chained up in the attic. Oh. Different movie.

As they approached the end of the corridor, Allison heard the familiar strains of afternoon cartoons. Now, that just couldn't be. Could it?

"ReBoot!" she heard Ethan yell.

Oh yeah. She entered the double doors at the end of the hall and came face-to-face with a television screen the size of Texas. Dot Matrix's digital curves filled up one entire wall. At least it was one of the early episodes, before Enzo and AndrAIa turned grown-up and everything went a notch darker.

Obviously the booming surround sound was muffling their entrance. Dex and Ethan sat on a huge tan suede sectional sofa. There was a tray of fancy appetizers on a pine coffee table, like rolled cream cheese on tortillas with ham and asparagus, which Ethan hated, and a half-consumed cheese ball with veggies and crackers, and two milkshakes in fancy glasses. At least Dex, or the cook, had a sense of healthy food for a kid. Not that she'd done so well. *Pasta pasta pasta* was the usual fare.

These little zingers hit her every time she saw the opulence of Dex's life.

And at that moment, as an Elvis-like robot recited binary code with a Captain Kirk accent during the talent show episode, Dex laughed. She hadn't really heard him laugh before. That struck her hard, too. She'd gone crazy in the kitchen with him, been to bed with him, romped all over the Grand Island estate with him on their one day and night together, besides the one ten years ago, and this was the first deep laugh from Dexter Needham she remembered hearing.

"Mom!" Ethan saw her first.

Dex turned and jumped up like someone had shocked him. "Allison! Bunny, what are you two doing here?" Dex grabbed a remote and punched the pause button.

"You've got *ReBoot* on tape?"

"DVD actually. I ordered it after Ethan's first visit. He told me it was his favorite show. I can see why." Dex was flustered.

That made Allison feel just the slightest bit better.

"Dexy, we've got big troubles," Bunny said. She

came in and plopped down on the sofa, grabbed an appetizer, and took a bite. "Not to mention we're starved because we didn't get to finish lunch, only a drink."

Allison came around the "pit" of sofas and gave Ethan a big hug. She sat down and kept hold of him, dropping her bag on the floor. Ethan put his arm around her middle and gave her a squeeze back.

"What's wrong, Mom?"

She pulled the tabloid out of her bag and handed it to Dex. "It looks like we've been found out. Bunny and I had to drive very quickly to get away from the reporters."

"Yeah, I didn't even get to finish my margarita," Bunny said with her mouth full of asparagus wraps.

"Well, that was a good thing because *you drove*, Bunny," Allison said.

She was still very upset at being chased. She was also very upset at Dex and the whole Needham family. She was also very hungry, too. "May I have one?"

"Oh, absolutely. Let me buzz the kitchen and have them send up some food. We've got soft drinks and iced tea and instant hot water up here for regular tea, if you want. Let me fix you something." Dex danced around the sofa to the back of the room, still holding the paper, to the mini-kitchen. He hit an intercom button on the counter. "Margaret, I've got two guests. Can you bring up something to eat? Whatever Mom and Dad had is fine."

"High tea. Cool." Bunny was munching a carrot.

"I'll have hot tea if you don't mind, Dex, and my friend Bunny needs a Diet Coke."

Dex nodded, but the headlines had grabbed him and he leaned on the counter and read the front splash cover first, then flipped to the inside, where even worse things dwelled: names, ages, more pictures, and lots of lies.

Allison got up and went around to Dex. He'd lost himself in the *Tattletale* article and forgotten about her. He kept reading while she bustled around him.

"Can I have a soda?" Ethan asked.

"Nope. It's poison, and it's *May I please* have a soda."

"Why are you letting Bunny drink it?"

"She's old. It's too late for her—and me."

Dex looked up to see Bunny stick her tongue out at Allison. Allison grabbed glasses out of the cupboard and a soda for Bunny out of the fridge while Dex finished reading. He pointed to a jug of lemonade in there, and she poured that for Ethan. She found the tea and cups and made herself a cup out of the instant hot water spigot.

"This is just . . . just too much. Why can't they leave us alone? What is so damn interesting about my family?" Dex looked up from the article and pushed his wire-rimmed glasses up his nose.

"Well, it is pretty freaky that Mom had me ten

years ago and I turned out to be your kid," Ethan said. "That's like . . . *Oprah.*"

"We don't watch *Oprah,*" Allison said to Dex.

"Grandma Trask does. It's really good sometimes. Do you think we'll be on *Oprah*?"

"Not if I can help it, son."

There was a silence that hung in the air like a freezing gust of wind after Dex spoke the word *son.*

"Bunny, why don't you let Ethan show you the room we are setting up for him? Ethan, would you mind showing Bunny the way?"

"Mom, you come, too, it's really cool. I got to pick the theme and I chose space. We're going to plot out the constellations on the ceiling and paint them with glow-in-the-dark paint."

"Your mother and I need to talk alone for a minute, Ethan."

"Yes, yes, you and Bunny go ahead, and while you're at it, go down to the kitchen and grab that tray of food they've got going. I'll see the room in a bit, I promise, Ethan," Allison said. She gave Ethan's hair a ruffle. Dex saw the edge of a volcano in her eyes, though, and he heard her keeping her voice calm for Ethan's sake.

"Come on, sport, I'm up for an adventure. After we see the room we can sneak in to the kitchen and stick lots of desserts on the food pile." Bunny got up and grabbed one more asparagus wrap, and her soda. "Let's go." She motioned to Ethan. He jumped up and followed.

"Okay, but you're next, Mom," Ethan said.

"I'm next. Go for it!"

They cleared out and Dex shut the double doors behind them.

He turned to face Allison, who still had that look—the volcano was about to blow.

"A room? You're setting up a room? According to the paper I read we'd need to discuss that in advance. That, and if he needs a teeth cleaning, or a *passport*? What is going on here, Dex? You can't just step in and take Ethan away from me. You might think you can, but he'll be a very unhappy boy. Do you care about Ethan at all, or is this purely for your own self-centered reasons?"

"You're right, I should have talked to you about the room. We should have talked about many things. The room is for him when he spends the night." Dex paused. He needed to be very straight with Allison. "Look, I have a son. I want to help him and give him all sorts of things he—"

"Hasn't had? Like love? And a mother that tried her hardest to make his life decent? I'm sorry if Ethan hasn't had all the luxuries you had growing up, but from what I can see, it hasn't improved your relationship with your mother that much. She pushes you around like a child."

"What are you talking about?"

"That joint custody proposal, and God knows what else."

"I hate to burst your illusions, but that was my own idea. Look, I know you've been running the show for the last ten years, but things have changed. I want to be involved in Ethan's life. I want to make decisions about his future. I want to pay for him to attend private schools."

"Oh, so since you're footing the bill, you get to make the decisions. You didn't say *help* in making decisions about his future, you said *make* decisions. That was a very telling slip, Dex. I'm still his mother." Allison smacked herself down on the sofa and pulled a throw blanket over herself. He could see she was curling up in a ball, and Dex needed to reach her somehow.

"And I'm his father. I'm not going to go away, Allison, I'm in for the long haul. You'll have to forgive my slip. I *do* mean I want to help make decisions." Dex crossed the room and sat next to her. He put his hand on hers.

"Look, Allison, I think deep down we probably both want the same thing for Ethan. You've been struggling for so many years to get him closer to those things: good schools, special programs, a better life in general. I don't know how to say this delicately, but I can make all that happen. I don't think you can even imagine the extent to which I can make Ethan's life better."

She pulled her hand away from him. "If you think I'm just going to hand him over to you, you are delusional. Besides, you'll get tired of this game and push Ethan aside after a year or so—or until you find something else to amuse yourself. Being a parent entails much more than writing checks, Skippy; you have to stick around. Not your strong suit as far as we've been concerned."

Dex took in a quick breath and felt his blood rise with anger. He had to try and remember Allison's experiences with her own father ran deep in her. He was going to try to be rational here, but . . . damn it. "That is just ridiculous. You can't believe I would have left you pregnant if I'd known. I'm sorry that our lives disconnected ten years ago. I can't undo any of that now. I realize you've had a bad time of it with your own father, but I'm not like that." He couldn't tell if he got through to her, she looked close to crying. She made him feel so much emotion. He wanted to hold her, or yell at her, or both. What could he possibly do to make her understand his side of things?

"Oh, your mother did such a great job on her fact finding, didn't she? Did she tell you how I took Ethan to the hospital at two in the morning with an ear infection and a hundred and four fever when he was nine months old? Did she tell you how many nights I've sat with him in a steamy bathroom for hours when he had the croup?"

"Allison, I've missed ten years of Ethan's life, tiny little moments that I can never get back: his first steps, his first day of school, just watching him grow. I would have been there if I'd known, for every one of those moments. Now here I am, and I can be there from here on out. I want that very much. I care about Ethan, even in the short time I've gotten to spend with him, he's made quite an impression on me."

"You're going to have to give me some time with all of this, Dex. It's all happened so fast. I came to your Fourth of July weekend expecting to maybe get a date if I was lucky, with some stable, well-off man. Heck, I would probably have accepted a date from the waiter. Instead my whole life got twisted, stapled, and . . . tied in a knot." Allison tucked her legs up on the sofa and leaned against the cushions, her head resting on her arm.

He saw pain on her face. He knew he had put it there, but there wasn't any way to erase what had happened between them, either years ago, or that weekend. It was unbelievable that they should have reached out to each other that day on Grand Island. It was like a part of each of them knew this other person held the key to an unopened door. A secret that had waited eleven years to be unlocked.

He wanted to say those words to her. But right now he had something else even more difficult on his mind. "The way things stand, we need to talk about something more pressing. Keeping Ethan safe."

"What?"

"That article in the *Tattletale* identifies Ethan as my son. His picture is in every supermarket and mini-mart in the country. Reporters chased you to my front gate." Dex reached for his drink and took a gulp to soothe his parched throat, and his anger at her words. The ice hit the glass with a sharp clink when he set it back down hard on the table.

Allison shifted herself upright. Her amber eyes were beautiful. Her face was beautiful. He could see her concern for her son—and that was beautiful, too. "Do you think he could really be in danger?"

"I wish I could say no, but there are some truly sick people out there, Alli. My cousin once received a threat saying his daughter Claire was being watched—it was a kidnapping threat."

"What did he do about it?"

"They contacted the police, they took the letter and tested it for prints and found nothing. They said unless they had actual contact or spotted someone watching the house, there was nothing they could do. The family hired bodyguards for both his children. Fortunately, nothing more occurred, and no more letters were received."

"Oh Dex, what are we going to do?"

"Short-term I'd say Ethan needs to stay here. We have a state-of-the-art security system, our staff is screened by my mother, and that's one hell of a screening."

Allison actually laughed a short, very tense laugh on that one. "Leave it to your mother to screen the staff. Isn't Bunny's house secure?"

"I'm afraid not as well. This property is completely gated with a guard at the entrance. We've got cameras scanning the perimeter."

"I had no idea. What's the big deal?"

"The work I do, for one thing. The pharmaceutical business is very big on having the first discovery. It's a multibillion-dollar industry. We have developed a few highly desirable methods and substances."

"Ethan stays here. I suppose that makes sense." Allison got up off the sofa, picked up her teacup, and took it over to the sink.

Something about her demeanor had changed. He wondered what he'd done now.

"But just for tonight. We'll talk about it again tomorrow. You better have a room made up for me, too, because I'm not leaving him here. And make it right next to his. Are there two rooms that adjoin in this place?" She set the cup down and turned to stare at him. He got up and walked over to her.

"Yes, there are two guest rooms with a door between them. Ethan's room is being painted anyway, so it's not ready for him to sleep in. Allison, I . . ." Words failed him. He had to touch her. He needed to hold her in his arms.

He came close to where she stood and pulled her in to him. He could feel her heart beating—racing. "Allison?"

"This all has to go on hold, Dex. We've got some serious problems to work through, and I'm not sure how I feel about any of this anymore." She had let him put his arms around her, but hadn't softened in his arms. Her distance made him want to break down the barrier she was putting between them. But he didn't know how.

"All right, Allison." He let her go, but stood

close to her. "Let's find Ethan. I'll have Mrs. Fisk get the rooms ready. I wonder where Margaret went to with that food?"

"I seem to remember Bunny saying they'd head for the kitchen. She's probably down there eating you out of house and home."

"Seems like you never get to have a decent meal around me. Except maybe a certain ham sandwich I have etched in my memory forever." He ran his hand down her bare arm. Her simple beige skirt and pretty white sleeveless knit top showed off her lovely figure. He wouldn't mind having her under his roof at all. Perhaps, just perhaps, they could find their way back to the beginning of whatever it was they'd started on Grand Island. Or maybe what they'd started eleven years ago. "I'll have to remedy that. We'll be having dinner about seven. I'd be honored if you'd both join us—since you're stuck here anyway."

"Us?"

"My parents are back from Grand Island."

"I see. Well, unless we can sneak a pizza past the security guards, I guess it's time to meet the folks." Allison shrugged. "Now, if you don't mind, I'd like to catch up with Ethan and Bunny."

Dex took Allison's hand. "Come with me. It's going to work out fine. I'll make sure of it. We just need some time." He led her out of the room. He just needed some time with her, too.

19

I Had the Craziest Dream

A rumbling sound woke Allison. She startled straight up in bed for the twentieth time. This time when she looked through the open door to the next room she could see Ethan's bed was empty. She threw back the covers and ran for the strange scraping noise that sounded like someone dragging a body across a wood floor.

Her bare feet made her silent as she moved through the halls. The morning light streaked through skylights and windows along the way. Her heart pounded, but her brain was fuzzy from waking up fast. She kept picturing that crazy wife in the attic getting loose and. . . .

This freakin' house was like a maze. There were stairways and hallways and doors everywhere. She got a little more frantic the closer she got to the sound. Finally, she hit the right room—or wing was more like it. By now she was hearing shrieks along with the noise. But they were more like laughter than panic. She flung open a set of double doors and stared into a huge room—it looked like a bowling alley or something. She couldn't even believe the sight that met her eyes.

First, Ethan streaked by her. "Hi Mom!" He was outfitted from head to toe: pads and bright clothes and a helmet. Then came Dex—Dex with Rollerblades on. Dex with a flame-designed helmet. He glanced up at her as he whizzed by, and looked as if he'd seen a ghost. He shrugged and grinned. To top it all off, next came Tutu. She had on purple spandex, leopard print pads, and matching leopard print Rollerblades.

"Woo hoo!" She whooshed by Allison and waved. The entire room had large pads lining the walls, and that was good, because Dex failed his U-turn and slammed into the wall. Allison figured this had something to do with the fact Dex turned ass-backward to look at her in her peasant-style cotton nightgown. That, and he didn't seem to be too good at in-line skating.

He got himself back together and rolled her way. She put her hands on her hips as he came near. "What the heck are you doing, Dex?" Allison tried to look serious, but she could hardly keep a straight face.

"It was all Tutu's doing. She had a crew setting up the wall pads this morning, I guess. After breakfast she dragged us up here. She's very adventurous for seventy."

"After breakfast? "What time is it anyway?"

"I don't know, noon?"

"How could you let me sleep so long? I've never slept that long in my entire life." Suddenly Allison felt very, very weird wandering the halls of Needham mansion in her nightgown at noon.

"You looked so peaceful. We didn't want to disturb you."

Ethan slowed down when he went past her this time. "Hey Mom, look at me!" Then he sped up again.

"Tutu said something about a boy needing toys. My mother must have called her yesterday afternoon. I assume Tutu went phone shopping after that. She popped up early this morning. Really, she's having so much fun, you can't stop her from going a little nuts."

The mention of yesterday and Dex's mother made Allison remember the dinner from hell. Talk about a little nuts. Naomi spent the long hour looking like she'd sucked a lemon. Dex and his dad just talked over sourpuss Naomi's head the whole time about genomes and genetic markers, and Ethan actually sounded like he knew what they were talking about.

Then Ethan had told her all about the wonderful musical Dex had taken him to. How colorful the sets were, and what a super experience it was. How he'd maybe like to play the trombone or the saxophone, and then they'd all talked about lessons and who was the best teacher in town, even Naomi.

Bunny's presence hadn't helped buffer the tension. And when Bunny left for her own house, she patted Allison's hand like she was leaving her at summer camp with the scary counselors. "Hang in there, Alli," she'd said, with that sympathetic look in her eye.

Some plans were made for Ethan to visit the office with Dex. What office, Allison hadn't any idea. She didn't think rich people had offices except in their houses—big fancy desks in big rooms to intimidate anyone who got too close to the family nut tree and needed to be paid off quickly, that kind of office.

Allison felt like she was being pushed down the tracks by a freight train and if she didn't move very fast, she'd get run over. The Needham Railroad. They probably actually had one of those.

And her son was on board, that was for sure.

Ethan and Grandmother Needham were racing each other down the long stretch.

"I'm going back to bed," Allison declared. She turned tail on Dex and walked back out the door. Her thin cotton nightgown billowed as she walked determinedly back toward her room, wherever that was.

Dex stuck his head out the doorway. "Since none of your clothes are here yet I had Nordstrom's send a few things over. I hope I got your size right. We'll talk about having your things packed up and moved over into our storage area for the time being. Oh *ohh*." Dex made some sort of move and ended up on his butt. She smiled to herself.

Allison tried to imagine the entire contents of her and Ethan's apartment being packed up by strangers into boxes and moved into some giant Needham warehouse. She stomped down the hall.

Well, it was her idea to stay here. Otherwise they'd pack her up and store *her* in some warehouse, and pull Ethan right in. The poor kid had no defenses against the Needhams'. They'd have him in a boarding school uniform before he knew what hit him, and Allison would never see him again. They sucked up whatever they wanted like a Kansas twister.

And speaking of Kansas twisters, the Wicked Witch of the West was flying down the hall toward her this very minute. Figures.

"Good morning, Naomi." She fake-smiled.

"Allison." Naomi fake smiled back. "Your room is the other direction." Naomi pointed her bony finger down the corridor the same direction she was going and kept walking past Allison. Well, it wasn't really bony.

"Thanks." Allison turned around and headed the right way. Damn it, that woman always caught her in her weakest moments: nightgowned, naked, or necking. She let Naomi get a good ways ahead, then kept her distance. When Naomi passed Allison's door she pointed again, without turning her head, perfectly aware Allison was trailing behind. Damn it.

* * *

Naomi fumed. Dex must be out of his mind. That must be it. She knew there was an uncle a few generations back on her husband's side who thought he was Harry Truman.

The woman slept till noon, then flounced around the house in her nightclothes with her uncombed hair sticking up like a wild thing.

Naomi had a very big headache. She'd been disturbed by her mother-in-law installing gymnasium pads on the walls of the upstairs reception hall, and again, Dex must be nuts, putting on roller skates and ruining her floors. Tutu and the boy, too.

Then there was the video game system delivered and set up in the TV room, the new basketball hoop going up outside, the tennis rackets, racketball equipment, and, well, her mother-in-law had gone insane, too. Clothes, toys, it wasn't right to shower a child with that amount of goods all at once.

Now she had to sit still for two hours and stew about it while Inez did her nails and Jodi did her hair. She had bridge club tonight, and no doubt everyone knew the entire story by now. At least she'd get out of this crazy house for the afternoon before she had to face another dinner with Dex's guests. Maybe she'd dine out tonight with Clarisse Van Cleve, then they could both go to bridge together.

Naomi was going to ask Clarisse about that boarding school she'd sent her granddaughter to last year. Whatever they did about schools had to be done very quickly this late in the year. As it was, they'd have to pull some strings to get the boy enrolled anywhere. He really should be in a good prep school. He was such a bright child. She'd actually hate to send him away. If he stayed here, she could watch over things more closely.

Right now she was going to take two aspirins, then call Jodi's salon and have them add a minifacial. That would make her feel better, surely.

After a hot shower Allison looked at herself in the full-length mirror. She was dressed in the pretty skirt and top Dex picked out for her. It was a different look for her: expensive, nice lines, a pale celery color that brought out her eyes. The fabric was some sort of fine knit, with white stripes on the edges. It hugged her curves very nicely.

Dex had done a good job. And the underwear he picked out was a total hoot: days of the week from Victoria's Secret. At least she had seven pairs of undies and seven matching bras in interesting colors. He must be a good judge of size, too. After all, he was a scientist, and good at measurements.

And a damn pushy, controlling scientist at that.

Now she was going to find her way around this barn if it was the last thing she did. Before they locked *her* in some attic, she better get all the escape routes down.

Allison took several pieces of stationery with a

big fat *N* on the top out of a writing desk in her room, and a pencil. She was going to make lists until she felt order return to her life.

What a beautiful room this was. She didn't know much about designers and all, but the floral pattern they'd picked and repeated in the rugs and overstuffed chair, bedding, and draperies was a very pleasing sunny yellow with deep rose-pink, lilac, and green in the print.

Before the lists, she needed one other thing. She drew a big square on the paper and made a mark for her room. X—You Are Here. Like at the mall. Then she gathered up her papers, marched out the door, and started diagramming hallways and landmarks: huge blue Chinese vase here, painting of a lady in yellow reading there.

It was all very English, she guessed. It was nice, but not exactly her style. She wasn't sure what her style was, but it was way less formal.

She followed a worker in a white jumpsuit down one hall and found the room Ethan had shown her—his room. Another worker was up on a scaffold painting stars on the blue ceiling. A young woman was taking measurements for window coverings, she assumed. It was really beautiful. Ethan would love it.

It hurt her inside to have someone else giving him so much. Allison knew it wasn't right. She should be glad. She opened a spacious walk-in closet door and found a large quantity of still-in-their-box toys, and a telescope. Someone was getting very carried away.

After an hour of wandering the halls, drawing rooms on her paper, and thinking about Dex and why she was here and feeling very confused and upset, she happened upon yet another installation relating to Ethan. The TV room was now fitted with video game components and a rack of games as high as her head. She riffled through the titles. Most were acceptable, but some were not. Had she been consulted? No. Did these people know anything about keeping a kid on track and not having his brain fried out with television and violent video games? No.

For some reason the sight of Kung Fu Space Fighters just pushed her over the edge.

She and Dexter Needham were going to have a little chat.

This time she maneuvered the halls like a champ, her cheater chart in her hand. And she started her list. First item was to get a pager for her kid. She wanted to be able to find him more easily than this, and Rusty had returned the one from the MIT trip. Second on the list was how long Dex was planning on keeping them prisoner. It had been about twenty-four hours so far and she was climbing the walls already.

She found them still in the upper reception hall, or whatever it was called, now the skating rink. They'd moved on to ramp action—well, Dex and

Ethan, anyway. Thank heavens Tutu was sitting this one out. Allison had never seen a woman Tutu's age so active and agile.

"Hey, Allison, help me get these contraptions off." Tutu waved her over.

"They are really having a blast. I hear you set this in motion." Tutu's skates had snap-locks and Allison bent down to unhook them, setting down her paper.

"I haven't had this much fun since never. These things are great. Having a kid around again is great. It's been a good thirty years since I got to go kid crazy. Naomi used to yell at me something fierce for overindulging Dex and Celia and little Eddie."

Allison blanched at the thought of her and Naomi having the same instincts about overindulging kids. But Tutu's face was all lit up, and you couldn't just yell at her and take all that fun away.

"I mean, what's all this funny money for if we can't use it to buy skates and basketballs?" Tutu said.

Allison pulled Tutu's skates off one at a time.

"Whew! That feels better. Good thing I got to lifting weights with Naomi's trainer. I'm one buff grandma!"

"Tutu, you are one cool great-grandma. I'm glad Ethan is getting to know you." Allison stood up and straightened out her skirt.

"Nice duds. Good color for you. And your cute

little sandals look great. We should paint those toenails of yours to match. I helped a little with the clothes, but Dex really picked them out. He had way too much fun with the underwear. We had a personal shopper bring it all over while you were sleeping. You sure had a good snooze, honey."

"I guess I was tired. Tutu, I need you to do me a favor. I'd like to talk to Dex alone when they finally give it up in here. Can you take Ethan and maybe watch a movie with him in the TV room?"

"We'll play Timesplitters 2 on the PlayStation."

"As long as it has an *E* on the box. Anything that says *M* or *A* is too violent for Ethan. *T* might be okay—but ask me first. He's only ten, after all."

"Gotcha. I just had the whole pile sent over. We'll give away the bad ones. The computer hasn't arrived yet, but you'll have to help me pick out some stuff for that. Dex just had them put on educational stuff."

The computer. The freakin' computer. Allison took a deep breath. She sat down next to Tutu on a side chair with a green velvet seat. "Tutu, we need to have that computer set up where someone can see Ethan use it. It has to have some parental controls set up and . . ." She just couldn't talk. It was too complicated to impart in one lump, and she was upset that buying a computer for Ethan was as easy as ordering a pizza for the Needham bunch.

"Wow, you're turning just as pink as Naomi does." Tutu patted her hand. "Don't worry, sweetie, we'll get the hang of it. You just go ahead and talk to Dex, I'll make sure Ethan stays busy. We'll read or something." Tutu winked.

Allison knew perfectly well they weren't going to read. But she also knew Ethan would have more fun than he'd had for years, so she gave up—as much as she was willing to give up right now anyway.

"Can you tell Dex I'll be in the kitchen? Once again I've missed a meal around here. I'm going down to make myself a salad or something."

"You bet. Don't let Margaret talk you into that lemon meringue pie she made. Us gals have to watch our figures, don't we?"

Allison got up. If she kept wearing dresses this tight, she sure would. It'd been weeks since she'd done any of the exercises Bunny insisted she had to do daily. Fortunately for her, when she was stressed, food was the last thing on her mind. On the other hand, lemon meringue was one of her top three favorites. "I'll try and resist, Tutu." Allison grabbed her map off the floor. Can't lose that.

As she crossed the room she watched Ethan do some ramp moves that were pretty darn amazing. Dex came rolling behind him and, well . . . not bad for a thirty-something science nerd, really. He seemed to be getting the hang of it. Allison waved to them, and went in search of the kitchen. She had her map, and knew how to use it.

Dex knew he was going to regret spending over two hours on in-line skates. He knew he'd dream of the motion all night, and he knew his muscles would scream at him later. Running and tennis didn't use the same set as slamming into a wall full-speed or taking a ramp. Ethan had just about mastered the darn things in an hour.

He didn't care about later. He was having a blast. The time they'd spent playing had slipped away without his once thinking of some patent or some business arrangement. He liked that feeling. It was similar to the timelessness he fell into when he worked in the lab alone.

He skated over to Tutu, who had her feet up and was chugging down her bottled water.

"This was a great idea, Tutu. Thanks. Ethan loved it."

"Looks like you had a pretty good time, too," she said.

"I did. I feel like a kid again. Remember when you and Grandfather put in that rope swing over the water on Grand Island? Celia and Edward and I spent every high tide that summer swinging out over the water and letting go. I'll never forget that. Even when we were teenagers we kept it up. At night the phosphorus would splash up around us and glow. You came down and watched us a few times, remember?"

"I remember. I'm glad you do, too. Have some fun, Dexy, life is too short to stay cooped up in your lab. Your work is important, but now you've got Ethan and, well, darn it, it's just time for you to get some balance. Do ya get me, Dex?"

"I get you, Grandma. And you're one heck of a skater. Talk about balance."

"Speaking of balance, Alli was here." Tutu flexed her toes and smiled.

"I saw her. That outfit turned out pretty good. Thanks for the help, partner."

"She wants to talk to you. I'm gonna keep Ethan entertained for a few hours. She's in the kitchen getting some late lunch. She's a little ruffled around the edges, I think."

"Hmmm, I suppose we've moved a little fast. Well, I'll get it all patched up and set right. Thank you for keeping an eye on Ethan for a while."

"I'll keep him busy till dinner. We're gonna do something educational."

"You're going to play video games and watch *Harry Potter* again, aren't you?"

"I'm not tellin'."

"We'll see you at dinner. Maybe I'll take Allison on a tour of the house so she can find her way around."

"Oh she's finding her way all right. She's a smart cookie."

Dex gave Tutu a smile and waved as he skated over to Ethan. He'd let him know what was going on. Then he'd better get these wheels off and practice walking again.

Allison was eating a huge piece of lemon meringue pie when Dex walked in the kitchen. She looked surprised to see him. She also looked extremely pretty. Her reddish hair fell in graceful waves to her shoulders. Her bare arms were tan, and her long legs looked smooth and shapely.

"You summoned me?" Dex sat down next to her at the kitchen counter. Margaret got out a plate and cut him a piece of pie without asking. "Margaret, this is too pretty to eat."

"Pish," she said, and smiled at him. She went back to chopping up a large pineapple.

Allison set down her fork. Dex picked his up. He took a big bite of the pie. It tasted heavenly. "Wow," he said between mouthfuls.

"I'm glad you're enjoying yourself, Dex. You Needhams' seem to dive head-first into everything."

Dex laughed. "Today I did for sure. It's a good thing I had a helmet on." He glanced at her and wished he had one on now, because she looked like she was going to hit him with a rolling pin or some nearby object. Kitchens were dangerous. In more ways than one. He had a flashback of Allison in the kitchen on Grand Island. A very, very hot flashback.

"We have things to discuss. I have a list." She tapped the table with her fingernails, and Dex saw she did indeed have a list, and some other things: some sort of drawing done on Needham stationery.

He pulled it out from under her fingers. "What's this?"

"*Give me that.*" She grabbed for it, but he kept it away from her. "It's my escape plan."

He looked at her out-of-proportion odd drawing

of the first- and second-floor layout. "We have a map of the house you can have. We make them up for the staff." He smiled. He liked her drawings.

"Oh good, I'll be needing that when you give me a job around here. Will I be the upstairs maid or the scullery girl? Frankly, it would be an improvement on pacing the halls and seeing the truckloads of entertainment items brought in to keep Ethan from noticing I'm still alive."

Dex noticed Margaret smirk somewhere around the scullery girl part. That was about the time he was thinking of Allison in a very short French maid's uniform with a feather duster.

"Allison, it's only been a day. I thought maybe you'd like to rest a bit. You've worked very hard for the last what, fifteen years? Wouldn't you like to have a day off and relax?" He took another bite of pie.

"Relax in the House of Needham? Very funny, Dex. I have a few things on my mind."

"Perhaps we should discuss this elsewhere." He eyed Margaret, who looked as if she was going to laugh out loud any minute. She kept cutting pineapple into uniform chunks and throwing them into a white ceramic bowl.

"If you'll give me my map back, I might be able to find *elsewhere*." Allison drummed her fingertips on the table over her list.

"Margaret, where does Mrs. Fisk keep that house map?"

"Kitchen office file drawer. Look under *B* for

Bellevue House." Margaret pointed with her long knife.

Dex finished his last bite of pie.

"Just give me mine back. I have special notes." Allison glared at him. Dex kept the map out of her reach and read her scribbles.

"Like *left at ugly statue?* You should be careful what you write on paper, Allison. You never know who will find it." He grinned at her.

"It's you that should be careful what you write on paper, Dex, and by the way, I haven't signed any of that, so as it stands, you are not officially recognized as existing. How about that?"

Dex lost his smile. He handed her papers back to her and got up. "Thank you, Margaret," he said to her. "Come with me," he said to Allison.

She followed him out the kitchen door. At least she didn't battle him this time.

20

Someone To Watch Over Me

A long, silent walk ensued. Finally he opened the door to the sitting room adjoining his bedroom.

"Have a seat." He gestured toward the small table and two wingback chairs next to the fireplace. Then he locked the door. If they were going to have it out, this time no one would be walking in on them unexpectedly. Besides, he figured it was about time to turn the tables on Allison. Balance and unbalance. It was all just like an equation and it had a solution, just like any other equation. *X* equals Allison set straight.

"Okay, I'm just going to start with my list. First, I'd like you to give Ethan a beeper so I can find him in this maze. One with a text feature so we can write the room in. I've logged more miles just locating him today than I've walked in a month."

"Sounds reasonable, and sort of interesting. There is an intercom system built into the walls of every room, also. I'll show it to you. But the beeper can be between the two of you and that's fun."

Allison didn't look happy about his answer, which confused him. What *do* women want?

"How insane is it that I'm sitting here asking you for a beeper to find my son? I can hardly stand it."

"I honestly don't get what you are upset about, Allison. I'm trying to understand, but all I see is Ethan having a good time getting to know us, and you not having a good time. What can I do to make things better for you?"

"I don't know, take back your biological contribution and put our life back the way it was?" She twisted herself up in the chair and kicked off her shoes.

"Back to hardly paying the rent and not having enough money to give Ethan the educational environment he obviously would thrive in?"

"You see? That's what I mean."

Dex rubbed his forehead and leaned on the fireplace. What the hell was she talking about?

"We haven't even signed this agreement you had drawn up, and you're deciding where Ethan should go to school, what Ethan should watch on TV, and how he should spend his school vacations. I can't just hand him over to you on the mere fact you happen to be the sperm donor. I've been making decisions about his life since before he was born. I can't just stop. You can't make me stop. I won't let you!" She leaned forward in her chair and raised her voice for emphasis.

"The nature of that paper was for us to share in decisions. I don't care if you are paying for them or not, you have failed to consult me on a single thing. If this is what you call joint custody, I think I'm going to have to take Ethan out of here and hire myself a lawyer on Bunny's money. Since I'm unemployed at present, I can certainly keep an eye on Ethan whether we've been plastered in a gossip rag nationwide or not."

Ah, the *L* word. Lawyer. But at least she made some sense this time.

"Which brings me to the fact that keeping Ethan locked up in here isn't healthy. Rich people have kids. They go places. Look at Bill and Melinda. Look at Prince freakin' Charles."

"Bodyguards."

"So get one." Allison smacked back in the chair. "And by the way, keeping *me* locked up in here is *really* not healthy."

"I can see that." Dex flipped on the gas fireplace. The room had taken on a chill. A little warmth would be good.

"So what's it going to be, Dex?"

"Is there a decision involved? There is no way I'm going to step out of the picture. I can see your point about discussing major decisions with you. I've been rather impulsive."

"Not just major decisions, all decisions. Like what video games are acceptable and whether it's wise to buy a child so many toys and amusements all at once. Do you want Ethan to become a spoiled, pampered rich boy? Part of who he is now has to do with us working together to make our life better."

"You were struggling to survive. That's the flip side of what I'm doing. Surely Ethan has suffered from knowing there was barely enough money to pay for books. He told me how much he wanted a computer but he didn't want to tell you because he knew you'd work extra hours to try and get it for him or just hurt inside knowing you couldn't save up the money."

"Not *everyone* is wealthy. The rest of the world is out there struggling while you're in here cozy and warm. Your electric bill is probably equal to a working man's yearly wages."

"Didn't you always want to be free of it, Allison?"

She didn't answer. She turned her head to the chair side and let her hair fall in front of her cheek. He saw her brush a tear away.

"Didn't you?"

"Yes. I did. Are you happy now? Ethan's had a horrible life. You've stepped in now and everything will be just peachy. You can just push me out of the way and write lots of checks. I'm sure you know everything there is to know about raising a child. Or you could hire someone to do that part. Maybe marry one of your snobby girlfriends and buy me off. Wasn't that pretty much the idea with the house and the hundred-thousand-a-month support check?

"Boy, Dex, you don't fall far from the Needham

family nut tree. And that part about if I remarry, then you'd be off the hook. Brilliant clause. Only we both know my chances of remarrying are pretty slim with my background. That means you'd be stuck with my bills for a really long time—maybe forever."

Dex listened to her whole speech. Then he reached over and pulled her out of the chair, into his arms. "I do not want to push you out of the way, lock you up, pay you off, or make you vanish. I want you here. I want you right here." He tipped her chin up and kissed her hard and deep. He wanted her to feel his words.

She stayed very still for a moment, letting him kiss her. Then she pushed him away and looked into his eyes with confusion and anger and hurt written in the lines and edges of her face. Years of pain and loss: loss of her father, and her mother, and even Rusty, were contained in this woman. She'd lost her childhood, and the kind of joy that comes when a person is free from struggle. Ethan had given her the only happiness she'd ever known.

He knew what had to happen. She had to give up something so deeply carved into her makeup that it would be a miracle if he got her to do it.

She had to stop fighting the world and surrender to him.

He put his arms back around her. "I'm not going to let anything happen to you and Ethan ever again, Allison. I'll make sure you are taken care of no matter what happens."

She let out a single cry. He gathered her to him and just held her close. He'd been circling around her for days now, trying to find the door back in to her heart. How she ever let her guard down long enough to make love to him on Grand Island was a mystery. The woman who let herself open up to emotion and pleasure for one amazing night was still in there, waiting to get out again. She'd been like a tidal wave that washed over him and changed him forever, sweeping his own years of loneliness aside.

He'd thought if he just let her work things through she'd find her way back to him. But he underestimated the demons she had fought for so many years. She needed help. She needed him to break down the walls and carry her out.

He stroked her hair and curled a strand behind her ear. He ran his fingertips over her temple as he listened to her fight back the tears, lose her fight, and sob against his chest.

He could never know the kind of pain she'd gone through. His life hadn't fallen that way. He thought about his parents and felt grateful, suddenly, for their presence in his life and their efforts to create a supportive family. His brother and sister were always there for him. He even had grandparents to guide and support him.

These things, more than the fortune he was born into, or the vast amounts of money he made himself, were the things that made his life privileged.

Now he could give that to Ethan . . . and Allison, too, if she'd let him.

He felt her take a deep breath in and let a ragged sigh out. He smoothed her hair and kissed her tear-moistened cheek.

"Come on, we'll just lie down for a while." He put his arm around her, handed her a pile of tissues from the table, and took her to his bed in the next room. She blew her nose and left a trail of tearstained tissues across the room. He smiled to himself. Her funny habits were so consistent.

They lay down together on top of the down coverlet, his arms supporting her, for quite a while, silence smoothing over their emotions. He kept stroking her temples quietly until he felt her breathing even out.

And then she came to him. She pulled him into a kiss that became more and more intense. Her mouth opened to his, and he explored her—warm and giving and full of desire. His hand brushed over her side and up to her breast lightly. He heard her take in a sharp breath as he gently touched her nipple with his thumb. Then he wanted to make her cry with pleasure—not sorrow—so bad it made him ache.

Slowly he touched her, pushing up her clothing, taking each piece off. He left her bra and panties on and used them to filter his hot breath on her breasts, and between her legs and back until she writhed under his mouth. She entwined her arms around his neck and pulled him into her kiss. Her mouth was so hot, her kisses so amazingly sweet and hot at the same time.

She pulled at his shirt and he stripped it off, along with his pants and remaining clothes. He gently removed her bra and she slid her panties off. He reached for his condoms from the bedside table. She ran her hands over his chest and across his back, pulling him in to her.

He let her feel him against her—how hard and excited she'd made him. Their bodies, flesh-to-flesh, created waves of desire through him that made his head spin and his emotion rise to heights he'd never known possible. He let her roll the condom onto him, and her touch was like fire over his body and his mind. Then he made her slow down.

"Slow down, slow down," he whispered softly in her ear as he reached his fingertips into her sweetness. Her cry was pleasure this time. She was molten hot and wet inside and he could hardly stop himself from thrusting his throbbing erection deep into her, but he waited and stroked her until he felt her explode and throb around his fingers. He took her nipple in his mouth as she came and she cried out for him.

She wrapped herself around him and pressed hard, hard against his heat as waves of pleasure still rolled through her. He kept his fingertips on the wet nipple he'd had in his mouth and slid down to her till he could part her legs and put his tongue on the burning pearl of flesh that made her scream out loud and press herself against his mouth. He slipped his fingers inside her as she peaked again. He truly had never felt anything like her openness and passion. It surrounded him and made his vision blur into a darkness that made him so hard he couldn't bear it anymore.

He pulled her legs around him as he moved up and slid his burning erection inside her. Her breast sweet in his mouth, her hands pressed him deeper and deeper inside. He moved his mouth to her mouth, and the wetness of her tongue drove the rest of his mind to the edge of sanity. He fell into the spell of her body and her hips moving against him, thrusting him deeper each time.

Then she stopped moving. He heard her breath, ragged and wild. He held very still. A deep, aching cry came from within her, and when it reached a scream he knew she'd let go in a way she never had before.

He moved once, pressing so deep inside her he could feel the thunder that rumbled through her body until it became his own and he could no longer control his own release. He gathered her and held her close as hot fire poured out of him and shook his body, and their bodies felt eternally connected for a time until their hearts slowed. He lay on her, inside her, feeling the throb of pleasure, feeling her heart beating and her breath against his neck.

He moved finally and gathered her against him, her back to his front. He stroked her body with long, slow, loving strokes. Her hair was silky and wild and he buried his face in the scent of it.

"If we made love like this every day we'd forget to have any problems," she whispered.

"That could be arranged," he said softly.

21

Until the Real Thing Comes Along

For the first time since she'd been here she was actually enjoying dinner. Of course, a woman who'd been made love to like Dex made love to her only hours ago would probably enjoy just about anything.

Her cheeks were flushed; she knew it. She and Dex had showered in his roomy shower, and it had turned into a long, long shower. Apparently the Needhams had very large hot water tanks because he'd backed her against the cool white tiles and done her crazy all over again, standing up. And truly, she'd never felt a man fit into her the way Dex fit into her.

She could think all these things while she ate scallops sautéed in white wine and shallots resting on a bed of angel-hair pasta with Asian vegetables on the side because she and Dex were the only ones at the huge dining table. Margaret's daughter Anna kept bringing new delights to the table. Before the scallops came a bright salad with fruit and raspberry vinaigrette, and a bowl of some amazing broth with tiny straw mushrooms and a few scallions floating in it.

She reached for the crystal wine goblet Dex had filled with very mellow white Bordeaux, he said. She was sort of drunk from good sex and good food and good wine. She took another sip anyway.

She knew when this all wore off she was going to get upset again, but for now she was just going to enjoy herself—a very odd feeling, but worth exploring.

"Dex, I feel so good I think I could rationally discuss schools for Ethan without screaming. Do you want to try it?"

"Hmm, maybe a quickie. I was thinking either Northwest School or Washington Academy. Washington Academy is more science-oriented."

"What color are the uniforms?"

"You're kidding, right?"

She took another sip of wine. "Nope, lay it on me."

"Navy blazer, gray slacks, white shirt with a very interesting light blue navy and green striped tie. That's Washington Academy. Northwest is no uniforms.

"Okay, that's too deep. I can't decide based on dress code. Is there lemon meringue pie for dessert?"

"I think Tutu and Ethan ate it all after their dinner. They went to watch *Harry Potter II* and fell asleep on the TV room sofa. Mrs. Fisk says she got them both to bed."

"And your mother and father?"

"Friday is mother's bridge night, and she dines out with friends. Father is in Scotland golfing. Grandfather went, too."

"Golfing in Scotland. Got it. Where do your sister and brother live?"

"Edward and Nora live on Mercer Island. Celia and Warren have a beautiful place in Issaquah. We're all pretty close by. Of course my Grandmother Tutu and grandfather spend most of the year in the Grand Island house. That's their place; they just let the whole family use it."

"Of course. You know, Dex, when I pictured life beyond my recently departed status, it never got this big and grand. It was a pretty simple deal. Nice house, a car that ran whenever you stuck the key in it and turned it on, just sort of basic stuff: no bills, mortgage paid off. Maybe a little left over to help single moms like me with their food bills or school supplies for their kids."

"Having a simple life actually sounds very nice. It's extremely strange for me because I was born into this. Trust fund, all that jazz. I've stayed here with my parents because hey, it's a huge house. I wasn't married, and I built a lab here."

"Where is the *office*?"

"Needham Labs? Downtown Bellevue in the

Needham Building, you know. That's where my initial experiments and theories get taken to another level with lots of other lab workers. And we have several research and development people on staff besides me."

"Needham Building. How silly. Of course, I've seen it." Allison suddenly got the big picture; the twenty-story building that housed the labs, Dex's research, the whole shebang.

Dex leaned in close. "Come back to bed with me," he whispered.

The wine had made Allison's head fuzzy. Or something had. She thought of a few reasons why she shouldn't, but they faded away. "Okay, but have me back in my room by six A.M. so Ethan doesn't miss me."

"We can do that. Alarm clocks, roosters, we've got them all."

"You've got a rooster?"

"Somewhere around here. We may have had him for dinner."

"We had scallops."

"You look extremely beautiful in that dress. Can I get you out of it again?"

"You are . . . bad," she whispered.

"It's a recently acquired trait."

The light was already coming through the window when she crawled back into her yellow floral sheets. She'd walked very quietly through the hallways and even managed to find her way without her map. Not that she could sleep anymore, but she stretched out in the bed and pulled the covers around her neck. She felt like that little girl in *The Little Princess*, Sara Crewe, when the neighbor man filled the room with beautiful things and warm coverlets and she woke up thinking she was in a dream.

"Nice one, Mom," Ethan giggled.

Oh brother. She blushed even though he couldn't see her. Well, for all he knew she'd been wandering the halls aimlessly, which seemed like the only thing for her to do around here.

"Come on, jump over here," she said. He brought a blanket and padded over the bare floor and pretty carpets to her bed. He lay on top of her down comforter, his blanket wrapped around him, his head on the pillow next to her. They stared at each other and giggled.

"Cool place, isn't it?" he said. His eyes were wide open.

"Big place, for sure."

"It's kind of like going to summer camp."

"Yeah, but with servants. In real summer camp the kids work and do stuff. This is more like a luxury resort. You've never been to one of those, but this is what it's like. There's something we need to talk about, Ethan. Dex and his grandma got a little carried away with the toys and stuff. Normally kids don't get this amount of . . . stuff all at once."

"I know. I was freaked out at first but I figured it can stay here for Uncle Edward's kids, and Aunt Celia's kids when they have them."

"I suppose that's right. So you get that it's not all just for you?"

"Sure it is, but I'll be careful with it and make it last." Ethan's face was calm and happy. She decided he hadn't been warped too much yet.

"We've got to decide about schools for you. I have no idea how long we are staying here, but Dex has offered to send you to private school, and that seems like a very good idea. We'll visit a couple and you can see what you think."

"I want to invite a few friends from my old school over here if I'm going to leave it—sort of to say goodbye. And Dad—Rusty. He *has* to see this place."

"We can do that. We'll talk to Dex at breakfast. It's so weird having people cook for you, isn't it? Breakfast is better because you can sort of get your own off the big buffet table."

"The food is great."

"Let's get dressed and escape the house. There's a huge patch of land around us. And a pool. We could swim. It's outside in its own little glass house."

Ethan popped up. "Let's go! Swimsuits under clothes. Did you get a bunch of new clothes? I did. What's going to happen to our old stuff?"

"It's supposed to get packed up today. I think I'll

have Bunny take me over there. You don't mind being here when I'm not, do you?"

"Mom, there's tons of stuff to do. I found a totally awesome library yesterday and my computer is going to arrive any day now. Tutu said I could order a bunch of books. I did find some, though, from when Dex was a kid. *Treasure Island*, I love that story. Tutu showed me."

"Okay. You tell me the really important stuff you want from your room and I'll make sure it's in one box." Allison eased herself out of bed. A swim would feel wonderful. She wasn't sure if there was a bathing suit in the clothes she'd been given, but she figured there'd be a bunch in the pool house.

Tutu was in the pool doing laps. Allison found a red one-piece in the dressing room that sort of fit. Ethan took a big cannonball jump in the water and splashed her good. "Hey!"

"Jump in, Mom, it's great."

She stuck her toe in the water, then slid herself in. It wasn't the warmest pool ever, but it was July, and it was already hot outside. She swam over to Tutu, who had stopped and was resting on the side of the pool.

"Hey, Alli, what's shakin' besides you and Dex?"

"Oh my God, does everyone in the house know?"

"It's a big house, but not that big."

"What, where we echoing through the walls?"

"Dumbwaiters. Don't worry, I kept the movie cranked up way high. And Naomi came in late. She sleeps with earplugs and a mask anyhow." Tutu grinned at her. "You're only young and sexy once, ya know."

"This whole thing is just ass-backward, Tutu."

"Pretty typical for the Needham men. The sex is great, they go to work and make lots of money, you can play to your heart's content, and they are a fun bunch underneath it all. I'd call that a pretty good deal."

Allison squeezed the water out of her ponytail with one hand. "I know, but I'm used to working hard myself."

"Lookit me, Mom! Tutu!" Ethan was up on the high dive. She felt very nervous about that, but she'd learned long ago to keep a lid on it unless there was real danger. Ethan knew how to dive. He took a jump and did a pretty decent job of it with just a partial belly flop at the end.

"Woo hoo!" she yelled when he emerged. He was obviously going to do that about twenty times in a row until he mastered whatever it was he felt like mastering.

"Find something," Tutu said. "I have my garden club and I help with the Needham Foundation."

"I'm in a very awkward position here, Tutu, I've lost my job, I have no money. That alone is making me completely nuts. I can't ask Dex for walking-around money. I feel very trapped."

"It's a big cage. But I know what you mean. Kick your legs like this, it's great for keeping them toned." Tutu flutter-kicked out behind her while she held on to the pool side. Allison did the same.

Tutu went on. "I was a telephone operator before I married. I went to a training high school. I didn't go to college. But I had me a skill so if my husband went off to war or some crazy thing like that and got himself killed I'd be able to support myself. I had Dexter II, Dex's father, by the time I was nineteen. That was back in the fifties. I had three kids right in a row. You met Randall. And there's another son living in California. Lloyd. Three boys.

"What great times those were. Then my husband got rich inventing medicine and we built a nice little house on this property. It's just back yonder behind those maples." She pointed to the west. "Sometimes I go over there and remember our good times. There weren't many neighbors back then, and no fences. We had a big spread, and I kept a couple horses for the kids.

"It's the guest house now. Though why the hell we need a guest house I have no idea, there are so many rooms in the big house. I guess Naomi likes to put her relatives up there when they come visit because her mother drives her nuts." Tutu laughed big and kicked harder.

"Man, this is killer exercise, Tutu. Are you talking about that English Tudor house over there? That's huge."

"It sure was at the time. We'd lived in a little bungalow-type house before that. But Dex's father, Dex the first, when he got even richer, he wanted to build this big place so we could all live together. Turns out Gramdpa and I like the Grand Island house lots better. The sea air agrees with me. The gardens are better, and it was so much fun for the grandkids. Yee haw, Ethan, that was a good one!" Tutu yelled in Ethan's direction.

The splash from Ethan's flopped dive rolled over their way.

"Celia's trying, I heard."

"Poor thing, I pray for her every day that she gets a baby. If she can't have one, we'll all help her adopt."

"She's got great doctors. I think it will happen. She looked very healthy at the party."

"See? Look at you. You fit in here just dandy."

"Don't let Naomi hear you say that."

"She'll come round. So like I said, let us take care of you for a while. You've earned a break. I'll slip you some pocket money and you just go find something to do."

"I can't take money from you, Tutu."

"Why not? Do my laundry if it makes you feel better. Just figure you won a prize and it's just been ten years coming. Now it's here."

"Ed McMahon was a little late with the ten-million-dollar giveaway?" Allison quit kicking and took a rest.

"Right."

"Tutu?"

"Yes dear?"

"You are way cool. Will you show me your old house? I want to see it."

"Sure." She finally quit her kicks. "Race me to the end of the pool. We'll get Ethan and dry off—and go for a walk."

Now, this was a house. The outside had stones covering the bottom half and creamy white stucco siding with a little bit of English trim. There were eyebrow windows and the roof tiles were red.

"This looks like the house in Alice in Wonderland, Mom, don't eat any mushrooms, you'll pop out the top."

"Haw, haw. Stay where I can see you, Mad Hatter."

Tutu took a key from inside a fake rock that blended with the other landscape rocks.

"What are you all up to?" Dex's voice boomed out, so close she jumped. He smiled at her when she turned and looked in his eyes. It gave her a jitterbug stomach—a flip-flop she hadn't felt in a million years. She supposed he'd gotten to her with all his fabulous kisses and other talents.

"Dex, you scared the bejeebers out of us." Tutu swung open one side of the double front door. "We're snooping. Got anyone locked up in here?"

"Not today. Let me get the lights for you. Ethan, I see you and your mom found the pool."

"I'm working on my diving," Ethan said.

"Aunt Celia is a champ. She can give you some pointers. They're coming out in a few weeks."

"I want to have some of my school friends out, Dex. Can we do that?" Ethan asked.

Allison was surprised how bold he was. But kids are like that because they don't think so much about things—just blurt them out.

"And my dad. Rusty. My other dad. I want him to see your house."

And the blurting was still rolling along, Allison noticed. She decided to just stay out of this one.

"Sure. It's Saturday, why don't we call him and your friends. They can all come over. We'll have a pizza and swim in the pool. Or swim and eat pizza—the other way around." Dex laughed.

Pretty smooth on Dex's part. She admired his finesse, among other things. They wandered through the house with Tutu telling tales. She showed Allison a wall in the kitchen with markings of her three boys' heights. Dexter II, Randall, and Lloyd.

The house was sunny and well kept. The furniture had sheets draped over it and Tutu pulled back a few to show Allison some real classic pieces: channel-stitched sculpted mohair chairs in deep rose-red, pillows with Yellowstone Park embroidered on them; tacky stuff that had gone beyond its time and become collectible. There was a jade green horse-head lamp.

Ethan ran up to her. "We're going back so I can call Dad."

Boy howdy, Allison had no idea how this dad

thing was going to work out. Dex, Dad, whatever. She figured on letting them work it out. "Sure. Tutu and I are going to stay here for a while."

"Bye!" Ethan waved. He had a towel wrapped around his shoulders, and his hair was sticking up all over. That boy was just way cute.

"Bye," Dex echoed.

"Go, leave us women in peace."

"Look here, these were my mother's dishes from the twenties." Tutu called her to the kitchen, which had creamy white cabinets and a wallpaper border of black and cream checks and red cherries. All the dishware was bright and funky—so amazingly homey for a Needham residence.

After they washed out a few of the colorful Blue Ridge cups and brewed some tea for themselves, Allison and Tutu talked. By the time they left she had fallen in love with the house and its history and the way the rooms rambled around. There were window seats and five bedrooms, and lots of closets.

And there were memories. Tutu's memories and her husband's and even the three boys'.

"Tutu, I want to stay in this house for a while. I'm not good with big huge mansions. Can I?"

"Sure. We'll tell Naomi so she doesn't get spooked. She spooks easy. Then we'll call up a cleaning crew and get the dust out."

"Oh no, I can do it myself."

"Well, you could, but then you wouldn't be giving some other woman twenty-five bucks an hour to feed her kids and pay her rent."

Allison thought about that for a while and decided that was a good idea. "Okay, but I'll do your laundry anyway. I have to *do* something. Anything."

"I was joking, dear. Don't you have a house full of stuff to move?"

"What about Ethan's friends?"

"Dex and I can handle them."

"When is the last time you had four ten-year-olds running around?"

"Forty years, but that's okay. We'll hired a lifeguard for the day and Margaret can whip up a mean pizza."

"Okay, you're on. I'll call Bunny and have her pick me up."

"Here, dear." Tutu opened her Gucci backpack and pulled out her wallet. "Close your eyes and hold out your hand. This won't hurt a bit. We're practically family, and I can't have you out there without a ha'penny or a farthing or whatever they called it in that song."

Allison closed her eyes and held out her hand. It did hurt. She looked down to see three hundred dollars in her palm.

"I . . ."

"Ack. No talking. Girls need mad money. Stick that in your bra. We gals have to hang together. And I have one other thing for you. I had it made when Dex and I had so much fun shopping." She pulled out a shiny silver MasterCard. It read *Allison Jennings* across the bottom. "Now buy yourself some clothes. I don't care if they are Kmart or

Anne Klein. And get that great-grandson of mine some stuff—socks and shorts. If you don't do it, I will, and I'll buy out the whole dang store."

"I'll—"

"Ack—no talking allowed." Tutu repeated. Then she pressed the key to the house into Allison's hand.

"Wow" was all Bunny could say. Big burly moving men were taking boxes of books out to a truck when they pulled up to Allison's old apartment. She and Bunny arrived in the nick of time, as far as Allison was concerned. She should have been there earlier.

"Stop." She walked quickly through the apartment with the head mover following her. "That sofa and these chairs all go to St. Vincent's. That wooden rocker can come with us. The beds go to St. Vincent's. This one side table can come with us. The rest of the furniture can go to St. Vincent's as well."

The mover put blue tape on the pieces that were coming with them. Allison was keeping just two things that had belonged to her mother. She was scared to death letting go of her entire motley pile of furniture, but in her pocket was the shiny gold key to her future home. If Dex wanted to give her a house, she'd found the one. She'd be right next door, Ethan could come and go at either place, and she'd have her own space. It was already filled with furniture, and memories, and Tutu's love.

"Did you see that one? His name is Joe." Bunny had a gleam in her eye.

"Behave, Bunny. Help me with this stuff. I promised Ethan I'd put his books and his new microscope where he could find them. And Brown Bear." Allison held up a worn-out teddy bear with a red bow tie and made him dance for Bunny.

"That's just too cute. Trish has a Raggedy Ann my mother sent her. It's a good thing we got here. I think this whole thing is going to take them about twenty minutes. The kitchen's packed and the living room—well, there were just books in there after your furniture purge, which I highly approve of, by the way. So what's the plan?"

Allison had kept quiet about the house till now. She reached into her shorts pocket and held up the key.

"Where, where! You know I love houses. How could you pick a place out without me? When did you find it?" Bunny jumped up and down and jiggled, attracting some attention from the movers, who smiled at her from then on out.

"I found it about an hour ago. It's the cottage next to the main house. Dex's grandmother's house."

"I've been in there. Celia had a huge sleepover, and Naomi put us out there with a nanny. The nanny got drunk and we permed her hair. I think it all fell out. It was very homey. Aren't you sleeping in the mansion?"

"I need some space."

"We better get you back over there and establish territory before you have to move stuff twice."

"Wait, I have to find my jeans. I need my jeans. I've got one two-piece dress and this outfit and that's all. Except for Tutu's credit card." Allison walked to her room and rummaged through the boxes. She emptied one and started putting a few things in it. "And the contents of my top dresser drawer. No man should be going through this stuff. And my toothbrush." She carefully placed her personal items in the box, tucked some clothes on top, then headed for the bathroom, dancing around Bunny, who was following her like a sheepdog.

"Lucille Needham gave you her credit card? You could charge Columbia on a Needham account. Let's go buy a car."

"No thanks, but we might do a little shopping later. We can go to Bellevue Mall. I've only walked it, never shopped it. We were Target people."

"I can't believe what I'm hearing. You're going to let Lucille buy you clothes? I had to lie and tell you it was a birthday present," Bunny said.

"You lied to me?" Allison looked at Bunny and made a funny, chastising face at her. "Here, carry this." Allison put a big box in Bunny's hands.

"*Moi*? I don't think so. Oh fellas! Over here. Load this in the Jag trunk for us, won't you?" Bunny smiled, batted her eyelashes, and cocked her head at Alli. Three moving men appeared instantly and removed the box from Bunny's hands. "Walk this way, boys." She wiggled her way out the apartment door, followed by all three. Now why they all three had to go with her, Allison couldn't figure.

If Allison been a smarter gal she'd have learned to use her feminine wiles much better over the years. Then again, she'd managed to catch the interest of Dex Needham. She just wasn't sure if that was because she accidentally had his baby, or because he truly wanted her. And for what, exactly? As she and Bunny used to say about Bunny's many boyfriends, hey, the sex was great but now what?

Allison decided not to think about that and just enjoy the thought of having a house of her own. She needed to create a home for Ethan besides the Great Hall of Needhams, even if it was in their backyard.

But she was going to call Bunny's lawyer and tell him she'd accept joint custody. She'd take a quarter of what he offered and pay off all her back bills, get what she needed for the house, and get on her feet. After all, her life had been turned upside down. Then she'd cut herself off from his funding. They could look it over again in a year.

If she had a new, better job, she could stand on her own. She'd really be able to make progress with no rent. She'd do it for Ethan. And for herself. She'd finally come to see that if she let this opportunity slip out of her grasp, she'd be a huge fool. That was after Bunny practically smacked her with her Prada bag to get her to see reason. She cited labor and childbirth as a good trade-off for a few measly months' worth of support and a house.

She had a point. Allison didn't see twenty-five thousand a month as measly, though. She could live on eight hundred bucks a month, and had proven that a few times. There were mice involved, and holes in the wall that had to be filled with rags, but she'd done it. And probably the popcorn she'd lived on was not considered a staple food. Of course, that was before Ethan was born.

Allison didn't even need child support since they were going to live right in the shadow of the big house. Dex was obviously hell-bent on paying for every pair of Nikes and every saxophone lesson Ethan could possibly need. She took a big breath and sighed to herself.

And who was she to say no to that?

22

Takin' a Chance on Love

She and Bunny had already instructed the moving company to come around to the cottage. The cottage they called it—a five-bedroom, four-thousand-square-foot cottage.

She unlocked the front door. At least here there wasn't a reporter camped out in the street, as when they'd gone to her apartment. The guy'd had the nerve to come up to them on the street and ask questions. Bunny had growled at him to go away, and he finally did, after snapping one picture.

Allison made Bunny help her take dust sheets off the living room furniture. Bunny took off one and plopped down in the chair, tossing the sheet on the floor.

"Whew, that was hard work. Look at this. I almost broke a nail." She stared at her perfect French-manicured fingernail.

With her bright pink slacks, matching silk sleeveless top, and orange and pink Jimmy Choo high-heeled sandals, Bunny wasn't exactly dressed for dust. Allison smiled at her. "Get off your hot-pink ass and help me."

"Bitch."

"Lazy."

"Oh, fine. Can't you get people in for this?" Bunny got up, complaining.

"It's Saturday. We can at least get these sheets off and make it look like we live here."

Allison looked up to see Naomi Needham standing in the open doorway just as those words came out of her mouth.

"Ahhh! You scared the hell out of me, Naomi." Bunny put her hand to her heart. "I guess I'm just used to you sneaking up on Celia and me to catch us smoking or nipping at the gin."

Naomi actually smiled. "And to think I trusted you with my daughter."

"We've been through that already, Naomi, old news. Remember? Celia turned out fine, I went bad, but here I am, spunky as ever."

"Yes, spunky as ever." Naomi turned her attention to Allison, which Allison was hoping somehow to bypass, but there you go. "My mother-in-law informs me you have decided to move in here."

"I was going to speak to you about it today. I hope that's acceptable?" Allison asked.

" 'Scuse me, ma'am." Muscle Mover took this moment to show up behind Naomi. So much for

Allison looking like she hadn't actually started moving in before asking.

"Oh, the first bedroom on the left upstairs is the boy's room. The master bedroom at the end of the hall is mine. You can stack any unknowns in the dining room," Allison directed him.

"I'm going in the kitchen and see if there's any gin." Bunny vanished. Traitor.

Naomi moved to one side, and that funny smile came back. "Looks like you're already in." She walked through the small entry and into the living room where Allison stood. Naomi seemed lost in thought for a few minutes. She walked along the edge of the room, fluffed the lace curtains surrounding the window seat, and ran her fingers over the pretty limestone fireplace mantel.

"We'll have our cleaning people come in Monday."

"Tutu mentioned that. I'm very grateful."

"I used to have a pair of candlesticks that looked lovely on that mantel. They're French faïence . . . pottery. They might be in the main house. I'll have Mrs. Fisk find them for you."

Allison had to hang on to the back of the sofa. "That's very kind of you. Did you ever live here?"

"Dex's father and I lived in this house for five years while they built the main house. It has good memories for me. I had it decorated differently, of course. We put the original things back after we moved to the main residence. Or shall I say, Tutu did. She had fun recreating the cottage the way it used to be."

It was so out of character for Naomi to reveal personal things to her. Of course, they hadn't really had a chance to talk much, just the occasional threatening and bribing.

"There are some obvious advantages to me taking this house. Dex's offer was a bit too much. I just couldn't accept a house from him. The family already owns this one, so no large expenditures and furnishings and all that have to happen for me. Plus Ethan can just go between the two houses, and we won't have to worry about his safety. It's just not acceptable for him to move in with Dex while I'm in another house somewhere else. We have lived together his whole life. We need each other."

"I agree. This is a good arrangement. I wasn't aware of what Dex had offered you. He refused to let me take part in the legal arrangements."

That fact made Allison feel three notches better about Dex Needham, oddly enough. She assumed Naomi had orchestrated most of the legal agreement's content. "Why are we agreeing?" She immediately wished she hadn't said that.

"I don't know. It's very odd, isn't it?" Naomi smiled. "Tutu told me you asked her to stop buying so much for the boy."

"I don't want him thinking he's going to be showered with gifts like that on a regular basis. I hope I didn't hurt her feelings," Allison added.

"I don't think so. I told her the same thing."

Allison came around the sofa and sat on the draped sheet. "Thank you." This was just too *Twilight Zone* to last, so she'd better say that before things got ugly.

"Is it noon yet? I made gin slings." Bunny came out with a tray and three glasses, set them on the coffee table, and grabbed one for herself. "I'm exhausted watching those moving men."

More men came in the door. Several of them winked at Bunny.

Both Allison and Naomi took a glass and found seats. Naomi probably needed a drink as much as Allison did.

"I'll have Margaret send some lunch over," Naomi said as she emerged from her gin sling sip.

"I think she's making pizza for a bunch of Ethan's friends. My ex-husband is coming over today. Ethan asked for him."

Naomi groaned. "Well, we better hide out in here then. We'll have Margaret make us some shrimp Caesar salads. She makes the best Caesar dressing I've ever tasted."

Us? Allison stared at Naomi. Lunching with Naomi. Bunny stared at Allison, then scrunched in her chair and sucked gin. Allison gave her a look that conveyed the fact that if Bunny left her here alone with Naomi she would kill her in her sleep. Bunny nodded. It was great to have a friend like Bunny who could read facial sign language.

* * *

Dex and Rusty and Ethan and Jack and Eli and Dylan all jumped in the pool at once. Tutu clapped. "Wild men! Now go!"

Dex struck out for the far side of the pool, followed by four small boys and Rusty. He slowed down a bit and let them all catch up. When they got to the end he was neck-and-neck with Rusty. He thought about the dynamics of the moment and decided to hang back and let Rusty win. Then came Ethan, then the other boys almost simultaneously.

"Rusty Trask in first place, Dex Needham in second, Ethan third, Jack in fourth, and a tie with Eli and Dylan for fifth place. Come out for prizes!" Tutu was at a table with tall plastic glasses of lemonade and a plate of big sugar cookies.

Dex grabbed his towel and dried off. "We haven't had pizza yet," he commented as Tutu handed him a cookie for second prize.

"Shhh. Don't tell anyone." Tutu winked. She handed out cookies to the other boys and Rusty.

Dex parked himself at one of the poolside tables and watched the boys inhale cookies, then jump back in the pool. Rusty wasn't far behind.

The guy was really doing a decent job with a tough situation. They'd had a chance to talk while the boys were splashing in the water earlier. Rusty had told him they'd just take it one day at a time and not get all knotted up about it. They talked about Rusty spending time with Ethan.

He was a very likable fellow, and Dex thanked God for that. He'd heard of cases where the paternity claim turned into a nightmare with the custodial father. They'd discussed Rusty signing the change of parental rights forms, and he seemed amenable to the agreement.

All the same, Dex could see Rusty cared a great deal about Ethan, and Dex told Rusty he was determined to keep the contact going between them. They'd make sure to include Rusty on a regular basis. And Dex had decided to give Rusty a hand with the ownership of the garage he worked at. Dex figured it was the least he could do. He'd talk to him about the details later.

They'd discussed schools, and Rusty admitted Dex was the best thing that ever happened to Ethan—like a miracle, he said, because that boy's mind was amazing. Then the kids dragged them into the pool for a race, and that was the end of it.

Men were so practical about things when given a chance. Why couldn't women be more like that?

Take his mother.

Just as Dex thought that, three women appeared in swimsuits, and one of them was his mother. She must have thought to swim some laps and forgotten about Ethan's little party.

"We're here to help."

Dex just stared at her.

"Shut your mouth dear, it's unbecoming."

Bunny and Allison were behind her. Allison had

on a red swimsuit that showed off her ample curves extremely well. What a figure on that girl. And to think he'd had her in his arms, in his bed, in . . . Dex chugged some cold lemonade.

"I'm here to drink," Bunny said. "Give me that lemonade; I've got a little friend for it." Bunny had on a two-piece black number Dex recognized from the guest suit pile.

She had something in a silver flask, and when Dex handed her the extra glass of lemonade he'd brought with him, she poured a rather large amount of the flask contents in, sat down next to him, and crossed her dainty sandaled feet in front of her.

"Hot today, isn't it?" Bunny's eyes were dancing with glee. "Gawd, I hope I don't get a waffle pattern on my butt."

"Hey, Dex." Allison sat in the next seat over. Her eyes were big, like a scared cat's.

"I'll just go chat with Tutu and get some more lemonade." Naomi left for the end of the pool where the snacks were laid out.

"You girls are scaring me," Dex said.

"Your mother is scaring us. We think she's gone over the rainbow."

"Why?"

"She drank gin slings and ordered shrimp Caesars and ate lunch with us and did the dishes. She did the dishes," Allison said.

"I've seen her do that before. It's like she can't stand people waiting on her anymore, and she'll just roll up her sleeves and stick on an apron. Mrs. Fisk just gets out of the way. Margaret, too," Dex replied.

"Dex, I'm moving into the cottage," Allison blurted out.

Naomi returned with another lemonade and a paper plate full of cookies. When Dex gave her a look, for once she wisely went back to the other end of the pool.

"And my mother approved?"

"Yes." Allison stared at him with the same amazement she saw on his face. Matching amazement.

"Wow. Something's gone very wrong. Maybe she's ill."

"She said it was very wise of me not to incur the extra expense of a new residence when this one was perfect for my needs."

"Is she drunk?"

"Just a little. We did eat lunch. And there's one other thing. I got a job. It doesn't start till fall, when Ethan will be back in school. I'm going to work for the Needham Foundation. Your mother hired me."

"My mother gave you a job?"

"Yes. Your mom said I had years of management experience, and years of experience as a single mother, and she's going to create a position where I can set up programs to help single moms get some training and have their day care paid for. I think that will be great. I have lots of ideas. We'll discuss them sometime."

"That would be wonderful."

"That's what I thought. And I get paid. I told her I was going nuts after working so many years. She seemed to understand."

Dex tried to gather all the facts in, but none of them added up to his mother having a change of heart. He didn't believe it. She was up to something.

"You heard me, I like her." Naomi set her lemonade down on the table.

Tutu smelled gin on Naomi's breath. She almost laughed. "Well, you should. She's a peach."

"She could have signed those papers Dex drew up and accepted all that money he threw at her. He was way too generous."

"I thought you didn't read them," Tutu said.

"Get real, Lucille, Jeff Tilden sent me a copy over by messenger the same day. It was a family concern how Dex chose to handle this situation. It had to do with our assets." Naomi nibbled on a cookie calmly.

"And here I thought you were mellowing."

"Hardly. Business is business. I said Dex wouldn't let me participate, not that I hadn't checked up on him."

"You're nothing if not consistent, Naomi."

"My friend Clarisse and I had a long talk last night. Did you know her daughter had to go to rehab and her granddaughter Lissie is living with them, raising all sorts of hell? Clarisse had her put in a boarding school. It's all costing her a fortune.

What a mess. And the father of Lissie was trying to extort money out of the family for damages or some trumped-up legal garbage."

"My heavens."

"It just made me think. Things could be worse. The girl has some good qualities. We can shape her up and make a decent Needham out of her. She stood up to you about overindulging the boy, and she turned me down on several occasions when I—"

"What, tried to buy her off? Naomi, really."

"So I'm overprotective."

"You've left out a little detail." Tutu leaned back in her chair with her glass of lemonade, the ice cubes tinkling.

"What?"

"Dex hasn't asked her to marry him."

"What's keeping him anyway? He's completely smitten with her. He's sneaking her into his room at night."

Tutu leaned forward. "You remember what we had to do to get your Dexter Sr. to marry you?"

"You promised you'd never bring that up again in our lifetime."

"Get real, Naomi. These Needham men need a push. And that's your specialty, dear."

Naomi tapped her fingernails on the glass tabletop, thinking. "We'll need Celia."

"Celia has to be trained sometime."

"She's already had his child, so that's out."

"It worked for you, but I don't picture Allison playing along with that."

Naomi looked at her sternly. "You promised."

Tutu put her finger to her lips and silenced herself. It was great to have a trump card to throw at Naomi every once in awhile. The fact that she'd gotten herself pregnant after Dexter II had dated her for three years was a good card. Never mind it was she who had suggested it. After all, a three-year engagement was enough already.

They sure threw that wedding together fast!

What amazed her was how the entire family had math amnesia when it came to Dex's birth date. Of course, the family spread the rumor he came early, and no one seemed to notice he was a strapping, healthy little lad at seven pounds.

"We could try the direct approach. Just ask him," Tutu suggested.

"I'm pretty sure it's the time frame here. They've only known each other a few weeks. Not counting the one night eleven years ago. That's just not long enough for a Needham man. Remember how we had to work on Edward to marry Nora? For heaven sakes, you'd think marriage was a disease."

"Dexter Sr. and I only knew each other three weeks."

"That was in the fifties. All you had to do was hold out sex and they'd get around to *engaged* much faster. And your wedding was a year later."

"In my case it was the other way around. Dexter Sr. knew he'd better marry me before someone else found out what a hot mama I was."

Naomi rolled her eyes. "Watch me not hear you say that. I hate to admit it, but I think we might be out of our league on this one. It's just too soon."

"We'll just drop hints like rose petals all over the place and see if the two of them can work it out."

"You mean leave it to them completely?"

"It's an idea," Tutu said. "Just dropping hints."

"But what if . . . ?"

"Rose petals." Tutu said again. She picked up her gin-spiked lemonade, courtesy of Bunny, and sipped.

23

In the Mood

Dex straightened his bow tie and looked in the hall mirror before he headed out the door. God knew if he was going to be able to pull this off.

He'd told Allison he was going to take her out on a date, no matter what. She had agreed, saying she'd walked the perimeter of their twenty acres enough times and needed to get outside the gate. No stupid, pushy reporter was going to stand in her way.

It had been a week since she moved into the cottage, and she'd been so busy with the house, he had hardly seen her. She said she and Ethan needed to bond with the house. Bond with the house? He didn't get that.

He missed her in so many ways, it was amazing. Her smile, her way of making him crazy, her strange sense of humor, and her soft, soft body next to his. He didn't know if he could take another day or another night without her. She was in his head every minute. He sometimes thought he caught her fragrance on the air.

Last night he'd stared out his bedroom window at the cottage for an hour trying to figure it all out.

He hadn't been able to work in his lab all week. He'd tried, but couldn't get himself to focus on anything besides Allison. He'd had to call Doug Yoshida, his top researcher from the labs, to come and mind things. For the first time in many years, he'd seen that a few weeks' vacation didn't cause the havoc he thought it might. Of course, since he had no life, it had never occurred to him to take time off, except for major holidays and that pesky Fourth of July house party every year.

Finding out he had a son was a very good reason to take some time off. He'd seen Ethan every day, and they'd set up a chessboard in the library and had a regular Tuesday and Thursday three o'clock game scheduled, complete with a tray of sandwiches from Margaret.

Being out of his mind was also a good reason. This love thing, it must be chemical. He was fascinated with the amount of obsession possessing him. His body felt like it was going through withdrawal, not having her in his arms to kiss and hold and make love to every night.

Allison had been up to something, but she wouldn't tell him what. She said they'd discuss it tonight.

At first he liked her idea of the cottage, and he

was glad she finally signed the agreement and got those pesky lawyers out of the way, even if she did take only a small portion of the monthly support. She obviously had ethics. Way too much stubborn pride, too.

But now he wanted her back. He was being pushed aside by a house.

He readied his bunch of roses Tutu had sent over by the bushel from Grand Island. They were a very nice lavender color—called Sterling Silver, she'd said. He hoped Allison liked them. He hoped she bought this whole charade he was about to play out. He could see several flaws in the plan that might make her run in the other direction.

But he had no choice. He had to have her.

He knocked on the door. There was a long pause, and then Mrs. Fisk opened it.

"Lovely." She smiled at him. "Do come in."

"Are you visiting?"

"Miss Jennings and I have been having a discussion about home management and other matters that don't concern you. I'm going to walk Master Ethan back to the main house now."

Mrs. Fisk always had loads of attitude, but she needed it to hold her own with Dex's mother.

"Hey, Dex." Ethan had a large box of some kind of toy in his arms. "Grandma Naomi and I are going to build a model of the Brooklyn Bridge. She says I need to learn engineering basics." Ethan shrugged and smiled.

Grandma Naomi. Oh my God. Dex practically

died laughing inside his head. "Oh she does, does she? She's very good at putting things together. You'll have fun."

Mrs. Fisk slipped on her usual navy-blue sweater and put her hand gently on Ethan's shoulder. "Off we go then. Your mother has a date."

"A date? Wow, that's incredibly weird. I thought they were just going to talk, talk, talk again. No wonder she's all decked out. Are you going to kiss her?"

What's a billionaire to do? "Yes, I'm going to kiss her. Is that okay?"

"Go for it. I mean, obviously, you've had some sort of encounter before. Otherwise I wouldn't exist."

It was like talking to Dr. Spock. "A very clinical analysis, young man."

"Cheerie-o, we're off to a great supper tonight. Margaret made fried chicken, and in this heat." She gave Ethan a gentle guide out the door. Saved by Mrs. Fisk. Ethan waved and winked. Sheesh.

Dex stepped into the living room through the open archway. The place looked amazing: sort of a retro forties-fifties thing with deep red and purple cut velvet and wild patterns on throw pillows. The lights were dimmed. A pair of candlesticks were lit on the fireplace mantel. He remembered them from when he lived here with his parents as a very small boy.

"Cocktail?" He turned at the sound of her voice.

Allison stood in the archway that led to the dining room, holding an empty martini glass.

Black dress. Very good black dress. Very short, tight, high-neck black dress, which brought out her lively red hair and dangerous-looking gold eyes. Very high high-heels with a few black straps holding them on very cute feet. Dex adjusted his shirt collar.

She slunk. No kidding, slunk over to him. Slink, slank, slunk. Her arms went around his neck, and she kissed him. Not just your average hello kiss, but one of those body-press kisses where her ample cleavage burned a hole through his shirt and her hips . . . well, he ran his hands down the back of her dress, which had about no back at all, and over her luscious rear end, and pressed her into him.

His aroused state went up five notches. She gave a little grind with her hips while her tongue played with the ridge of his teeth and danced around in his mouth.

He moaned out loud when she did that little grind. It was involuntary on his part. He wanted to throw her on the sofa and push up that dress and do her right there. He ran his hands over her again. She had no panties on. He groaned as she ruffled his hair with her fingers and kissed him deeper.

Now, how the hell was he going to get her out of here? Maybe he could just have her now and think about it later. But then he'd want her again and again.

He pulled his mouth off her like a suction cup and gasped for air . . . and sanity. "My, my it's certainly hot tonight, isn't it? I'll take you up on that cocktail."

Her eyes opened wider and didn't blink. She slowly extracted herself from him.

"Can we put these in some water?" He picked up his somewhat rumpled roses off the floor where he'd dropped them, needing both hands for her greeting.

"Sure," she said flatly. She took the bouquet from him.

He adjusted his tie and did his best to walk to a chair in the dining room so his goodies could cool off in peace. Friction was not his friend right now.

He heard her heels click their way to the kitchen over the dark wood floors. The dining room looked the same as he remembered; clean lines, 1940s blond wood. She'd put some things in the display case: thick cream-colored pottery vases in various shapes. They were quite nice. He was desperate to focus himself away from wanting her so bad it was killing him. He had to get her to their destination.

Bunny had specifically told him a secret about Allison, and he was going to pull off this thing—this memorable thing—so they could laugh about it for years.

Okay, she'd gotten all dolled up, sexier than any known moment in her life, put on the *do me* shoes, cleared out the house, used all her female stuff, and he didn't bite? Allison wrapped the sheer black coat that went with her hot black dress a little tighter around herself. Not that she was cold, oh no. She'd been away from her Sexy Dexy too long and had really wanted some wild stuff.

Instead, she'd made two gin slings, her new favorite summertime drink, and he'd sloshed it down like water, grabbed her arm, and dragged her out to his ancient Mercedes for a drive.

"Exactly where are we going?"

"Whatever happened to your Nova?"

"Rusty found an engine for it, and it's all over at the garage, I guess. He works on it in his spare time."

"What car would you get if you could have any car?"

"Don't buy me a freakin' car, Dex. Just quit it. Now, we are going on this date like normal people, right? Dinner, I hope?"

"I was just asking, Miss Snappish."

"I'm not telling. You have bad habits. You buy things."

"That's not fair. Look at this car. I've had it since after high school."

"Yeah, what's up with that, Dex?"

"It was a good year. I like this car."

"I suppose that's a good thing. Expensive cars are insane. Even Bunny had a domestic engine installed in her Jag to keep from having all those costly repairs on that persnickety foreign engine."

At least Dex had her focused on something besides where they were going for the last ten miles, because now they were here, and now she'd yell, but it would be worth it.

"What in the *holy hell* are you thinking?"

Here it comes. He grinned while he turned the car into the parking lot. He came to a stop and set the brake.

"Like, what? I'm going to go in and make peace with Tim and get my job back?"

"It's under new management now."

"Which nephew did Uncle Percival give the job to this time?"

"Let's go find out. I believe your last paycheck is here."

"I don't care about my check. No way I'm going in there."

"Allison, I'm asking nicely. I'd like you to come in for a minute. Then we'll be on our way. In case you've forgotten, we met here."

"You'll have to drag me."

Dex opened his door, got out of the car and looked back at her. "Come on, follow me. You'll be glad. We'll pick up your check and donate it to charity. That will feel terrific. Won't it?"

"No."

"I'm coming to get you now, Allison."

He shut his door and ran for her side. She slid over and hit the lock buttons. My God, she was being difficult. He figured she'd protest, but not this much. He hit the unlock button on his keys and swung her door open before she could click it locked again.

Dex dove in the car after her. "You are the most stubborn woman I have ever met. You'll thank me for this later." He lifted her out of the car very quickly, legs first.

"*Noooooo!*"

She was pretty light over his shoulder, but she was wiggly and noisy. "Is this how you want to go in? Ass-backward?" He gave her behind a light, playful smack.

"Put me down this instant!"

"I don't think so. I know the owner, and he won't mind."

Dex stopped at the front door and punched in a security code. She kept twisting around to see what he was doing, making his work very difficult.

"Dex! Have you lost your marbles?"

Finally the green light blinked and he opened the door. As soon as he was inside with her he turned around and punched a button. Lock-down. He set her on her feet.

"My God, woman, has anyone ever told you you're sort of a handful?"

Allison turned herself around in a three-hundred-sixty-degree circle very slowly, while she readjusted her dress. The light was very dim, but she could see that the Tasty Freeze had been transformed. It was oh-so-fifties, and oh-so-authentic. In the center of the black and white checked linoleum floor was a table for two with a white linen cloth draped to the floor, candles, silverware, the whole nine yards. Two fancy chairs with velvet seats awaited them. Soft violin music played in the background.

What an idiot she was. Here he'd planned this cute dinner at the place they'd met.

"Oh Dex, I'm so sorry. I just didn't think. This *is* the place we met, all those years ago." She went to him and hugged him. He gave her a smile so she'd know he wasn't mad at her. And a soft kiss that made her lips tingle.

A man came out of the back wearing a chef's uniform. He was drying his hands on a Tasty Freeze towel.

"Good evening, Mr. Needham. Would you like a glass of champagne to start with?"

He had a French accent. Wow. A real French chef.

"That would be fine, Mitchell."

"Would mademoiselle care to sit?"

Allison turned around, and Dex took off her wrap.

Mitchell held her chair out for her, and she slid in. Dex took his place across from her. Mitchell took Allison's wrap, tapped his hat, and left the room.

"Dex, you're a real surprise."

He took her hand. "It's you that's a real surprise, Allison."

"That's for sure. I'm sure finding out you had a son was about as shocking as it gets."

"It was, but equally as shocking was finding out you were such a delightful, sexy, bright woman. I obviously made the biggest mistake of my life eleven years ago when I didn't recognize that fact and pursue you to the ends of the earth."

Allison was speechless. Mitchell returned with the champagne bottle and poured out two glasses for them. She went right for it and took a sip, probably very uncool in the wine world—wasn't someone supposed to sniff a cork or something? But the little bubbles were streaming up the tall crystal flute and looked very fun. Plus she suddenly had a case of the jitterbugs again.

"Thank you, Mitchell, we'll ring when we're ready."

Mitchell gave another bow and left.

"We'll ring?"

Dex pointed to a small bell on the table. She was less than observant tonight, probably because her mind was on *sex* instead. But that was one pretty speech Dex had made. It was like these little bubbles. It kind of went into your bloodstream and danced the tango or the cha-cha or something.

She felt herself getting fuzzy. A nice fuzzy. But she must be fuzzier than she thought because she kept seeing Dex on his knee. She blinked it away a few times, but he was still there. He took her hand. She started to laugh. He started to laugh.

"There's no way I can do this with you laughing. Now stop it," he laughed.

"I . . . can't." She couldn't. It got worse. He held

on to the side of the table for support, and she slapped the tabletop and cracked up again.

"Allison, Allison, how can I ask you to marry me if we can't stop laughing?" He said that through tears streaming down his face.

"What? You can't be serious," she said. She sobered up quickly.

"Of course I'm serious!" He wiped his eyes. "Bunny said very clearly that you said the only way you'd ever remarry is if the richest man in the entire state of Washington fell to his knees at the Tasty Freeze and proposed to you. I'm just carrying that out to the letter."

"Oh my God. You're kidding, aren't you? You don't actually want to marry me—after two weeks?"

Dex got up off the floor and dusted off his knees. He sat down in his chair and took a drink of champagne. "That was the idea. I explained it pretty well a few minutes ago, didn't I?"

"You can't just marry me because I had your son."

"I realize that. Since when does a simple proposal have to be so difficult?"

"Since we met—or re-met—on the Fourth of July." Allison stood up and paced around the table.

"Allison, sit down, you're making me dizzy."

She thumped back in her seat.

"See how well we get along when you surrender to my wisdom?"

Allison rolled her eyes. "Would that be the obey part of the wedding ceremony?"

"Exactly."

"And would you be expecting more little heirs?"

"I would. At least one more."

"Any particular sex?"

"No preference."

"You don't even know if I snore."

"Yes, I do. You don't. But I do. Is that going to be a problem?"

She folded her arms across her chest. "It might."

"Well, in that case I'll just have to take the ring back."

"Ring?"

"Yes, the ring." He picked up the brass bell on the table and revealed a very sparkly, very large, round diamond about the size of . . . Cleveland.

"So clever." She reached for it. He snatched it away.

"Eh eh, you said no thanks."

"No, I didn't. I said it might matter if you snore. We can always get you one of those nose strips or something. Besides, I sleep like a log. Are you going to make me sign some prenuptial nightmare?"

"It's too late for that. You had my baby."

"Oh, Dex." She put her arms on the table and smacked her forehead down on them. "What's wrong with me that I can't say yes to a filthy rich, good-looking, extremely nice guy when he wants to marry me after only a few *weeks?*"

"I have a few ideas, but we could get you a therapist if you like."

"A head shrinker? You're not going to have me put away, are you?"

"We'll just keep you in the attic. It's done in all the best families. So you think I'm extremely nice?"

"Very. Would you come and live with me in the cottage?"

"Sure."

"I know it's silly, with that huge house right there, but I can't wrap my head around living in such a big place."

"We can work out the logistics. So, you are considering accepting?"

"Can I just see the ring?"

He held it just out of her reach. He smiled a big smile. God, he was handsome. He was teasing her. He was being very patient with her.

"I guess . . ." She swallowed hard. "I could be . . . engaged." She thought she'd pass out just saying it out loud.

"That gets you the Crackerjack prize anyway." He took her hand and slipped the ring on her finger. It fit perfectly. She looked at him, puzzled.

"I calibrated the circumference of your finger while you weren't paying attention."

"You're such a nerd, Dex. But you're so good in bed."

"It's all science to me, darling."

"Oh, say that again. Darling." She stared at the ring, unable to believe it was real.

"Darling. Are you hungry?"

"Ring that bell, darling."

Dex rang the bell.

"By the way, what did you do to the Tasty Freeze?"

"I bought it."

"No. Why?"

"So I could fire Tim."

"I like what you've done to the place."

"We get free ice cream for life."

"Wow, my wildest dream come true." Allison made a face.

"We'll get into that later, after Mitchell goes home for the evening."

"Oh, that's right, you've got a weakness for marshmallow cream."

"I have a weakness for you, Allison."

"Say 'Allison darling.' "

"Allison darling."

"You see how well we get along when you surrender to my wisdom?" She smiled at him.

"We'll talk about surrender later when you're covered with chocolate syrup."

"What will the *Tattler* say about this?"

Dex kissed her fingertips. "*Sexy Dexy Meets His Match.*"

24

The Glory Of Love

One Year Later

Mr. and Mrs. Dexter Needham II
request the honor of your presence
at the wedding of
Dexter Needham III
to
Allison Louise Jennings
4th of July
Eight-thirty in the Evening
Grand Island

Her brother, Ben, was giving her away wearing his dress Navy uniform. He was so tall and good-looking. Bunny was standing with Celia, and even Trishy Tiger, all dressed up looking so almost-cute in her red sailor dress. Bunny said never to say that to Trish, or she'd scream. Even so, the dresses were lovely, and Bunny and Celia looked fabulous in red.

They'd set up the wedding on the expansive back veranda, and Naomi had done one heck of a job. Red and white striped bows with floral accents were on the end of every aisle, and the gazebo they'd set up for the minister was festooned with red, white, and blue florals and ribbons that were truly beyond elegant. Torches lit the edges of the veranda as the sun faded.

As she walked down the aisle on Ben's arm, she could see Tutu with her truly magnificent hat, next to Grampa Dex. That woman should live in hats. Naomi and her husband were watching her. She could not believe the moment when Naomi put a handkerchief to her eye. Someone must have given that woman a mellow pill. Or a gin sling.

Celia, not her usual slim self after giving birth to twins, still looked great, and Warren had them both in a baby carriage in the second row. Actually there was another carriage there as well, because Edward and Nora had brought their new baby son. Allison looked at the nervous dads with binkies ready in case a three-way squeal went out.

She was trying not to look at Dex in case she started to cry. But the closer she got, the more amazing Dex and Ethan looked in their suits and red bow ties.

Rusty winked at her and made a funny face when she went by, the brat. Pamela gave her a thumbs-up. Their girls had pink lace dresses on, and Pamela held the littlest one, who was determined to squirm away. She finally plopped her in Rusty's lap and smoothed out her matching pink dress.

"Ready, sis?" Ben whispered.

"Ready as I'll ever be."

The sun was about to set, and the sky was streaked with color. Dex came forward and took her hand. She picked up her fairy-tale princess skirts that glittered with crystals and pearls in the fading light and stepped up inside the gazebo with him.

Dex leaned over and whispered to her. "Just say 'I do' when he asks. Don't argue with the man. And if you say 'obey,' I will, too."

She smirked at him. "I do, I do, I do."

"Very good, Mrs. Needham."

Allison handed Bunny her red and white rose bouquet and took Dex's hands in hers.

"Dearly beloved . . ." the minister began.

Allison and Dex stood in ready position again.

"Go for it, Mrs. Needham." Dex gave Allison a thumbs-up and winked at her.

"There's no way I'm letting you hit that damn ball at me. I'll give birth right here."

"I've had lots of lessons now, Babs. It's going to be okay."

"I swear, Babs, I've seen it myself," Dex said.

Allison made her first toss and nailed the serve. It rocketed cross-court. Babs stretched for the return and missed.

"Tough miss there, Babsy," Reg said.

"My balance is all off. I can't do this preggers, damn it."

"Okay, we're out." Reggie strolled off the court. "I'm getting my wife a cool drink, and no martinis this year."

"Admit it was good before you go, Babs," Allison said.

"Oh, crap, it was good. I'll give you that because you got married last night. At least you didn't bean me this time." She gave Allison a nasty look.

"I really like that Babs stays the same no matter what's up in her life."

"Me, too. And Reg. They're a perfect couple."

"Do you think people say that about us?"

Dex came over and put his arm around his wife. "No, but that's their problem."

"What do they say, she's not in his league?"

"No, they say I don't deserve you."

"Very funny."

They walked toward the house together. Celia and Warren were stretched out on chaises sunning themselves on the expansive lawn. They were exhausted after the wedding yesterday and another sleepless night. Tutu had Celia's two babies in her lap in another chaise and was talking to them in a funny voice. They seemed to understand everything she was saying.

"They're very bright, aren't they?" Tutu said.

Ethan ran across the lawn to them. "Hey, Dad,

Edward wants to know if you'll watch Tommy while he tracks down Aunt Nora." He'd started calling him Dad, or Dad *the second* sometimes, in funny moments after Christmas—after Allison had agreed to actually marry him instead of just being engaged forever. It was one of the best feelings he'd ever had in his life. He had a family. He had a son and a wife.

He looked up on the terrace and saw Edward waving to him, holding his new son close. It was raining babies around here. It seemed to him that the last Fourth of July he and Allison weren't the only ones romping around the Grand Island house!

His sister was so happy she could hardly talk about it without crying again. They all teased her and hugged her a million times and had baby showers for three months straight it seemed like.

Ethan sat down next to Tutu on the chaise and started playing with baby Karen Lynn. Or was it baby Kimberly Marie? He couldn't tell them apart.

"Celia, you've got to paint those babies' toenails so I can tell them apart," Dex said.

"You find me some completely natural nail polish and I will." Celia shaded her eyes from the sun as Dex stood next to her. "When are you two going to jump in the baby pool?"

"Are we jumping there?" Allison looked at him.

"We better jump fast, we're not getting any younger," Dex said.

"Oh, do it, Mom. But it has to be a boy. No offense, Aunt Celia, I've just done too much Malibu Barbie time with my stepsisters."

"Ethan, we can't choose the sex, it just happens."

"Well, actually, there is a method. It has to do with centrifuging the . . . sample and separating the male and female elements. The success rate is very high for boys. And there are some timing methods and other factors. But we can get about a ninety-eight percent ratio if we follow the guidelines to the letter."

"See?" Ethan smiled.

"What am I? A petri dish?"

"Ask me. I took hormone shots for six months before we conceived. I'm a pincushion!" Celia said.

"Ask me. I had to give them to her," Warren laughed.

"We'll discuss this later tonight," Allison said, making a goofy face at Dex, indicating she'd rather not do this in front of Ethan.

"Are you two going on a honeymoon or what?" Celia asked.

"We're already on one. We'll get around to it eventually," Dex answered.

"Just go somewhere secluded. They won't find you. We only had that one helicopter buzz by yesterday, and I think the whole idea of hiring a PR firm to handle press releases the way we want them was brilliant," Celia said.

"That was Naomi's idea." Allison looked up at the house and saw Naomi standing on the second-floor balcony. She waved at her. Maybe she would have a baby, just so she could call Naomi *Granny* to her face. Allison giggled.

Naomi Needham waved back at Allison. She surveyed her little kingdom. Her children were happy. That's all she ever wanted. And her grandchildren were everywhere. She could almost see Tutu's point of view when she walked into Petite Bateau in downtown Seattle and found the French layette wear. Overindulging was a grandparent's delight, for certain. And all the clerks at FAO Schwarz knew her by sight now. They'd started putting aside Muffy Vanderbear outfits for her, for heaven's sake.

And Ethan, well, he looked so handsome in that school uniform, she had to buy one of those digital cameras so she could e-mail his picture to her own mother. And the babies, and the wedding, which was really perfection, she'd have to give Mrs. Fisk a huge bonus for helping Allison and her pull it together between December and July.

Her husband came up behind her, and she gave a little jump.

"Did I startle you, dear? Sorry."

"That's all right," she said.

"Lovely party."

"Yes, it is." Naomi turned and put her arms around her husband. "Thank you, dear." And she really meant that. He had stayed by her the whole time she'd gone over the edge and tried too hard to control everything. And here he was, waiting, when she came back to her senses.

"You're welcome, Naomi."

They walked back inside, arm in arm, and closed the French doors behind them.